"Wonderful . . . had me laughing out loud."
—*USA Today* bestselling author Nancy Warren

"One of the best new voices in women's fiction."
—*New York Times* bestselling
author Jennifer Crusie

"Fresh, funny, and quirky, an absolute delight."
—Annette Blair, national bestselling
author of *The Scot, the Witch,
and the Wardrobe*

"With laugh-out-loud scenes and lovable characters, I don't have
to be clairvoyant to know you'll read this book in one sitting."
—Beverly Bartlett,
author of *Cover Girl Confidential*

"[A] lively and entertaining read, packed with humor, romance,
and magically human characters."

—Wendy French,
author of *sMothering*

unpredictable

Eileen Cook

BERKLEY BOOKS, NEW YORK

THE BERKLEY PUBLISHING GROUP
Published by the Penguin Group
Penguin Group (USA) Inc.
375 Hudson Street, New York, New York 10014, USA
Penguin Group (Canada), 90 Eglinton Avenue East, Suite 700, Toronto, Ontario M4P 2Y3, Canada
(a division of Pearson Penguin Canada Inc.)
Penguin Books Ltd., 80 Strand, London WC2R 0RL, England
Penguin Group Ireland, 25 St. Stephen's Green, Dublin 2, Ireland
(a division of Penguin Books Ltd.)
Penguin Group (Australia), 250 Camberwell Road, Camberwell, Victoria 3124, Australia
(a division of Pearson Australia Group Pty. Ltd.)
Penguin Books India Pvt. Ltd., 11 Community Centre, Panchsheel Park, New Delhi—110 017, India
Penguin Group (NZ), 67 Apollo Drive, Rosedale, North Shore 0632, New Zealand
(a division of Pearson New Zealand Ltd.)
Penguin Books (South Africa) (Pty.) Ltd., 24 Sturdee Avenue, Rosebank, Johannesburg 2196, South
Africa

Penguin Books Ltd., Registered Offices: 80 Strand, London WC2R 0RL, England

This is a work of fiction. Names, characters, places, and incidents either are the product of the author's imagination or are used fictitiously, and any resemblance to actual persons, living or dead, business establishments, events, or locales is entirely coincidental. The publisher does not have any control over and does not assume any responsibility for author or third-party websites or their content.

PRINTING HISTORY
Berkley trade paperback edition / February 2008

Library of Congress Cataloging-in-Publication Data

Cook, Eileen.
    Unpredictable / Eileen Cook.—Berkley trade pbk. ed.
        p.   cm.
    ISBN 13: 978-0-425-21396-4 (alk. paper)
    I. Title.
    PR9199.4.C65845I6   2007
    813'.6—dc22

                                        2006043019

PRINTED IN THE UNITED STATES OF AMERICA

10   9   8   7   6   5   4   3   2   1

ACKNOWLEDGMENTS

At the risk of sounding like an Oscar speech that goes on way too long, I would like to thank a few people for all their help.

To my family, especially my parents, Jane and Ken McIntosh, who shared with me their love of reading and sense of humor. Thank you for making me who I am today and I'm sorry about smashing up the car when I was sixteen.

To friends who provided support by reading early drafts, cheered me on, and supplied chocolate or martinis as needed: Maribeth Ruckman, Alan Donald, Laura Sullivan, Allison Klundt, Marion Abramo, and Tara Immell. A special thanks to Jamie Hillegonds, who believes everything is possible and provides kicks in the ass until you do it. I wouldn't have written this without her.

To writing and English teachers past and present, in particular Ivan Coyote, who suggested that if I ever wanted to be published I might try sending things off. Thanks to my writing group and my critique partner, Brooke Chapman, who has energy to spare and time to listen.

When I started writing I had a dream agent in mind and I was lucky enough to get her; thanks to Rachel Vater who is the perfect blend of agent, coach, and friend. Working with the entire team at Berkley has been a privilege; a special thanks to my editor, Kate Seaver, and her assistant, Allison Brandau, who guided this book to publication.

Big thanks to CSICOP (www.csicop.org) and Skepchicks (www. skepchicks.org) who taught me that critical thinking can be fun.

To readers and bookstore owners, thanks for your passion for books and your willingness to give a new author a try. Drop me a line at my website and tell me what you thought: www.eileencook.com.

Most important: Thanks to my husband, Bob, the ultimate skeptic, who always believed in me, this book, and our future.

One

CAPRICORN
Today will bring new adventures—be willing to step outside your more quiet nature. Don't be risk-averse—it's time to seize what you want. Others may be nervous with this new you, but stay the course and they will come to appreciate you more.

I want to go on the record as saying that I have a perfectly good reason for breaking into my boyfriend's apartment building. Okay, technically according to the *law* it wouldn't be considered a good reason. It's not like the place is on fire with children or puppies trapped inside, however my life is teetering on the edge of disaster, which clearly constitutes some kind of emergency. I would also point out that *technically*:

- I'm not breaking into his apartment but only the building's *laundry room*, which, as anyone would tell you, hardly counts as a crime at all.

- As we have lived together for six years before he moved out, in many ways any place of his is a place of mine, as well.

- Not to mention I didn't *break* anything to gain entry, so it's more like just "entering."

Doug would point out that *technically* he is no longer my boyfriend, as he broke up with me, but that is a situation I plan to remedy. He seems to be laboring under the idea that I'm going to walk away from a six-year relationship with a smile, a kiss on the cheek, and a promise to be friends. Obviously, I'm not the crazy one here. If I'm caught I can't imagine there's a court in the world that would convict me.

Of course, part of the plan is to *not* get caught, which is why I'm currently crouching under the utility sink in the laundry room, clutching Doug's socks. Not all of his socks, just one from each pair that was in the dryer. This is my plan: steal his socks in an effort to slowly drive him insane or, better yet, drive him back home. He's the kind of guy who values familiar routines. When he realizes how out of sync his life is without me, as demonstrated by his woeful lack of matching socks, he will recognize my value. I'm counting on it. However, I *hadn't* counted on him coming down to the laundry room. At home, when I could actually get him to put in a load of laundry—an event about as regular as a solar eclipse—he would put everything into the dryer and leave them there, knowing that the laundry fairy would eventually fold them and return them to their proper place. Not that I minded doing the laundry. He's got a stressful job; I didn't mind taking care of things. But the point is, in the six years we lived together he never once emptied the dryer. So why is it that here, in his new home, he's become so timely?

Doug told me he was leaving me in our laundry room, which, if you knew Doug, is just so typical. He likes to check things off his to-do list. As he's not the kind to wait for the right moment, I should consider myself lucky I wasn't in the bathroom when the breakup urge struck him. Doug likes his underwear folded into this tight origami shape the way his mother used to do it for him. Leg, leg, crotch, fold over; leg, leg, crotch, fold over. I'd done this for so long I could've done it in my sleep, and it had gotten to the point where I did it to my own panties without even thinking about it. On the day we broke up I was standing there creating my one-millionth underwear nugget and thinking about what I needed to get from the store, when he came in and told me that he was leaving. I thought he meant leaving to go the store so I asked him to pick up some milk and laundry detergent. I didn't get it.

I never saw it coming. That makes me sound pathetic, doesn't it? Honestly, I knew we had our issues, what long-term relationship doesn't, but I still thought we were happy. I was happy. After six years I'd been lulled into a false sense of safety. I thought we were destined to be together. I felt like the person who had won the relationship lottery. We'd had a big talk about how it was time to move our relationship to "the next level." I actually believed this might mean it was the year he was going to give me a ring. Apparently, what he meant by "next level" was his own apartment.

It's all about expectations, I guess. One thing I definitely expected was that if our relationship was going down the tubes, we would have talked about it once or twice before it was all over. As it was, there was no argument, no big crying jag where I could lie dramatically across the sofa, beg him not to leave, and end up screaming that he was a bastard. He never mentioned a thing until that morning when he came to the laundry room, said he was leaving, took his clean underwear from my hands, and walked out the door.

How could he decide to leave? This is the guy who would stand in front of an open refrigerator yelling that there was no mustard until I got up and showed him. He'd look at it like he'd never seen a squeeze bottle of mustard before and accuse me of not putting it in the "right" spot. This is a man who couldn't find a condiment in a four-cubic-foot refrigerator. How is he going to live on his own? More important, why does he *want* to live on his own? Every time I bring it up he says that he needs his space, and that he really loves me but isn't sure he is *in love* with me anymore. What the heck does that mean? That's the kind of line that usually ends up with someone choking on a steak knife. He's never been a guy to really talk about his feelings. I started to wonder if he was just having the premarriage jitters. I don't want him to throw away our entire relationship because of nerves.

I'm willing to admit that when he first left, I wasn't sure I was going to make it. It was two days before Valentine's Day. February is the worst month in Vancouver, nothing but nonstop rain, the kind of rain that makes you start thinking about taking up ark-building as a hobby just in case. The only bright spot in February is Valentine's Day, and this year even that was taken from me. Continuing to breathe in and out seemed to be too much effort. I just couldn't walk away without knowing more, so I started spying on him. Scratch that. *Spying* sounds really negative. It sounds better to say I was *looking out* for him, sort of like a social experiment. He moved out three weeks ago, and watching him has become my newest hobby. I have invested six years in this relationship and most of my life dreaming of a happily ever after. I'm not giving up without an explanation. He'll thank me for my dedication once we're back together.

This is only the second time that I've actually been in the building. Mostly I park out front and down a ways and watch the building. So far I have seen him have two pizzas delivered and accept one package from FedEx. He looks good, but he needs a haircut. What he really needs to realize is how much he wants me, how he can't live without me. When he didn't seem to be coming to this realization on his own, I knew I would have to up the ante, so I began Operation Drive Him Home, aptly titled since it started with the car. I found the extra set of keys to his Mercedes. When he first picked it up at the dealership, they gave him two sets. When he moved out, he left one buried in the junk drawer and he'd forgotten all about it. I started by going to his office and moving his car over a few parking spots. I've done this five times, culminating in moving it a full level down in the parking garage. Now, when I have one of those nights where I start feeling sorry for myself, I picture him in my mind. He's standing there with his briefcase, looking at where he left the car, starting to panic, and then he sees it three or four spaces over. He realizes in that moment that his life is falling apart, that he needs me. It's a small thing, but it really does make me feel better.

My best friend, Jane, who can be counted on to bring ice cream in times of emotional turmoil—and not the cheap, store brand, but the full cream and fat-laden designer brand— thinks I am brilliant. To be precise, she said something along the lines of "You're insane," but I know what she meant was "crazy like a fox," which means clever.

Doug rented an apartment in a modern chrome-and-glass high-rise. The first time I got into the building, someone was walking ahead of me, and I just followed them through the front door. I checked out the lobby: pretty typical, wall of gun-metal gray mailboxes, a few dusty spider plants (fake) and art that looked like it was painted by a kindergartener, with big splotches of primary colors that appeared angry and slightly pornographic. I found a flyer for the building. They targeted themselves to the "urban single," which I know means a pick-'em-up place. Basically, it's a giant glass phallic symbol, inhabited by men with receding hairlines and young women pumped full of silicone looking for a man with a stable job. Doug fits in. He's losing his hair—it's not receding, nor does he have a bald spot—but it's just sort of thinning all over. His head resembles a dandelion, like if you gave it a big puff, his hair would go spinning off his head and blow around. I shouldn't say that, because it makes him sound dorky when he's actually a really attractive guy and a good catch. He keeps himself in great shape. He plays in baseball, basketball, and hockey leagues, and when he can't get a group of guys together, he goes to the gym. He has a great smile. As a kid, he stood too close behind a friend up at bat who ended up whacking him right in the face. His tooth cut his mouth open and he still has this tiny white scar that runs through his upper lip. It makes his smile slightly crooked and utterly charming. Whenever he goes somewhere he's one of those people you find in the center of the action. He's definitely got the stable job bit down. He works in the financial district as a personal investment advisor. His dad owns the company and someday he'll take over. As someone who doesn't even balance her own checking account, I find his job very impressive.

I snuck into Doug's building tonight to steal his socks. Phase two of Operation Drive Him Home was carefully planned. Moving his car wasn't working. It was time to up the ante. I packed several Holt Renfrew and Coach shopping bags full of crumpled-up tissue paper, and stood next to the front door, waiting. When I saw someone come out of the elevator, I juggled the bags and searched my handbag as if trying to find my key. I smiled, tossed my hair, and generally used my high school theater talents to make myself into a harried, overburdened, expensive-shopping-bag-carrying urban single. I gave a few deep sighs and wrinkled my brow as if in deep concentration similar to that of world leaders pondering the decision to launch tactile missiles. When a woman in an acid green designer yoga outfit came through the door, she held it open for me. I whispered "thanks," and slid inside.

I slipped down to the bowels of the building into the clearly marked laundry room. There was a fitness room next door that had hip-hop music blaring so loud I could see the sound waves as they passed through the wall into the laundry room. I dumped the shopping bags into a large trash can and started checking out the bank of washers and dryers. I knew Doug would do his laundry tonight, because it's Sunday, and on the last Monday of every month his office has a big project review meeting. Doug likes to be all decked out. He actually lays out his clothes for the week, making an outfit on a hanger for each day, including underwear and socks. Living with someone for so long means I know more about him than he might expect— I plan to use this knowledge to my advantage.

The room is white: white walls, white tile floor, white washers and dryers. And *clean*, so clean you could perform surgery on the folding tables. It makes me wonder what happened to all the lint bunnies that should be lurking in the corners. They must have all emigrated to my house. There are eight washers and eight dryers, all but one going full speed tonight. (Sunday is apparently a big laundry night for the urban single.) I open up each dryer and grope about, looking for familiar laundry, *Khakis and cotton dress shirts*; no. *Leopard-print thong and matching bra*; no. *Rainbow assortment of day-of-the-week panties*; no. *White boxers with dark socks*. Until—bingo. Colors with whites, I should have known. His underwear is already starting to take on a gray pallor. Bleach would fix that, but I'm not going to tell him. If he gets into an accident and is caught with bad, meat-gray shorts, it won't be on my head. When we lived together I bleached, color-sorted, and added fabric softener (not that I'm bragging). I pull socks out of the dryer and fight the urge to make sock balls. Instead, I find pairs and toss one sock from each pair back in and stuff the others in my handbag. I shut the dryer door just in time to hear Doug laugh in the hallway.

Until I'd heard him laughing, I hadn't really given any thought to what I would do if I saw him. The image of Doug in a laundry room was so foreign that I hadn't been capable of picturing it. After all, he'd already broken up with me. What other reason could he have for entering such a room? I consider trying to stuff myself into the one empty dryer, but decide against it. Damn, this place is lit up brightly. Who needs this much light to do laundry? I consider standing next to the wall to try to blend in to the surroundings, but even Doug, who appears to have perfected the art of ignoring me, is likely to notice me here. Then suddenly, I see it. On the back wall there is a large (white, of course) industrial sink, and below it is a shelf stacked with white cotton muslin laundry bags. I dive to the floor, pull the bags out, and tuck myself in, then pull the bags back over me.

The door opens and Doug walks into the laundry room. He's talking to some blonde woman who looks like she's a model for a catalog targeted to impossibly tall Swedish women with melon-sized breasts. She laughs—*shrieks*, really, at something Doug must have said, and her teeth look like evenly spaced white Chicklet gum. I hate her.

"Oh, Douglas, you have such a wicked sense of humor!" She punches him playfully on the arm and I consider punching her, playfully of course, right in those perfect teeth. *Who calls him Douglas? He hates to be called Douglas, except apparently, by tall, blonde, melon-breasted models.*

"I just call 'em like I see 'em," Doug says, giving his "aw, shucks" grin. He's holding his laundry basket, *our* laundry basket. When did he take that? I bought it at Winners. It's a knockoff of an expensive designer laundry basket. It's not important that it's a faux designer. The point is, I like that laundry basket. I don't remember it being in his pile of divided things when he moved out. The bastard must have sneaked back into the house to take it! He has been sneaking in and out of our house! I feel violated. How *dare* he slink in and out of our house. What else has he taken? I've got to remember to call a locksmith tomorrow. If he thinks he can just come and go simply because he pays for some of it, he's got another think coming. I long to tell him off right now and snatch that basket right out of his smug little hands, but I'm hiding under his laundry room sink and I expect he would want me to explain that fact first.

"Why don't you call me later?" Melon Tits says, as Doug pulls his laundry—minus the one-half of his socks that are in my handbag—into the stolen laundry basket. I see him flush at the neck. Melon Tits has gone too far. Now Doug will tell her that he prefers to be called Doug, not Douglas. And that he's just out of a very serious long-term relationship. And that his heart is broken, that he's not sure if he's over me, and that he's seriously considering us getting back together. And that he dislikes pushy women and that she needs to just back off.

"I think I'll save myself the call and just ask you out to dinner now," Doug says, trying to look cool by leaning against the dryer. Who is he kidding? Melon Tits laughs and flips her hair. She has on a matching gym outfit that looks like it's designed for the red carpet rather than for actually sweating. I mean who works out without a sports bra and she's not wearing one—sports or otherwise. I'm trying to give her the benefit of the doubt; maybe all her bras are in the wash, but I have my suspicions. She's actually licking her lips now, like this is an audition for a porno. "Of course, you probably already knew I was going to ask you that," he adds. She gives him another playful shove and I consider how it would feel to give *her* a playful shove off Lions Gate Bridge.

"Are you making fun of me?" She flips her hair again. I'm shocked she hasn't developed carpal tunnel syndrome with all that hair flipping. You would think her wrists would give out or that she would have developed weird-looking, bulky arm muscles. "I shouldn't have told you that I see psychics. Now you think I'm crazy." I nod to myself. *Go ahead, Doug, tell her she's crazy. Then run away. Run home, in fact.*

"No, I don't think you're crazy. I imagine there's a lot more to the psychic phenomena then we know. I've thought about going to a psychic before. If you're going to that psychic fair this weekend, you'll have to ask them about me and what I should do with my life."

"You've got yourself a deal," she says. Doug is smiling and I suppress the urge to throw the ant trap that is pressing into my head at him, right into his leering smile. I am most likely breathing in deadly ant poison right now, while my boyfriend woos another woman. There are tears in my eyes, and I concentrate on trying to suck them back into my eyes by will alone. I refuse to cry over this. She pulls her laundry out of the dryer, including the leopard-print thong and matching bra. I should have known. She pulls each item out of the dryer slowly, making sure Doug gets a good look. All that's missing is some bump-and-grind music to do her dirty laundry dance to. Poor thing has to put up with the hip-hop music leaking in from next door. Honestly, she has more fancy underwear than a Victoria's Secret store. Where are her fat-day undies with the broken elastic? She must wash those in the sink in her apartment. She saves her trashy underwear peep show for the public laundry room. Doug is practically drooling onto his clean shorts and T-shirts.

"So . . . back to dinner. Where do you want to go?" she asks.

"I'm open. Do you like seafood? We could go for a walk in

Stanley Park and then head over to the Fish House." I would
like to point out here that when I said I wanted to go to the
Fish House for *our anniversary*, Doug said it was too fussy
and expensive. Apparently, for laundry dates it's the perfect
place to go. Melon Tits folds her bits and pieces of string she
uses as underwear into dainty piles in her real designer clothing basket.

"I *love* the food there," M.T. gushes. "Have you had their
crab cakes? Yum. I don't eat red meat, you know. I'm a nut for
organic veggies, and the chef there does a super-tasty veggie
grill thing." The Melon touches Doug's arm and they walk out
of the laundry room.

I think I'll continue to lie under the sink for awhile. It's
sort of nice and quiet here. The cotton muslin laundry bags
smell like Bounce dryer sheets. I love that smell. If it weren't
for the ant poison seeping directly into my brain, I could
lie here all night. Suddenly, the sock mission of Operation
Drive Him Home seems pointless. The reason Doug suddenly
needed his own space is now crystal clear: He couldn't fit both
me *and* the Melon into his life. With those breasts of hers,
there simply wouldn't be room for me. He's clearly looking
for a new adventure. It's not like I'm unattractive, I'm just sort
of all-around average: average height, average brown hair,
and average-sized boobs. My hair is curly, which everyone
says they want until they realize that *curly* is just a nice word
for *uncontrollable*. As a curse from my Irish heritage, my
nose and cheeks are covered with freckles. I used to try to
cover them with makeup, but then I realized I would need
foundation caked an inch thick to hide them. Even if I stuffed
my Wonderbra I wouldn't be able to compete. I sniff a few

times and wipe my nose on one of Doug's socks. I am working myself into a proper cry when I notice a pair of shoes, connected to a set of legs right in front of me. I hadn't heard anyone else come in. I try to sniff quietly, but it's too late. This guy bends over and peers at me.

"Are you okay?" This strikes me as a stupid question, so I choose not to justify it with an answer. "Do you need me to call someone?" he asks. He's got a slight Scottish accent that makes the words run together in such a soothing way that it makes me want to close my eyes and go to sleep. However, he clearly isn't going to go away and leave me to my slow, ant-poison-to-the-brain suicide plan—he's going to keep talking until I respond. I crawl out from under the sink and take a few deep breaths. I rub my right temple and can tell the ant trap made a round dent in my skin. Perfect. Now in addition to my emotional scars, I have a physical one.

"No, thanks, I'm fine."

"You're fine?" he repeats. Apparently he has some kind of hearing difficulty. I notice he's cocking his head to the side like a confused dog.

"Yep, fine. I was just doing some laundry, and had all these socks that had lost their mates—you know how that happens?" He nods. "These socks have had mates for years and years. They were living their day-to-day lives, not suspecting that anything was going to change—then *wham*, they find themselves coming out of the dryer all alone. I mean, what good is one sock? Now that they are mateless, they've got nothing. You might as well dump them in the trash." I toss a wad of Doug's socks into the trash, but then can't bear it and grab them back again. He hands me a pressed linen handkerchief. I don't know anyone who carries these things anymore except old men, but he's not old. Maybe midthirties. He's a bit shorter than me and wears thick-rimmed Buddy Holly glasses that make his blue eyes stand out. I blow my nose in his handkerchief and start to hand it back to him, then realize he probably doesn't want it back coated in crazy lady snot.

"Are you sure you don't want me to call anyone? I could walk you back to your apartment if you'd like."

"I don't live here," I say before I realize it doesn't sound too good. Now he's going to think I'm some crazy lady with a sock fetish who has broken into the building, which, technically speaking, I might be. "I was just visiting a friend," I offer.

"I'm Nick McKenna. I'm on the tenth floor."

"Sophie Kintock." We shake hands, and it's all very civilized except for the fact that he met me crying into a wad of socks. "Well, I guess I should be going." I try to give him what I hope looks like a confident smile and head for the door. I glance back and see him standing there holding his laundry basket watching me. I notice that he was the khakis and cotton dress shirts owner. At least he knows to sort his colors.

I leave the apartment building and slip down the alley to my car. It's starting to rain, or rather, the rain is resuming. I drop Doug's socks along the alley, one every few meters, a cotton trail back to the building. I hang on to the last one. I don't know why. I tell myself that no matter how depressed I get, I will not sleep with his sock like some kind of sad, twisted memento of our relationship. But at the same time, I want to keep it. The night wasn't a total waste. Tomorrow he'll still have to go to the meeting in mismatched socks.

Two

AQUARIUS
A close friend tells you information you don't want to hear. Be
willing to listen and keep an open mind.

"Doug has another girlfriend?!" Jane asks, holding a Starbucks
venti nonfat latte in one hand and pushing a behemoth SUV
of a stroller in the other. Her two-year-old son Ethan rolls back
and forth inside as Jane makes an effort to convince him to go
back to sleep. The mini-Hummer of a baby carriage barely fits
in the store where I work and looks capable of summiting Ever-
est. None of this, however, impresses Ethan, who is concentrat-
ing on thrusting his two-year-old body against the restraints in
a bid to escape. Me, I *dream* of being pushed around in a giant
La-Z-Boy while shopping, but no such luck.

"I knew something was up when he left. He was looking to
meet someone else. He's been bewitched by that creature. Poor
guy probably never knew what hit him. I'm telling you, he was
totally hypnotized by those giant breasts. Everywhere I looked,
there they were." I smile at a customer entering the store. "Let
me know if I can help you find anything," I call out.

Stack of Books, where I work, is known in today's book market as a niche store. We specialize in hard-to-find, obscure books. If you're looking for something that's out of print, or has approximately ten copies available in the entire world, then we're your salvation. In today's giant-box bookstore market, even *that's* not enough, so we're also in the research business. We take requests on everything, from a designer wanting to know more about Victorian dining rooms, to a student needing to hunt down a copy of a First Nations land treaty for a paper, to government officials looking to find a quote that will work perfectly in their next speech. If it hadn't been for the research, I probably wouldn't have gotten this job. Every so often it comes in handy to have changed my major in school about half a dozen times. I know a little about a lot; it's a wide, but very shallow pool of knowledge. It's not a high-powered career, but then again I have a degree in English literature, which doesn't exactly qualify me for a high status corner office in the financial district. My dad used to argue that I should major in something that would lead to a job. Didn't I know that the English factory was laying people off? Har-de-har. A real funnyman, my dad.

The store is small, very small, smaller than the dorm room Jane and I shared in college. The two side walls are lined—floor to ceiling—with books. Judith, who owns the place, had wooden ladders installed with slide rails so that you can reach the upper shelves. A few years ago I helped Judith refinish a couple of old wooden tables that now sit in the middle of the room, stacked with books. Along the back wall is our "office," an L-shaped counter with an antique cash register, and a state-of-the-art computer for client records, inventory, and Internet searches. A pot of tea is on all the time, and the regular customers have learned to help themselves. I spend my days selling books and looking things up in our collection of research texts or online. For a book nut, it's pretty much a dream job. I get paid to track down the strangest pieces of trivia—it's like living in a crossword puzzle. Judith is a great boss. She doesn't care if Jane comes in and hangs out as long as the customers get what they need.

"So, have you made him get his junk out of the house?" Jane asks. She pulls open her purse to find a snack for Ethan. At any given time she carries around enough food to lay out a full buffet at an Italian wedding. She's got Tupperware full of Cheerios, juice boxes, grapes (cut in half to avoid choking), a baggie full of animal crackers, graham crackers, sandwiched peanut butter, and some raisins that look like they have been buried in the bottom of her bag since her first child, Amanda, was born five years ago.

If you had told me during college that Jane would be a stay-at-home mom, I would have laughed until beer came out my nose. Jane was the one who taught me to drink martinis, had her hair died ebony black to match her eyeliner, and blew these amazing smoke rings with her clove cigarettes. She'd planned to move to New York and be a fashion designer, but gave it all up for home and hearth. You'd think it would have made her bitter, but Jane's one of those people who actually *likes* her life. She and Jeremy got married right after graduation.

Jeremy got a job with a high-tech company out in Vancouver, and the two of them moved a few weeks after their wedding. I was living back home in Traverse City, Michigan, waiting tables, which is about the extent of jobs that are available to people who have a degree in English literature. Turns out my ability to analyze great literary works was not in demand. My dad mentioned this frequently. He was trying to get me a job in the customer service department of the insurance company where he worked. Waiting tables was boring to me, but it felt like an "in-betweener" job, a job meant to be a pit stop before going on to do greater things. Answering phones all day, talking to people who were desperately trying to understand their insurance policy felt like signing on to a permanent position in purgatory. Rather than face that reality, I ran away to Vancouver to visit Jane and Jeremy. Once I got here, it hit me. If Jane could live here, so could I.

I'd always wanted to live in Europe, someplace exotic like London or Paris. However, Canada had several key advantages: it wasn't too far; I already had a friend who lived there; they speak English (although with an admittedly funny sort of accent); it's a safe country; the cost of living wouldn't require me to sell off my own organs; and perhaps most valuable, I had a job offer that didn't require me to ask who ordered the soup. Despite the fact that everyone thinks of Canada as just like America but cleaner, it's actually a pretty interesting place, and it still does count as a foreign country. I lead everyone back home to believe the place is crawling with Canadian cultural icons, Mounties, wild bears, moose, snow, and mountains. This is not technically 100 percent true. I've never seen a bear or moose, but I have seen snow and mountains. The Mounties hardly ever wear those dreamy red uniforms (perhaps someone figured out target red was a poor choice for law enforcement) but you can't have everything.

When I visited Jane and Jeremy in Vancouver, I fell in love

with the place. It wasn't how I imagined Canada to be. I'd had in mind a sort of snow-filled vista, complete with dog sleds and attractive burly men in lumberjack outfits. I figured there would be a lot of maple syrup, bacon, and pudgy people wearing plaid wool hats with ear flaps. The first shocker for me was that Vancouver wasn't cold. I'd just assumed all of Canada was cold. Honestly, do you ever see pictures of Canada when it isn't covered with snow? As it turns out, Vancouver is on the west coast and has the same weather as Seattle—mild, with sufficient amounts of rain to make you wonder if you're living in Atlantis.

The city looks like a Disney theme park. It has clean, gleaming high rises with a public transportation system called the SkyTrain, which is your basic Disney monorail. Plus everyone is Disney-employee nice, smiling, excusing themselves if they bump into you, and generally looking like at any time they'd like to pause and break into a rendition of "It's a Small World." Even though it was unnaturally clean and friendly, it was still a real city, complete with trendy boutiques, designer stores, Chinatown, theatres, a hockey team, and restaurants that serve every kind of food you can imagine. For a girl who grew up in a small town that practically declared a civic holiday when a new fast food restaurant opened, it was amazing.

Moving here wasn't all learning to like hockey and sushi; there were pesky differences between Canada and America I hadn't counted on. For one, Canada actually uses the metric system. In seventh grade my math teacher tried to instill fear into our hearts that America would surrender its comfort with gallons, feet, and pounds for the tidy, precise metric option. We snorted with laughter, confident that our country would never let logic rule over familiarity. Canada, apparently, did not share our values and changed their system in one fell swoop. One day they were driving around at so many miles per hour and the next it was all kilometers and centipedes or something like that.

My first day in Vancouver I trooped down to the local grocery store to find that everything weighed amounts in terms that meant nothing to me. Prepacked items weren't *too* complicated, after all I just had to look at the size of them to make a guess, but the deli counter presented problems. Behind the glass were mounded piles of lunch meat all priced per one hundred grams. I had no idea how much a gram might be, let alone a hundred of them. A hundred of anything sounded like a whole lot to me. When my number was called I stepped up and requested twenty-five grams of the turkey breast. The deli clerk raised one eyebrow asking if I was sure. I could hear one of my fellow shoppers snicker. There was no way I was going to admit that I didn't know what I was doing.

I tried to look like a huffy shopper who was not used to being questioned by someone in a hairnet. The clerk shrugged and using her clear plastic tongs, peeled one slice of turkey off the pile and placed it on the wax paper covering the scale. She looked at the measurement, picked it up again, and tore it in half. She measured again and then wrapped it up carefully in the deli paper and slid it across the counter, asking if I needed anything else. I slunk home, made a conversion table on my computer, and carried it everywhere for three years.

Eventually Vancouver became my home instead of an exotic locale. I now know my way around the confusing mix of one-way streets. I know the best places to buy sushi, Thai peppers, homemade cranberry scones, and funky handmade jewelry. I've started to say "eh" like a native. Sometimes I feel like an undercover agent—no one looking at me or meeting me for the first time would know I wasn't a Vancouver native. No one seems able to tell that I don't quite fit in. At least, I don't think they can. Besides, if I'm being honest, I haven't felt like I fit in at any point in my life, so why worry now?

Jane and Jeremy didn't seem concerned about fitting in. They had their kids here, which I guess technically makes them part Canadian. Jane went from a martini-drinking party girl to looking like an ad for a Land's End catalog. She's got two kids, has the words to *Goodnight Moon* memorized, and makes homemade soup—no recipe required. Even more annoying, she and Jeremy are the perfect couple. He brings her flowers every Thursday and they drop the kids with a sitter on Fridays so they can have a date night. Jane has the metabolism of a ferret and eats whatever she wants. A few years ago she took up Boxercise and now has the defined arms you see on female action heroes. She quit smoking years ago and is now annoyingly devoid of irritating habits. I would hate her if she weren't my best friend in the whole world.

She and I munch on Ethan's Cheerios, while he focuses his energy on trying to mash grape halves into his hair. I know she wants me to say that I've told Doug to get all of his things out.

"No, I don't want to do anything too quickly. I think once this puffed-up breast fascination gets out of his system, he's going to want to come back," I announce, tossing O's into the air and catching them in my mouth.

"Do you think it's a good idea for you to be counting on that?"

"Well, I don't plan on just giving up. You know how long

we've been together?" I pause dramatically. "*Forever*, that's how long. You know how Doug is, he hates change. Remember how he dragged his feet on us moving in together?"

"That's what I mean. Doug has always been a bit commitment-phobic. Maybe it's time to move on."

"Easier said than done. It's ugly out here. I'm thirty-one. If I have to start over, date, filter through the losers, decide on, and acquire someone else, I'll never make it. Can you even imagine how long it would take to find someone else I liked and then begin another relationship? At that point, I might as well admit that I'm never going to settle down. Starting over is the same as giving up, and I am not a quitter. Doug and I are perfect together. He's just having a case of the whimwhams . . . nerves." I look at her carefully, and it occurs to me that most of the fights I've had with Jane over the past few years have been about Doug. "You don't think Doug and I belong together, do you?"

She rolls her eyes. "I have nothing against Doug. He's a nice guy. I just think you two want different things. You're attracted to Doug because he's everything you wanted—stable home life, stable job. He *knows* he's stable, and he's terrified that stable means boring. It doesn't make him the wrong guy, just the wrong guy for you." Ethan lets out one of those yells that only toddlers are capable of—high, shrill, and on the brink of shattering glass. "Listen, I've got to get the kid home. We need to pick up Amanda from preschool." She gives me a hug and then moves toward the door.

I have an urge to beg her to stay. I don't want to be alone. The thing I miss most about Doug being gone is having company. Not that Doug and I stayed up into the wee hours in deep philosophical conversations—he was usually busy watching sports—but it was nice having him around. When I would read something funny I could look up and share it with someone. Laughing in an empty house sounds sad. Last night I played an old Air Supply CD while crying into the sock I stole. I'm considering naming it. While the sock *has* been a nice emotional tampon, it doesn't make for great conversation. It's not like I can take the sock out on dates.

Jane is trying to steer her humungous stroller out the front door, and a customer on his way in helps her out. He walks in and stops when he sees me. He looks familiar, but I can't place him for a second. Then it comes to me: It's the same guy, Nick, from the laundry room. My stomach does a slow roll and I find myself touching my temple to see if the ant-trap mark is still there.

"Wow. Fancy meeting you again," I manage to say. He looks at me with wide eyes. Maybe it's just his glasses, but I don't think so. "Sophie Kintock," I offer, in case he's blocked the entire incident from his mind. A girl can hope, after all.

"Yes, of course. I'm glad to see you're feeling better."

"Oh, yeah, back on my medication again—world of difference," I say, laughing until I realize he doesn't think I'm joking. He's being careful to leave a clear path for himself to the door. "Just a hysterical woman joke there," I explain. I clear my throat and decide to skip being amusing and go straight to professional. "What can I do for you? Are you looking for a particular book?"

"Yes and no. I'm looking for a book, but also for some assistance with research. One of my colleagues at the university gave me the name of this place." He looks around a bit distrustfully, as if his colleague had sent him astray on purpose in a diabolical plot to destroy his academic standing.

"Sure, We do a lot for instructors." You could tell he was a professor. He had the look: glasses, complete with fingerprints in the corner of the lenses; leather briefcase stuffed to the max, and pens sticking out of his shirt pocket. You would swear they all shopped at some kind of uniform store for the academically inclined and fashion challenged. But you could also tell that with a makeover, he would be *dreamy*. For now, though, he's doing a great impression of Clark Kent. I pull out our research binder that contains blank forms. "What do you teach?"

"Statistics."

"Ugh, I hated math in school."

"Not math—statistics," he says, smiling, as if there were a difference anyone but the most geeky would consider. It is a good thing he's got that smile-and-accent thing working for him. I can't imagine his math skills are a chick magnet.

"I hope you aren't looking for any kind of math research. Excuse me—*statistical* research."

"No. I'm looking for information on a psychic."

I look him over: curly dark hair, khaki pants in need of pressing, and I decide he's cute, in a rumpled, smart-boy kind of way, but that he doesn't look like the type to be interested in psychics.

"You're into psychics? I wouldn't think stats and psychic mumbo jumbo would mix."

"No, I'm a member of CSICOP, the Committee for Scientific Investigation of Claims of the Paranormal. We're a group of skeptics. Scientists, mostly. We investigate paranormal claims. We look for logical explanations to what's portrayed as extraordinary. I'm working on an article on psychics for our newsmagazine. In particular, I'm writing about a fellow named Gary Krull, who just came out with a book."

"Let me guess . . . that's the book you're looking for?"

"It's called *Connections*. It became a moderate bestseller, and his popularity has grown as a result. He has a half-baked syndicated column that appears in the paper, 'Lost but Not Forgotten.' He's doing the upcoming psychic fair. I'm hoping to investigate him a bit further, since he's right here in my own backyard."

"How do you know he's not really psychic?"

Nick rolls his eyes as if I had asked how he knew the tooth fairy wasn't real. "I don't know for a fact, but I have more information to lead me to believe that he's a fake than I do to believe he's a true psychic. A member of CSICOP offers one million dollars to any individual who's willing to demonstrate their psychic skills under controlled scientific conditions. That offer has been open for years, but so far no one's claimed it. Krull hasn't even tried. Most psychics rely on a few basic tricks. One is the general reading, sort of taking logical guesses based on visual cues and what the person tells you, and building on hits. The trick is to toss out enough general items that people start applying the information to their own lives."

"That sounds too easy. Isn't it possible that it works and that you just don't understand it?" I ask.

He sighs deeply. I get the feeling he spends a lot of time trying to convince people of this issue. "For what it's worth, simple tricks seem to work. People forget what was said that doesn't apply and remember only the things the so-called psychic got right." He looks at me. "I hope I haven't offended you. I tend to get a bit rabid on the subject."

"No offense taken. I've never been a big believer in magic."

"Just the tragic tale of mismatched socks?" He says with a half smile.

"So, what can we do for you?" I say, bringing him back to the matter at hand. I am slightly annoyed he would bring up the sock topic.

"I need to get some more background information on Krull. It's mostly sifting through press clippings. I'd do it, except that I won't have enough time before the fair this weekend."

"Your time crunch is our gain," I say as I write down what he wants to know. I do a quick check on our computer. "We don't carry *Connections*, but I can order it and have it by the day after tomorrow. If you could write down anything I've forgotten here." I pass the form across the counter. "When do you need the research by?"

"Is Friday asking too much?"

"No, but it'll cost you our rush rate."

"No problem." He writes all his contact information on the form. He uses his own silver fountain pen. I notice that he's put down every conceivable phone number, home, work, cell. I'm surprised he didn't provide GPS coordinates. When he leaves the store, it seems quieter. I decide I might as well get started on his research now. Maybe I'll discover something interesting, like how to put a curse on Melon Tits. A girl can dream.

The idea of going home after work and wandering around alone is almost too bleak to consider. I wonder if maybe I should go out to a movie, some kind of documentary or a girlie film, something that would make Doug scratch his eyes out. Whenever I'd pick a movie, he'd act like I was asking him to attend a fifteen-hour cinematic experience on the making of cheese. If something didn't blow up, get shot, have model-thin women undressing or morphing into Victoria's Secret–inspired aliens in the opening credits, then it wasn't Doug's kind of film.

I refuse to lie around all night feeling sorry for myself. I should take myself out to dinner, someplace nice, someplace expensive. I'll bring a book, something serious, and order a nice glass of red wine. The waitress will have to ask me several times for my order. I'll be so engrossed in my book that I won't hear her and we will both laugh over it. Other women, struggling to make conversation with the man across from them, will look over and admire my independent spirit. They'll be thinking about how lucky I am to be so confident and happy in my own company. The meal will be fantastic. I'll debate staying for dessert, but with great willpower, well on the way to being the new, thin me, will turn down the decadent treat and go to a movie instead. I'll see a documentary showing at the Fifth Avenue Cinema. It'll be a perfect night, the kind I would never have had if I were going home to make dinner for Doug. If he can move on, so can I.

Three

PISCES
Today's events will lead you to question your decisions—learn to trust yourself. Others will try to erode your confidence—listen to your inner voice, not the negative comments of others.

The restaurant is busier than I expected. *Who knew so many people went out to dinner on a Monday night? Don't these people have homes to go to?* I stand next to the hostess stand with my book under my arm. I chose *Pride and Prejudice*. I've read it about a thousand times. It's like visiting an old friend, and plus, it's literature. People see you reading Jane Austen and you look smart and classy. I'm willing to bet that Melon Tits hasn't read Austen. I strongly suspect that she doesn't read at all. She's obviously the kind of person who watches reality television. I, on the other hand, don't watch that junk. Okay, I've watched *some* reality shows, but only to laugh at how bad TV has gotten. It's not like I'm really into any of them. Okay, maybe *Project Runway*, but that's it. I've got my standards.

"Do you have a reservation?" the hostess asks. I can't think of what to say because I'm too busy focusing on how impossibly thin she is. If I held my book behind her back there's a good chance I could read the text right through her. My wrists are larger than her thighs. No adult person can be this small. She must be violating some kind of child-labor laws or else she's some kind of fashion pygmy. I'm surprised she could get a job in a restaurant; she's a walking ad for famine relief. It looks to me like she hasn't even been in the same room as food for a considerable period of time. I suppress the urge to offer to sponsor her.

"No, I don't have a reservation. I didn't think I would need one."

"Yes, well, I'll try and squeeze you in. How many in the rest of your party?"

"Uh, there is no rest of the party. It's just me." I hold my book up for her to see. I try to look worldly and smart, like a type of college professor who has spent the day educating our nation's young or who has finished a translation of an ancient manuscript.

"You're eating alone?" she asks, eyes widening. If her cheek-bones weren't jutting out of her face, her eyes would be at risk for tumbling out of their sockets and smacking onto the floor. She's looking at me like I've asked her to do something obscene with the vegetables.

"Yes, please," I say, lowering my voice. I'm starting to think that I may have been better off going to McDonalds, to hell with the diet. Ronald never acts as if eating a Quarter Pounder alone is a social faux pas. The hostess looks around for another staff member. She seems totally at a loss. You would think a high-caliber place like this would provide some training for their staff.

"Um, wait right here. I think we have a two-top you can

have." She looks around, confused. "I'll be right back." She smiles, but doesn't meet my eyes. She's acting like no one has ever come in here alone before. There must be other people who dine by themselves; you see it in the movies all the time.

I peer through the potted ferns into the main dining room. There isn't a single table with only one person occupying it. There are tables full of laughing couples, families, large groups of people who must be friends. Hang on—I breathe a sigh of relief—at the back there's a guy eating alone. I look closer. OH MY GOD! I spin around and try and catch my breath. Doug's sitting back there by himself. I debate about what to do. *Should I go up to him, smile, and say, "Looks like we're both alone tonight, care to join me?"* No, something sexier, like, *"Want some company instead of dinner?"* No, not my style. Maybe something more direct: *"We came here alone, we could go home together."* No, I couldn't carry that off. I'll just go to my table, sit, eat, and read like I imagined, pretend I didn't see him. Then, Doug, seeing my comfort with myself and the way other people are looking at me like a woman of mystery, will realize his mistake. He'll come to the table, bend down, and he'll stammer a bit. "Sophie," he'll whisper, "Ah, Sophie . . . I . . ."

Hang on. Who is that? Someone just sat down with Doug. He's not alone. Oh God, someone else is joining him. I am practically crawling through the ferns in order to get a better look. It's Melon, from the laundry room. They went out for dinner just last night! *Two nights in a row?* What, is she incapable of cooking? He leans over and kisses her on the cheek. I can hear him call her "Melanie" as he hands her flowers. He never buys flowers. He says they're a waste of money, since they just die. Makes me wonder why he spends money on beer since he just pisses it away.

Oh god. He and this Melanie creature are going to see me eating alone. I won't look like an intellectual woman of mystery, I'll look like someone who couldn't find anyone to go to dinner with, except for a book she's read a hundred times before. I'm leaving. I don't need this. The whole thing was a mistake. He hasn't seen me, so I'll just slip out and pick up some Thai food.

Ahh! He's looking over here! I drop to my knees. He can't see me down here. Everything's fine, I think. He couldn't have seen me. I would've been just a glimpse of a face through the ferns. There's no way that he would suspect it was me. I'll just stay down here for a moment, long enough for him to get distracted, and then I'll leave. No problem.

Crap. Famine Girl's bony ankles, above shoes that surely cost more than my monthly salary, are right in front of me. I look up and see that she's holding a menu in her skinny arms.

"Miss? Your table is ready." I think she is trying to act like I'm not down on my hands and knees in front of her hostess stand. If she was ill prepared for a woman who wants to eat alone, she must now be totally at a loss with what to do with one crawling around on the floor. I am quite certain that most food-service training programs do not cover this topic. "Is everything all right, Miss?" She looks around for reinforcements.

"Yes, of course. Everything's fine. I, uh, just dropped my book." I hold it up.

"Oh, okay." She stands there for a moment but I remain on my knees. "Um, do you need some help getting up?"

"No," I say, trying to appear offended. "I'm fine. I just want to take a moment to, uh, pray. You don't have anything against someone who likes to pray before a meal, do you?" I clasp my hands together and bow my head. I suspect the hostess is wondering that if she ran for it I could chase her down before she reached the safety of the kitchen. "Look, maybe it would be best if I left. Can you get the door?"

She nods, a little overenthusiastically, and steps carefully around me to hold the door open. I crawl out on my hands and knees with as much dignity as I can muster. Very little, as it turns out. Once outside, I stand up quickly and move away from the restaurant's windows. I lean against the brick wall and breathe deeply. That was close.

I open my eyes and I see it. Doug's Mercedes, parked right in front of the restaurant. Across the street is a tow-away zone. I suddenly decide to believe in destiny, karma, direct messages from God, whatever you want to call it. So much for being practical—now is the time to put your faith in a higher power. I close my eyes and ask God for a message, a sign. I shake my handbag, and hear them in there—Doug's extra set of keys rolling around at the bottom of the bag with my own. I shake the bag again. The keys give another satisfying clank in the bottom of my bag. Operation Drive Him Home is morphing into Operation Teach Him a Lesson.

I think things happen for a reason. And that reason is pure, glorious revenge. Really, I have no choice; we're talking divine intervention. I jump into the car and rev up the engine.

I move the Mercedes across the street, park it, and get out. As I start to walk away, I risk taking a look behind me to see a traffic cop pull up next to Doug's car. He's already on his little shoulder radio calling in a tow truck. Perfect. I give him a small wave and skip down the street toward the theater.

Four

ARIES

The answer to a problem you've been working on will present itself today in an unexpected way. Find a way to pamper yourself;
you have a sensitive side that deserves special care.

I plan to get to work early so I can get started on the research
for Nick. (That, and the fact that I can't sleep because I keep
worrying that Doug saw me last night and is planning to have
me arrested this morning for harassment.) I was planning to
have a hard-boiled egg for breakfast, but all this worry has
made me hungry. I'll get back on my diet this afternoon, I tell
myself, but for right now I think I'll make an apple crisp. After all, apple crisp has all kinds of breakfast ingredients in it:
apples, oatmeal, and butter, which *is* a form of milk. See?
Fruit, fiber, and dairy. It's very balanced, when you get right
down to it. I take a shower while it's in the oven and by the
time I dry my hair, the smell of baking apples and cinnamon
fills the house. I scoop up a big plate and turn on the morning
news.

The weather forecast calls for more rain. The government is over budget. Traffic is bad. I swear, sometimes the news is exactly the same no matter what day you watch it. I pull Mac, my Scottish terrier, onto my lap. He's not known for snuggling. He's a more independent-minded dog. He likes affection, but on his own terms. Doug used to say Mac was more cat than dog. I believe he meant this to be an insult.

I'm ready to give up on the apple crisp, after eating roughly half of the pan. The secret to successful dieting is knowing when you have had enough. For lunch, I decide to bring my hard-boiled egg. The news ends and the cheerful morning announcer starts listing what activities and events are coming up. He mentions the psychic fair and I look up in time to see a photo of Gary Krull. He's a nondescript guy. He doesn't look like a psychic: no black cape, no wizard hat. He looks a bit effeminate, if you ask me, like he spends a significant amount of money on mustache-grooming and other hair products. Never trust a man who overmousses. Gary looks boringly normal with the exception of his hair fascination. Heck, *I* look like more of a psychic than he does. I wonder if Nick is right, that this guy *is* a fraud. From the little I've already read, it seems frightfully easy to fake psychic abilities. I wonder why Melon goes to a psychic. Advice on her love life? Do you need advice on love with breasts that size? Maybe a psychic told her she was going to meet the man of her dreams, so she focused in on Doug. All I need is for a psychic to tell her to drop him and I'll be all set. I sit up so fast the pan of apple crisp hits the floor. Mac jumps down to take advantage of the unexpected feast.

This is a ridiculous idea. I can't believe I'm even considering it, although there's no harm in just thinking about it. I'm pacing up and down in the living room. I make a list of the pros and cons of the idea. Faking psychic ability:

Cons:

- Is a lie

- Don't know how to do it

- Could get caught, resulting in certain humiliation

- Stooping to deceit in order to get Doug back is beneath me

- If it takes trickery to get Doug back, this might not bode well for the relationship

- Might not work

- May be illegal

- If it *is* illegal it could result in jail time stuck with roommate named "Stella," who would force me to be her girlfriend and give her bunion-coated feet foot rubs during lights-out. Will have to wear bland prisonwear and eat high-carb, tasteless food resulting in weight gain until I resemble a lumpy, shapeless potato. Once released from prison will be deported from Canada and have my "Canadian Girls Kick Ass" T-shirt taken from me. Will be forced to return to Michigan, and Dad will get me job as a janitor with his insurance company, as convicted felons can't work in customer service.

Pros of faking psychic ability:

• May get Doug back if it works

• Weight and exercise room in prison could inadvertently turn me into rock-solid, lean, mean babe if it doesn't work

Well, there you have it in black and white. The situation really couldn't be any clearer. The list has spoken.

Five

You find yourself fighting for what you believe in today. The way the cookie crumbles can teach you a lesson if you pay attention.

I have now left three frantic messages for Jane. She calls herself my best friend, but where is she in my hour of need? I'm at work, chewing down my thumbnails. I used to chew all my fingernails but broke myself of the habit years ago. Now I restrict myself to thumbnails only. I think this shows my great restraint. I've been on the computer all morning, making reams of notes. It's not really shirking work. Technically, all this research could be useful for Nick, as well.

When I see Jane in the window with Ethan on her hip, I run out to the sidewalk to meet her.

"Where have you been?! I've been calling you all morning!" I shriek. Jane backs up a step, thinking I've lost it. Ethan is looking at me with that wide-eyed kid look, as if I just stabbed his teddy bear. His lower lip pooches out and he starts to cry. Jane bounces him up and down on her hip.

"Why don't we go inside and you can tell me what's up?"

she says, using her soothing, calm-the-crazy voice that mothers of toddlers have perfected. She puts Ethan on the floor and pulls a few plastic Happy Meal toys out of her bag. She starts the tea kettle and gets the teacups out. "Okay, what's the problem?"

"No problem. It's perfect, in fact. I've figured out how I can get Doug back. His new girlfriend believes in psychics, right? I told you that, right? So she's going to be at that psychic fair this weekend. I'm going to go and tell her that it's her destiny to leave Doug. That horrible things will happen to her if she doesn't. Plagues, boils, Botox-resistant wrinkles, premature breast sagging. Very bad things. I'll convince her that he belongs with his ex-girlfriend and that she needs to set the universe right." Jane is giving me a look like I'm not making sense, when clearly this is a brilliant plan. I've made diagrams outlining the whole thing. "She won't know I'm his ex-girlfriend—I'll be a psychic," I clarify.

"You think you're a *psychic* now? Have you been drinking?" Jane sniffs the air near my mouth. I push her back.

"No, I haven't been drinking, and *no*, I don't think I'm a psychic. Pay attention! I'm only going to *pretend* to be a psychic. I've been reading up on it all morning. I can do this. I'll find out some information about Melanie—I already know a bunch of stuff—and then I'll do a reading for her, telling her it's her destiny to reunite Doug and his ex."

Jane is giving "the look," the one she saves for the kids when they have done something particularly nasty, like putting the cat in the dryer. She says she learned this look from her mother. When done correctly it can freeze a child in their tracks and is more effective than any high-volume yelling, and, unlike beating them, is completely legal. Instantly I feel about two inches tall.

"Uh-huh." Jane sits down next to me, and Ethan rushes over and climbs up her front like he is attacking a rock-climbing wall in a recreation center. Jane holds out her cup of hot tea, and never spills a drop, it doesn't even slosh in the cup. How does she do that? Does she have some kind of inner gyroscope that allows her to keep her balance? "You know, Sophie, I've known you a long time, over half my life, and no matter how long I've known you, no matter how many late-night talks, no matter how many times I've seen you in action—you always find some way to surprise me. Now back up and start at the beginning."

For a bright woman, Jane sometimes needs things spelled out for her. I lay the plan out in simple steps: Melanie believes in psychics. There is a psychic fair this weekend. All I need to do is be at the fair and manage to do a reading for her. I've been reading all this research on how psychics fake people out, and most of it seems to be simple tricks. I've got days to practice. I'll convince her that she needs to break it off with Doug, or I'll tell her to do all the things that I know drive him crazy. Either way, Doug and she break up, and Doug comes home. I forgive him, and everything goes back to normal.

I can tell Jane doesn't think it's a good idea. I base this on the fact that she has her face contorted as if I were offering a mystery item from the back of the fridge, like milk old enough to be toilet-trained. I'm already getting better at reading nonverbal cues, so I must have some natural talent for this. Jane used to be much more fun-loving. Ever since she became a parent, she's lost a lot of her devil-may-care ways.

"Okay, let's assume for a minute that this plan works, which, I have to be honest, I think is doubtful. Assuming it works and Doug comes home, why would you want him back?"

"What do you mean, why would I want him back? I love him."

"Do you love him, or the *idea* of him?"

"What's that supposed to mean?"

"I mean that since the moment you met Doug you always talked about how he was exactly what you'd dreamed of since you were a little girl. He was the very kind of guy that didn't even know you were alive in high school. When you guys moved in together, it was like the captain of the football team asked you to prom. Since then, you've arranged your whole life around what Doug wants."

"There's nothing wrong with trying to make the person you love happy." I sip my tea and try not to pout. This isn't going the way I planned.

"There is if it comes at your own expense." She looks out the window. "Remember how you didn't go to London last year when Judy offered to send you to that conference?"

I shrug. "You know how much Doug hates to fly. It would've been ten hours over there to see a bunch of old buildings and eat food that all tastes overboiled. It just seemed like a waste of time."

"That's what Doug thinks. You always talked about how great it would be to see London, and yet you didn't go, because he didn't want to go."

"Okay, you got me there. I didn't go because he didn't want to go—so what? We'll take a trip somewhere we *both* want to go to once we're back together."

"It's not just the trip, Sophie, it's everything. How long

have you been waiting for a wedding ring, to get married, to have kids? Doug doesn't want to settle down. He never has. I'm not saying he won't at some point, but certainly not now. It's not that he doesn't love you, but he never loved you the way you wanted him to."

I stand up with my mouth opening and closing. I can't believe she's saying this. "You never really liked Doug, did you? Well, to be honest he wasn't crazy about you, either. He thought you were pushy." I cross my arms over my chest.

"I don't care what he thinks of me. What I care about is that instead of moving on, you seem to be obsessed with getting him back."

"I'm not giving up."

"It's not a contest, Soph!"

"I know that. It's my life. It's easy for you to say I should just give up. What do *I* have then? You're married; you've got the perfect husband, perfect kids, perfect house in the 'burbs. I know you think you've done brilliantly with your life, but stop trying to micromanage mine. I'm going to do what I need to do." Ethan starts crying. Jane bends over and picks him up. We seem to have run out of things to say.

"I'm not telling you what to do. I was just trying to give you some advice." She puts Ethan in the stroller and looks at me. I hate when we fight, but I also detest this cool, I'm-just-giving-you-advice thing. Jane loves to hand out advice, but she's not one to take it. "Have you thought about the house?" she asks, breaking the silence.

"What about it?"

"Are you going to be able to afford it on your own?"

"Great, so now I've lost Doug and I'm going to be homeless.

This is a very reassuring conversation. We should do this more often." I turn away and rinse out my teacup in the sink.

"Don't be dramatic. I'm not saying you'll be homeless. I'm trying to think of the practicalities. Instead of worrying about Doug, you should be talking to the bank. Your name's on the mortgage, but Doug always covered the majority of the costs. He paid this month too, but how long is that going to keep up? Have you thought about how you're going to pay for it by yourself? I'm trying to help."

"I need him back. Help me with that, Jane."

"I don't think I can. I'm sorry." She wheels Ethan out the door. I hurl the muffin I'm holding against the wall and it falls to the floor in an explosion of crumbs. It will be impossible to pick them all up.

The pile of research documents is heaped on the desk. That's when it occurs to me: There may be someone else who can help.

Six

GEMINI

Be open to learning a new approach—the tried-and-true methods may need to be spiced up. Be on the lookout for someone who can be your mentor.

I park my car in the University of British Columbia's visitor lot, approximately one hundred kilometers away from the actual campus buildings. No wonder all the students look fit and trim, they have to hike a minimarathon from their cars to the classrooms. UBC doesn't look like a film setting of a college. It's sorely lacking in the ivy-covered brick buildings and is instead made up of modern glass and concrete. What it does have are views. It sits on the far west side of the city, jutting out into the ocean with the mountains and trees making a perfect backdrop. The main street of campus doesn't allow cars, it's filled with backpack-clad students in sweatshirts milling from building to building. On sunny days like today several of them are sitting on the lawns with their faces tilted up like baby birds. It's only March, but spring comes early to Vancouver.

Nick's office is located in the math building. It takes me a while to find it. Clearly, statistics professors do not qualify for corner office suites with a view. His office is down a dark narrow corridor. I have to stop to ask three students for directions in order to find it. His door has an engraved nameplate, NICHOLAS MCKENNA, PHD and is covered with cartoons from the *New Yorker* and the Far Side books. A few of them are funny, and others employ math humor that makes absolutely no sense to me. I hate jokes I don't understand. His door is cracked open, and when I knock, it swings wide.

His office is approximately the size of my hall closet. There's barely room for a desk, his chair, an unsteady-looking bookcase, and a tiny seat for a guest. One wall has a framed movie poster for *The Maltese Falcon*. The only way I can figure how they got the desk inside the office is by building it in there. There's a narrow window behind the desk, which is covered with papers and books. Clutter is something that clearly does not bother him. He looks up, and I can tell he's surprised to see me. His glasses slip down his nose, and he stands up, sits down, and then stands up again.

"Guess you weren't expecting me, huh?"

"Please, come in." He moves a pile of papers from the corner of the desk to the floor so he can see me. "Did you finish the research already? I would have come by to pick it up."

"Yep, I've got it here. There's a ton of stuff on the guy, but I just got the basics you were looking for. I didn't mind swinging by. Actually, I wanted to ask you some questions, and I thought it might be easier if I just dropped in."

"Certainly. No problem. I appreciate you getting this done so quickly. I stand in the presence of a master researcher. May I get you anything? We have coffee and tea in the main office."

I shake my head. He's really quite nice; I hope the kind of

nice that likes to help damsels in distress like myself. "I wanted to ask you about what makes people visit psychics."

He leans back in his chair and I can sense him slipping into lecturer mode. "People go for a number of reasons. The most common is for sheer entertainment value. They see it like a chance to peek into a Christmas present, to see what's in store for them. It's fun, a lark. They have a laugh or two. A smart psychic gives the person just enough information to make them more interested. Soon, some people find that they don't feel comfortable taking the next step unless they have an idea of what might be coming. The other reason's more bothersome to me: People who've had a loss, a death of someone in their life. If they feel they had unfinished business, they look for a way to make contact. They'll go to a psychic in the hopes of communicating."

"That's really sad."

"It's appalling. The psychic isn't really in touch with anyone or anything, except the customer's wallet. He'll toss out a bunch of platitudes and guesses. The person hears only what they want and they pay for the privilege of being taken advantage of."

"How are you so sure that the psychic isn't real? How do you go about investigating what they say?" I ask.

He leans back farther in his chair. I wait for it to tip over, but he's found the perfect balance point. "It's often not that hard if you're paying attention. Here, I'll show you." He leaves the room for a minute and comes back wheeling a TV on a trolley. It doesn't fit in the room so he parks it in the door, brushing past me to plug it in. I notice that he smells earthy and warm, like a cedar closet.

He slides a tape into the VCR. The video is of Gary Krull, the guy he has me researching. It's a video of a TV special where Krull's giving a psychic reading to a woman in front of what looks like a studio audience. He says he's talking to her husband who died. By the end of the tape, the woman's weeping and everyone in the audience is amazed. Frankly, so am I, and I don't usually go for these things. Nick hits pause on the tape.

"Now, what did Krull guess successfully?"

"Lots of things. He knew her husband died of cancer, that he was a big football fan, and that they used to fight over that. He knew the husband wasn't as affectionate as he should have been, and that she kept a picture of them close by." I sniff. It was quite sweet, actually.

"He didn't tell her any of those things." Nick crosses his arms over his chest.

"Yes, he did. I just watched him."

"Nope. Watch again. This time I'll pause it as we go." He rewinds the tape and starts it again. This time I see it. Krull opens with big generalities and lets the woman fill it in. Things like, she was there about a man, no? Her dad? No? Then she would shake her head and say it was her husband. Krull would latch on to that and go from there. Yes, he could see it was her husband now. Had he died quickly? She says no, it was cancer. Krull interrupts her to say that what he meant was, at the end, things went really quickly, and she agrees. He says her husband hated the hospital, but heck, who couldn't have guessed that? Krull guesses he liked sports, which—let's be honest—is also a pretty safe guess. He guessed basketball first. He was wrong more often than he was right, but you didn't notice when you watched him. I should take notes. Krull was slimy, but he was good.

"Amazing," I say when he stops the tape again.

"I guarantee if you ask the woman what Krull knew, she won't remember that she told him half of that information. She'll only remember that he knew all these remarkable things. He makes it sound like he just can't quite hear the voice from the afterlife, that he needs her help to understand. Did you notice when he would cock his head to the side like a dog who hears one of those supersonic whistles? It gives him time to read her body language and her response to what he's already said. Did you see how she would nod as he was tossing off guesses? That puts the pressure on the woman to help him out. That's how he knows he's on the right track. The smart psychics are natural people-watchers. They're also gamblers, they play the odds. A woman this age, crying before she even starts? You know there is a good chance this is about someone she lost—a father, a child, a husband. Remember how he says, 'I see a hospital'? That opening could be a million things, an illness, an accident. She fills it in for him."

"It sounds pretty easy."

"Like a lot of things, it looks easier than it is. But you're right. It's not very complicated. You have to come across as confident. More than half the battle is leading the person who's getting the reading to believe. You convince them that if you miss an important detail it's because they aren't doing their part."

"These people should have their heads examined."

"Maybe. Everyone believes in something, and a lot of people

want to believe in something special, so believing in psychics is easy. It's getting people to be critical thinkers that's hard."

"Do you think you could teach me how to do it?" I lean forward on the desk. He looks me in the eyes and frowns. I know he's hoping I want to be trained as a critical thinker, but he knows the truth.

"Why?" He sounds distrustful, and the story I had so carefully planned on the way over dries up on my tongue. This is one of those situations where the truth may be called for. It's a radical idea, but this is a high-risk kind of situation. And I can tell somehow that he's the kind of guy where truth may actually work. I take a deep breath and meet his gaze.

"What would you do if you were on the verge of losing everything you ever wanted? I don't want anything illegal or immoral, I just want to live happily ever after. I was almost there." I hold my thumb and finger up, almost touching. "I've got a chance to get it back, but I need your help."

"I'm not sure I understand. Can we start at the beginning? You want to learn how to fake psychic abilities because . . ." his voice trails off.

"Because I want my boyfriend back," I say. "He's dating a woman who believes in all this stuff. I want to give her a reading that tears them apart." He's giving me a quizzical look. I had high hopes that with his advanced education he would see the brilliance of the plan much sooner.

"You did understand the part where I explained that the group I belong to tries to discredit fake psychic phenomena? Training you to do it is a bit contradictory to our organizational values."

"I got that part. I can see where ethically, this presents you with a difficult dilemma."

"Can you clarify where the *dilemma* comes in? On one hand we have your idea, which is the opposite of everything we stand for, and on the other we have . . . ?"

"A matter of life and death. Generally speaking, most ethical codes allow for drastic measures in these types of cases."

"Life and death." He rubs his hand over his chin and taps his mouth. "I must have missed that part of the plan."

"My life. Death of my relationship. Serious stuff. The only person that this impacts would be his new girlfriend. Look at it this way: She already believes, so it's not like this plan moves a rational thinker over to the dark side. Not to mention that if this shakes her belief in psychics, it's a win for your side."

"Has it occurred to you there might be easier ways to win him back?"

I cross my arms and raise my eyebrows. *If he thinks he can come up with a better plan, let's hear it.*

He looks around the room for a moment. "Couldn't you just simply woo him back?"

"*Woo* him?" I ask. He nods. *This is the best he can come up with after a few decades of higher education?* I give a tired sigh. "I wooed. Trust me, I wooed for all I was worth. Wooing isn't going to do it."

He looks at me for a long moment. "You're not the type of woman who gives up easily, are you?" I can't tell if he admires this trait or sees it as a sign of deteriorating mental health. "You remind me of Katharine Hepburn—all business with a hint of trouble."

"I'm going to choose to take that as a compliment. So, do

you want to be my Spencer Tracy and get me out of the mess I'm in?" Wait. That almost sounded flirtatious. I change tactics and attempt to appeal to his scientific vanity. "The best part of the plan is that by helping me, you help yourself. You can write up the whole experience as an experiment, putting theory into action, so to speak. If you look at it that way, I don't know how you could pass up the opportunity."

"How very kind of you to think of me." He's smiling now, or it might be a smirk. "What makes you assume that if I help you, I have to get something out of it? Perhaps I would help from a misguided sense of chivalry."

"What makes you assume it would be misguided?" He laughs and stretches his arm across the desk to shake hands.

"I suspect I'll regret this decision, but you've got yourself a deal." I let out a squeal. To heck with the handshake. I lean over the desk and throw my arms around him, spilling piles of papers covered in formulas to the ground.

I leave with a huge smile on my face, practically skipping back to the car. Step one of the plan is in effect. Nick lent me a bag full of books and videos and we've set a date for training session number one. However, just to prove Jane wrong, that my head *isn't* always in the clouds, I've got a plan for the house, as well.

Seven

CANCER

You have to be willing to ask for what you want. Mixed messages should be avoided; clarify your intentions as soon as possible.

To: larrybeier@westcoastcreditunion.com
From: sophie@hotmail.com
Subject: Getting connected
Date: March 8, 2005

Hello:

I wanted to write to say thanks for all the kind things and "extra" customer service steps you and everyone at the bank take. I love how every teller stand has one of those pens attached by a little chain. I am impressed at how they are always full of ink, which is very handy when depositing a check. In all the years I've been visiting I don't remember ever coming across a dried-out pen. The chain also keeps people from putting it in their handbags by mistake. I know I almost did that once and the chain stopped me cold. I also have noticed that the deposit and withdrawal slips are always fully stocked in their little bins. Whenever I forget to fill in the date, the tellers do it for me without sending me to the back of the line for not fully completing the form. I appreciate how you mail out statements every month, even though until now I haven't taken the effort to write back. I happened to look through my statements today and have realized how much care and concern you have taken at keeping track of my money. I feel bad that I haven't taken the time to get to know you better before now, even though you have been assigned as my "personal" banker for several years.

I must admit that before today I wasn't aware that I even *had* a personal banker, but now that I know I am looking forward to getting to know you better. I imagine we might want to schedule regular lunch meetings where we can spend some time chatting and become good friends. Be sure to let me know your birthday and favorite color so I can make a note.

I imagine you have some kind of file about me there at the bank so you probably know lots already! You may not have heard that my boyfriend, Doug, and I are going through a "difficult" patch in our relationship. Are you married? As I'm sure you know, relationships go through these peaks and valleys. The important thing is to hang in there. Currently, Doug and I are not in agreement as to the best way to approach these difficulties. He may be considering selling our home, as he is unlikely to want to continue paying part of the mortgage now that he's moved out. Now, you and I know these kinds of major financial decisions should not be made lightly. What I was hoping you could do, as a favor for a friend, is to issue a statement saying that the bank has a hold, or some kind of financial restriction that would forbid us from selling the house. (I'll leave the exact reason up to you. I'm sure you can think of something.)

If this is not possible, would it be possible for me to refinance the house on my income alone? I have taken the liberty of crunching the numbers and think if we extended the mortgage from its current twenty-five years, to approximately seventy-nine, the payments would be low enough for me to cover on my own.

Looking forward to hearing from you soon. How about we get together for coffee?

Your friend,
Sophie Kintock

To: sophie@hotmail.com
From: larrybeier@westcoastcreditunion.com
Subject: Re: Getting connected

Date: March 8, 2005

Ms. Kintock,

Thank you for your kind comments about the service here at West Coast Credit Union. Everyone here sees customer service as a priority. I will pass your appreciation of the pens and stocked transaction slips on to the tellers.

I was sorry to hear about your current relationship discord, but regret that I am unable to issue a document from the bank forbidding the sale of your home. This would be considered *fraud*, and my manager would have a very negative view of me committing it on the bank's behalf. The bank does not have a current provision for a seventy-nine-year mortgage, although if you stop in I would be happy to meet with you to determine other options. As your personal banker, I am available to advise you on a range of financial services, including retirement, investment planning, and to how to lower your monthly banking charges. Feel free to call me and make an appointment at your convenience.

Sincerely,
Larry Beier

P.S. My birthday is July 16, my favorite color is blue, and yes, I am married. Thank you for asking.

To: larrybeier@westcoastcreditunion.com
From: sophie@hotmail.com
Subject: Re: Getting connected
Date: March 8, 2005

Larry—

I am in danger of losing my home. Do you really think that saving a few dollars on banking charges is going to help things? I wasn't asking you to commit "fraud," I was thinking of it more as a little white lie. I have to say I don't feel very supported by you; perhaps I should request that I be assigned to a different personal banker—one who is interested in my personal situation and who doesn't trivialize my concerns.

Ms. Kintock

To: sophie@hotmail.com
From: larrybeier@westcoastcreditunion.com
Subject: Re: Getting connected
Date: March 8, 2005

Does this mean you don't want to get together for coffee and chat?

Larry

Eight

LEO

Money troubles wear you down. The answers are out there, but
you have to be willing to seek them out. You may need a cooling-
off period before dealing with important issues.

Despite the fact that I never wanted to see Larry, my personal
banker with a wicked and slightly inappropriate sense of humor, I made an appointment. I needed to figure out exactly
where I stood. I had been the one keen on home ownership.
Perhaps as a warning sign of his commitment phobia, Doug
preferred renting. The housing market in Vancouver is completely insane. It requires a real commitment to get into the
market, like being willing to sell one of your own kidneys,
or killing off your parents for the life insurance money in order to make a down payment. Our parents were annoyingly
healthy and both of us were overly fond of our own kidneys. I
was reduced to reading the real estate sections of newspapers
like they were food magazines. I drooled over the pictures of
fully appointed kitchens and open floorplan kitchen/dining
rooms. We would go to open houses on the weekends and
dream about where we would put things if it was ours. Okay,

technically *I* was the one to go to the open houses. Doug felt stupid "tramping through people's homes."

Growing up I always lived in rented places; we moved every few years. I can think of nothing more comforting than owning my own house. Doug saw home ownership as less about stability and more about being locked down. I think he worried that as soon as he owned a place he would be offered something better or more exciting. However, Doug *was* interested in having more space and we figured it would be a good idea for me to have an investment. We agreed that if we could find something, we would put it in my name, but he would help cover the bulk of the payments.

I found our home by accident. Judith had asked me to drop some books off with an elderly woman who was a regular customer. When I did, she invited me into her home. It was the house time had forgotten. She must have last updated the place around 1966. The kitchen appliances were olive green. The carpets were made of six-inch-high shag; it practically tickled my knees as we walked through the room. The wallpaper had orange daisies the size of dinner plates. The woman had a *rotary phone*, I kid you not. The house was obviously getting to be too much for the woman to keep up. Her husband had died a year or two before. She wanted to move to be closer to her kids and grandkids, but she wasn't sure what to do about the house. I bought the house for a song. She thought Doug and I looked like a nice couple. I think she liked the idea of the two of us raising a family there the way she did.

The house is on the North Shore, just over Lions Gate Bridge from downtown Vancouver. The mountains begin on the North Shore, the houses clinging to the side. They look like they're at risk of sliding down into the ocean below. Even the air feels different compared to the city center; it's fresh and green. It feels like small town living right next door to a city. Buying the house in North Vancouver felt like graduating to grown-up status.

Now, it wasn't all fairy tales and romance. We ripped up the carpet before we moved in, but I had to live with that daisy wallpaper for over a year, so you can imagine the horror I felt when I peeled back the layer of daisy wallpaper to find yet another layer. This time, it was a sort of multicolored floral chintz, and it looked like someone threw up a garden on the wall. Below that, another layer, in a yellow stripe pattern. I started to fear I would keep peeling off layers until I was through the entire wall and staring into the backyard. I did most of the work myself. Doug isn't much for home chores. He likes the planning stages. He decks himself out in his "working guy" clothes. He takes elaborate measurements, and scribbles down complex NASA formulas before heading off to Home Hardware to purchase more supplies than would be required to build an entirely new house from scratch. He then pronounces himself done for the day and talks big about how he'll get down to it tomorrow. Invariably the following day there is some type of really big game or match that he's been waiting to watch—hockey, football, basketball, curling, or skiing. On one desperate occasion he tried to convince me he had been waiting all week to see this really big international dart championship. If all else fails, he sighs, rolls his eyes, and mumbles about working hard all week and just wanting a little break. It took me years to catch on, but now I just do it myself. He waits until I'm done, ambles in, and says something like,

"Geez, you should have called me. I could have helped." He says this with a straight face, as if he has been completely unaware of what I've been doing for the past two days.

All the work paid off though, and the house looks amazing. Martha Stewart would love it. I have truly made the house a home. My personal favorite touch? I took a small scrap of daisy wallpaper, framed it, and hung it in the kitchen. I'm telling you, people pay top dollar to fancy designers for original whimsical touches like that. Doug put his touches on the place, as well, mostly veto power over paint colors, an aversion to anything "too girly," and a passion for overstuffed leather furniture that looks like it was created for a family of giants. I don't want to move. I want to keep this house.

To achieve this, my banker, Larry, provide me with several options:

- Win the lottery

- Get a roommate, preferably someone like Doug who earns a large salary

- Ask for, and receive, a big, fat raise

- Consider a second . . . or third job

- Cut all my spending to the bone by eating on alternate days

- Refinance using the equity in the house, cash in my retirement savings to pay down the principal, and pray that the house continues to grow in value so that I don't have to subsist on dog kibble in my old age.

I bought a lotto ticket on the way home. After all, you never know, and you have to play to win. I didn't bother asking for the fat raise. I don't think I could bare the sound of Judith snorting and laughing before she realized I was serious. I like eating too much to give it up, and I dislike working too much to think of taking on another job. I did consider the idea of a roommate. To be honest, the only person I could stand to live with is Jane, who, despite the fact she might want to on some days, is highly unlikely to leave her husband and kids to bunk down with me. The other person I want to live with is, of course, Doug, who I am hoping will come to his senses and move back in—without Melanie. However, the bank and Mr. Larry "I can't commit bank fraud" Beier aren't willing to hold off on the house payments while we sort this out. This left me with the refinance option.

I felt awful cashing in my retirement accounts, like I had sold out my future. I tried to compare it to needing a costly organ transplant, a necessary evil. It felt like traveling back in time and seeing my mom scramble to pay the bills. I always swore that wouldn't be me. I was surprised to realize how easy it is to sell off what has taken me my entire adult life to save up. The point is, as horrible as it was, it's done. I've refinanced the house, which has me paying it off over the next thirty-five years with a payment schedule I can barely afford. The house is safely mine.

This is the first time I have completely relied on myself. When Doug and I work things out I'll take the money he puts toward the payment and double up on my retirement contribution. That should reduce my reliance on an elderly kibble intake. Besides, based on the dog food advertisements, the stuff is getting pretty tasty. Some of it even makes gravy when you add water.

Well. At least when I dine on kibble, it will be in my own home.

Nine

VIRGO
Surround yourself with peaceful colors and music. You've been
running around hectically—you need to create an environment
where you can take a break. Be prepared for an unexpected surprise.

The house is a disaster zone. There are piles of books and papers all over the dining room table. I'm sitting on the couch,
eating ice cream directly out of the carton. A spoonful for me,
and then one for Mac. I've got my bleach-stained sweatpants
on and my hair is pulled back with a headband that I've made
from Doug's sock. I've been working on a budget that cuts on
expenses so I can build my retirement account back up. Since
taking charge of my financial future, I feel empowered. If I
budget tightly, including buying food that is technically past the
expiration date, and knit my own clothing from yarn I make
using dog hair Mac has donated, I will be fine by retirement.

If the financial stress wasn't enough, I've been practicing
my psychic "skills" for what seems like every minute with
Nick. He's brought over tapes and more tapes of psychics and
made me read their various books, *Connections, Crossing
Over, Talking to Clouds*. We've done practice readings where

he imitates different people. He does a mean impression of a lovelorn teenage girl. He actually makes me laugh when he doesn't bore me with numbers. He's brought over sheets of demographic data and forced me to memorize common statistics so that I can make some safe guesses based on what I can tell about the person from first impressions. If I had studied this hard in college I would have earned a PhD.

The psychic fair is tomorrow, and I'm as ready as I'll ever be. The doorbell rings, and Mac lets out a single bark before going back to licking the side of the ice-cream carton. He's more of a lover than a fighter. If someone actually ever broke into the house, I doubt Mac would get up, unless the burglar had the poor sense to try to steal his treat jar. I open the door, and there stands Doug. I've dreamed of the moment when he would come back. However, I always imagined that I would be looking a bit better. I back away from the door. *Why did he have to come over now, when I look like something Mac dragged in from the yard?*

"Hey, Sophie. I'm sorry, I should have called." He's wearing one of his work suits. With his tie loosened, he looks slightly rumpled and utterly adorable.

"No, of course not. Don't be silly. This is your place, too." This is quite generous of me to say, seeing that technically, according to the bank, it's all mine. I try to project a winning smile. "C'mon in." Doug slips past me and walks into the living room. He lifts Mac to the floor and sits down on the couch. Mac is not amused, I've gotten quite lax in the no-dog-on-the-furniture rule since Doug left. Mac doesn't seem ready to go back to the floor. He furrows his giant, old man Scottie-dog eyebrows and fixes his look upon Doug, who is completely oblivious. I sit next to Doug, close, but not too close. Is this it? Has he decided to beg for my forgiveness and ask to come home? I lick my teeth to make sure there aren't any melting chocolate chips stuck in there.

"Are you doing okay? I'm worried about you." He puts his hand on my knee. It feels warm, like a fingered heating pad.

"What do you mean?" Then I look around and see the place from his view, the stacks of papers and books, the melting ice-cream container on the table. It looks like I'm turning into one of those women who starts hoarding paper and never leaves the house. They only discover her body, which was crushed under the trash, when the smell is noticed by the paperboy. "Oh, this." I give a little laugh and a vague wave. "It's been an insane week. I haven't done a thing around here." I flip my hair in a confident, Melanie Melon Breasts kind of way and the knotted sock falls into my lap. We both stare down at it lying there, a limp, brown exclamation point.

"I know this has been hard on you. I hope you know I wouldn't hurt you for the world. I just felt it was something that I had to do. We've been together so long and there was really only one direction our relationship was going. I love you, Soph." My breath catches. This is it. He's realized he's being an idiot. The fact that I'm wearing his old sock in my hair, the fact that the house is a mess doesn't matter. It isn't my house-keeping he loves, it's me. I feel myself starting to tear up a bit. Then, instead of taking me in his arms, he stands up quickly. Mac jumps, and with another dirty stare, ambles off to find a quieter place to resume his nap. (Emotional scenes upset his digestion.) "I knew this would be hard, but I didn't think it would be this hard." I consider making him beg to return, but I don't want to be cruel.

"It's okay. I think I know what you're here to say," I say, smiling shying.

"You always seemed to know what I was thinking before I did," he says, giving me a grateful look.

"I know you better than anyone." I stand up, too. We're kissing distance now. I'm trying to tilt my head slightly without looking like I'm puckering up.

"I would like you to meet her." I stop leaning in. My stomach starts taking a long bungee jump down.

"Meet who?"

"Melanie. She's a woman I've started seeing. I knew I needed a break, a chance to get my breath, but I didn't expect to meet anyone, it just sort of happened. I was going to bring her tonight, but she said it would be better if just you and I talked it over. I hate how I left things. Melanie says it creates bad karma. I want you to know how I feel about her, about how confused I've been."

"Uh-huh. You came over here to talk about your new *girlfriend*? You want *us* to have a deep discussion about your new *girlfriend*?" I have the sudden image of Melanie standing in the door in her perfectly matched outfit looking down her nose at me. "What happened to the part of the discussion where you didn't want to hurt me? What happened to talking about you loving me?" Doug looks surprised. "Sorry, maybe this sounds selfish, but I'm not sure I'm done talking about me. I'm not ready to move on to Melanie and how much you care for her quite yet." I can hear my voice getting shrill.

"Don't get upset. I needed some time to sort out how I was feeling. I realized you mean a lot to me, but I need to be sure of what I want. I know what you want. You want to turn us into my parents. But my future should also be what I want. I need some adventure, some excitement. I still want you in my life. I want us to be friends."

"So the way you decided to address our relationship problems was to start sleeping with someone else?" I shake my head "That's brilliant. You should write a book. I'm sure men all over the planet would read it. I wouldn't count on getting on *Oprah*, though." I pace back and forth. "I can't believe you. You want us to be *friends*? Has it occurred to you I might not *want* to be your friend?"

"I'm sorry, Soph. I had no idea how deeply this was affecting you. I've been so caught up in my own world I wasn't even thinking. I should have realized how losing me would devastate you." I stopped pacing.

"Devastate me? You don't need to worry about me. I'm doing just fine." Doug looks at me. It's very hard to project an image of confidence in stained sweats, a messy house, and your hair tied back with your ex's dirty sock. He's never going to want me if he thinks I'm pathetic. The doorbell rings again, and Mac gives another halfhearted bark. He wanders over to investigate. I hadn't fully shut the door when Doug came in, and with a push, Mac nudges it open with his nose. Nick is standing there with his battered briefcase and a bag of takeout Thai food.

"Sorry. I just thought I might bring over some dinner. It's been a long week." He holds up the bag of takeout as a visual explanation. Doug is looking for unexpected? I'll give him unexpected. I cross over to Nick in three strides and plant a kiss on him. It's a serious *Gone with the Wind* kind of kiss—the kind that can be used in emergency situations to resuscitate the near-dead by providing mouth-to-mouth. Nick staggers backward when I let go of him. His glasses are crooked and lipstick is smeared on his mouth.

"There you are, darling! I thought you would never get here," I say, staring into his eyes, trying to send psychic waves. After all, I've been practicing. Nick looks at me and then over at Doug. I can see awareness growing there. He's not a PhD for nothing.

"Well, muffin cakes, you know how bad traffic is this time of day." He kisses my cheek and takes a dog biscuit out of his pocket and leans down to give it to Mac. No wonder the dog loves him. He doesn't even have his own dog, and his pockets are still full of liver treats. He wraps his arm around my waist and smiles up at Doug, who is taller than him by at least half a foot. "I'm sorry, I didn't catch your name." Doug is standing there with his mouth open.

"My name's Doug."

"Ah yes, the ex. How awkward. Terribly sorry to just bust in on you, but the dog let me in. Sophie and I were planning a quiet evening together. It's been just a bear of a week. Do you want me to leave so you two can talk, Muffin?" *Muffin?* I make a mental note to talk to him about our imaginary love names. I've never pictured myself as the "Muffin" type.

"No, darling. Doug was just leaving. He came over to tell me how he's found someone else."

"Well, that's splendid. Wish you all the best." Nick takes a step to the side to let Doug pass. Doug is looking back and forth between Nick and me.

"I can't believe you're dating someone else. I don't know why. I didn't think . . ."

"I guess you didn't." The room goes quiet, except for Mac, who is nuzzling Nick's pant legs with loud snorts in the hope of another stinky organ treat.

"Well, I guess I'd better go." Doug walks out, silent and clearly shell shocked. Ha! Now he knows how it feels to be stabbed in the heart. I watch him walk down to the street and pause to look back at the house. His shoulders are hunched over and I want to run out and tell him it will all be okay, but I know I can't. I wait until I hear his car drive off and then give Nick a huge hug. He's brilliant. Plus, he brought dog cookies and takeout.

I could just kiss him all over again.

Ten

Trust your instincts and keep your ears open. You'll receive a message you've been waiting for if you pay attention. Others will look to you for guidance—be willing to share your wisdom.

The psychic fair is being held in the downtown Delta hotel. I wanted to wear my paisley wraparound skirt, black shawl, and big gypsy hoop earrings but Nick talked me out of the outfit. It turns out he was right. Everyone is dressed fairly normal. There are lots of black turtlenecks, and a few of the women went a bit heavy on the dark eyeliner, but that's the extent of the on-the-edge fashion. The event itself is in one of the hotel's large ballrooms. I take a tour around to try to get the lay of the land. By the door, there are tables stacked high with items for sale. These include any combination of the following:

- Crystals

- Books about crystals

- Books about people whose lives have been changed due to crystals

I browse the book tables for a while and hold various crystals while the saleswoman keeps asking if I "feel the vibe." She seems distraught that I'm not getting any vibes from anything. I finally lie and tell her that the purple stone I'm holding is definitely giving off some kind of energy. We were both relieved, until she pointed out that I was holding a keychain, which technically isn't supposed to be giving off any vibes. I buy it anyway.

The guy at the door gave me a diagram of the room, which shows the various table setups and which psychic can be located at which location. Turns out that the psychic business is more specialized than you might have imagined. There are psychics who specialize in either relationships, work, or health. The place is full, but not crowded. There doesn't seem to be any pushing or shoving, and everyone seems to be waiting their turn. I've positioned myself to the side of the door so I can watch people coming in. So far there's no sign of Melanie or her breasts. I concentrate on taking deep breaths and remind myself that I'm a trained "professional." When she finally walks in, I don't react. Instead, I just watch her. I'm not alone in this. Several other people turn around to watch her, too.

She is prom-queen perfect, tall, with long blonde hair that has clearly never suffered a bad perm. It looks like hair that belongs in a conditioner ad, the kind where a woman has an orgasm while using it. She's absolutely stunning. To say she is in good shape is an understatement. She looks like an Olympic athlete. All that healthy living can't possibly be good for you.

I feel like a balloon that has developed a slow leak. No wonder Doug is fascinated by her. Men all over the room are looking over at her, even the ones that I am certain are gay.

I suspect that when she attends funerals they nail the casket lid down to prevent the male corpse from popping up and giving a slow whistle. In high school, girls like her scared me. Who trusts someone who has intact self-esteem at that age? It's just not natural. I close my eyes and picture Doug, then I take a deep breath and wander over to her. I manage to "accidentally" bump into her, just the way I had practiced all week.

"Excuse me," she says. She and her friend have already visited the shopping table. They clearly found stones that vibed for them—they're weighed down by shopping bags. Her friend almost disappears in Melanie's shadow. She's dressed to kill, but after looking at the bright light of Melanie, you don't see her clearly. I touch Melanie's arm and then widen my eyes as far as they will go.

"You're in a relationship, aren't you?" I pause dramatically and look off to the side of her head as if I am seeing psychic waves coming off her skull. "His name is Dave, no Darren, wait, no—it's Doug." Melanie's friend is clearly shocked, her mouth is wide open. You could drive a Volkswagen into that gaping maw.

"His name is Douglas, actually. How did you know?" Melanie says.

"I'm a psychic. I'm supposed to be on break right now, though." I wave my hands vaguely toward the tables, hoping she doesn't look too closely. "My name is Emma Lulak. Don't tell me . . . you are Miranda? No, Mary? No wait—Melanie."

Her friend opens and closes her mouth like a guppy who has jumped out of the bowl in a bid for freedom. My alter ego psychic name is made up of my middle name and my mother's maiden name. I figured I would be able to remember it that way.

Plus my mom seemed to have eyes in the back of her head. She always knew when I had sneaked out of the house or borrowed her clothes. This is clearly some kind of parenting psychic skill. Who knows? Maybe it's genetic and she passed it down to me. I laugh conspiratorially like Melanie and I are close girlfriends, and I touch her arm again. "I'm sorry to just barge in on you. I just got such a huge vibe coming off of you about this. It must be some relationship."

"It is. He's the most amazing man I've ever met." Her friend still has her mouth open. You would think that her tongue would be drying out in there. She appears to be incapable of speech. It's a good thing she's cute because she's clearly not going to be known as the brilliant conversationalist of the two. I turn my head to the side again, like I am hearing something, maybe the distant musical tinkle of an ice-cream truck on a hot summer day.

"He's just out of a relationship, something long term." I squint as if trying to read the small line on the eye chart. "You're wondering if the two of you will last, if maybe he's the one." The last part is a guess. She could just be in it for laughs. Maybe the whole thing doesn't mean anything to her. In that case, I can be honest and tell her, woman-to-woman, to find someone else to play with, someone who isn't already taken. But her eyes start filling with tears. *Damn.* So much for thinking this was just a passing fancy.

"Will it last? Can you tell me that? I think he's amazing—I'm falling so hard for him."

"I'm sorry. I shouldn't be doing this. I was just going to get a cup of coffee. It's my break." Melanie grabs my hand and holds it to her chest. I fear it may get sucked in by the breasts of doom, but it just lies there. She clutches it so close I can feel her heart beating.

"No, please don't go. Can't you do a reading for me? I can wait, just tell me which table is yours, and I'll meet you there after your break." I smile and try not to lick my lips in anticipation. This is going exactly the way I had practiced with Nick.

"Tell you what: Let's go out to the lobby and find a quiet place to sit down. I'll do my best to do a reading for you." She and her friend give a little squeal like they've won a trip backstage to meet their favorite pop star. It's too easy, like taking candy from a baby. Just like Nick said, when people want to believe, they'll do all the hard work for you. I lead her and her friend to the lobby while trying to keep the grin off of my face.

Eleven

SCORPIO

Surround yourself with comfort today—put off major decisions and take time to regroup. Avoid office politics and unnecessary confrontations.

The last time I can remember believing in magic is when I was young. As a kid, I believed that Christmas trees were like people, with personalities and families. I would throw a fit when it came time to take it down. I felt like we had bonded over the holiday season. To this day, the smell of those Christmas tree–shaped air fresheners makes me relax. To avoid the histrionics I was capable of producing, my mom would employ a divide-and-conquer strategy. She would take me out shopping while she sent my Grandpa over to the house to dispose of the tree. When we got home, there would be a note from the tree with a few discarded needles telling me that he was sorry to leave without saying good-bye, but that he had to get back to his family in the forest. I saved those notes for years, until it struck me that if I could survive my dad leaving, I should be able to get over the trauma of the tree going to the chipper.

With the exception of the brief period of my life when

I believed in the souls of trees, I never believed in paranormal phenomena. I don't worry that the things that go bump in the night are ghosts. When I see a log in a lake I don't think it's the second coming of the Loch Ness monster. I'm not saying that I'm better than people who do believe. They believe in their fairy tales and I believe in mine, like true love forever. That's why I'm willing to use Melanie's beliefs to get what I want. All's fair in love and war.

When I practiced the reading with Nick I made a list of points that I wanted to slip into Melanie's reading:

- She and Doug were not meant to be together. The universe does not approve of this match. She shouldn't mess with the universe.

- Being with Doug is keeping her from meeting the true love of her life. In fact, the longer she stays with him, the less likely she is to connect with her *own* true love.

- If she doesn't meet up with her true love (because she's hanging on like a rottweiller with a death grip to Doug) then she's doomed to live the rest of her life alone. Her looks will slowly deteriorate until she's a lonely, wrinkled hag who smells like a litterbox because she lives with a bunch of cats.

Although these were my goals, Nick's were more simplistic:

- Provide general information on her family, health, and work.

- Determine how much of that general information is a hit versus a miss, and see how much information she provides to me, the "psychic."

- Let him write up the whole experience for his journal and be hailed as a god by his skeptical cronies.

I managed to meet both sets of our objectives and gave a bonus free reading to Melanie's open-mouthed friend Holly in under an hour. This must certainly be a psychic record. Assuming that Melanie follows through on my advice, and that the image of her with her breasts slowly deflating with age strikes home, Doug should be back with me in no time.

I was surprised at how easy it was once I got started. A few people had gathered around while I gave the reading and asked me to do theirs, too. I ended up being there for two hours. It was actually quite a lot of fun. Growing up I'd thought about being a counselor, and I'm starting to think that being a psychic isn't that much different. You listen to people and their problems, give some sage advice, and wind up with reminding them to follow their own heart and do what they think is best. How could it get any easier?

Twelve

Celebrate the small victories and share the joy with others. It will turn a personal victory into a party for all.

To: nickmckenna@ubc.ca.edu
From: sophie@hotmail.com
Subject: We are brilliant.
Date: March 13, 2005

Operation Psychic went without a hitch. I was able to waylay Melanie just the way we practiced. I gave her a brilliant reading. I was better than the so-called professionals! I fought off an urge to tell her that she was destined to find Yeti and must move to the mountains and live off grubs. I thought it might be going too far.

I picked up a crystal for you at the fair. In theory, it is vibing with energy from the pyramids. It looks like a plain purple rock, but it is a lovely rock and a memento of our adventure. I'll buy you dinner to celebrate. How

about tomorrow night around 5:30 at the Sand Bar on
Granville Island?

To: sophie@hotmail.com
From: nickmckenna@ubc.ca.edu
Subject: Re: We are brilliant.
Date: March 13, 2005

Congratulations. I am glad to hear that the reading went
so well. I hope that you were able to tape it as I would
like to transcribe part of it for the article I'm drafting. I
have to admit this is the most fun I've had with an investigation in a long time. I would be more than pleased
to join you for dinner, but certainly the vibing rock is a
suitable testament to your gratitude. There is no need
for you to buy dinner.

I'm glad you were able to hold off on the Yeti prediction. You don't want to be responsible for anyone moving to the mountains. I'm looking forward to seeing you.

To: nickmckenna@ubc.ca.edu
From: sophie@hotmail.com
Subject: Re: We are brilliant.
Date: March 13, 2005

Don't be a stick in the mud! She might benefit from a
few years away from civilization, or is it civilization that

would benefit from her being away? I didn't give any bad advice. I was wise, sage, and balanced. I promise I didn't try to fleece anyone from their life savings. See you at 5:30.

Thirteen

AQUARIUS
You'll find yourself thrown off your routine today. Use caution
in these unsteady times to avoid unexpected trips and falls.

I am not a morning person. My mother tells me that even as a
baby she would have to hold my alarm clock next to my ear
and rattle the crib before I would stir for a midnight feeding. I
have never been one of those people who describe themselves as
a "light sleeper." I hit a state much closer to coma than sleep. In
my opinion, one of the great things about being an adult, in addition to being able to make a dinner out of Skittles and cottage
cheese if you feel like it, is that you can structure your life any
way you want. My job at Stack of Books isn't going to make
me rich, but the store doesn't open until ten thirty, which means
I don't have to be at work until 10:29.

My ideal morning has me rolling out of bed around eight
or eight thirty. Then, still in my jammies, I go downstairs and
make some tea, and then read or watch a bit of TV while I wait
to fully wake up. Once awake, I like to take time to plan out
the day and make a nice, tidy to-do list. Then I take a hot

shower—hot enough to cook shellfish—and finally eat break-fast. Doug's a morning person. He jumps up when the alarm goes off and then heads straight into the shower. This used to irritate the hell out of me. No one should be that chipper in the morning. People should require some amount of time in order to really get in gear. The way I see it is, if you're sleeping well, you don't bounce right out of bed, you sort of ooze out. People who bounce most likely weren't sleeping soundly to start. They must lay there all night, slightly on edge, partially awake, waiting for the alarm. That can't be good for you.

So you can imagine, knowing how much I enjoy the morning hours, what joy I greeted the telephone with when it rang at 5:45. 5:45! Even Doug doesn't wake up at that hour. The phone rings two or three times before I can understand what it is. For the first few rings I just keep hitting the alarm clock, blaming it for the noise. Then I pull the clock plug out of the wall, but the sound continues. Finally, I've woken up enough to realize that it's the phone.

"Mrgh mhum um eg," I say, which is morning-speak for "Who is this and what do you want?"

"Sophie? Is that you?" Jane asks. How can she speak clearly at this hour? 5:45 is still middle-of-the-night time. Everyone knows that morning, even early morning, doesn't start until six a.m.

"Mmgh."

"You have to get up and read the paper. Have you read the paper?" *Is she kidding?* Read? My eyes aren't even fully open. There is some kind of gummy sleep snot still welding them together.

"Jane?" This one word is my first coherent, fully formed thought. It is a desperate bid to make a connection to the voice coming through the phone.

"Wake up! Go get your paper. I'll call you right back." Jane hangs up. I hold the receiver out for a moment and then hang it back up. I lean back. There is something she wanted me to do. I can't remember, it must not have been too important. I roll over and fall back to sleep.

RING! RING! RING!

"Are you looking at the paper?" she asks, while I try to remember her name. "Did you even get up and get the paper?"

"Look, I'm sleeping. You should be sleeping. Everyone is still sleeping. Call me later." I start to hang up, but her shrill voice erupts out of the receiver.

"Don't you hang up the phone! Trust me, this is important! Go get your paper." I realize that she is not going to go away. She's going to keep calling and calling. If I take the phone off the hook she will likely come over and pound on the door. She's that kind of person. Very focused, my friend Jane. I'm sure others would consider this an admirable trait.

"Okay. I'll get the paper." I drop the phone on the table. Mac is curled up on Doug's pillow in a tight dog ball. He raises his head and gives me the look that lets me know he is not amused to have been woken up. Mac is the kind of dog who has made sleep into a career. Later, when he's more alert, he'll punish me for waking him by chewing up an expensive shoe or by pooping in my laundry room.

I pull the paper off the stoop. It's pitch-black outside. Perhaps if Jane had looked outside she would have realized that it's the middle of the night. I shuffle out to the kitchen and un-roll the paper on the counter and one of the headlines stares up at me.

PSYCHIC SAVES FAMILY OF FOUR. For a moment I wonder why Jane woke me up for this. I wonder if there is some other article I should be looking at. Then I see the byline, Melanie Feehan. Melanie the Melon wrote the story. Who knew that she was capable of written language? Then I realize: *I* must be the psychic. I pick up the phone in the kitchen.

"Oh my god. I just saw it. I'll call you back." I hang up the phone, run to the bathroom, splash some ice-cold water on my face, and then pick up the paper.

Fourteen

PSYCHIC SAVES FAMILY OF FOUR

By Melanie Feehan,
Vancouver Sun Staff Writer

A chance meeting at the Vancouver psychic fair yesterday led to the saving of four lives in a house fire. Psychic Emma Lulak gave a reading in which she warned that she saw the family of Holly Hammond in a difficult, risky situation. She specifically mentioned they needed to check the batteries in their smoke detector. Following the reading, Ms. Hammond checked the smoke detector and found the batteries dead and replaced them. Last evening, a fire broke out in the Hammond home and when the alarm went off, the family was able to escape before fire consumed the house.

"If I hadn't checked the batteries that evening we wouldn't have had any warning. The fire was so fast that we barely had time to get out. We weren't able to save any of our things. Everything was destroyed. The important thing is that my husband and our two kids were able to get out safely. We're lucky to be alive. I owe my life to Ms. Lulak," Ms. Hammond said.

The fire started in the kitchen as a result of faulty wiring in a toaster oven. The fire caught quickly and spread to the window curtains. "The fabric of the curtains contained a chemical that results in a thick, noxious smoke," stated fire marshall Evan Hillegonds. "In most fatal fires, victims succumb to smoke inhalation rather than being burned by the fire. Proper use and maintenance of smoke detectors is often a family's best protection against tragedy."

Psychics, and psychic phenomena, are experiencing a wave of popularity, which can be seen in the success of TV shows such as *Crossing Over* and *Beyond and Back*. Psychics such as John Edwards and Sylvia Brown have gained celebrity status. Polls show that 60 percent of us believe in some form of psychic ability. Psychic fairs, such as the one held at the Delta Pinnacle Hotel, are sold out with legions of people looking for insight into their futures, or for a way to get in touch with their pasts.

"I believe that interest in psychic phenomena is growing as a result of society's urge to get in touch with some type of higher meaning. Many people come to our readings looking for an opportunity to make a connection and to find meaning in what seems like a meaningless world. A good reading allows you to make sense of a difficult situation, and in some cases, it is truly a miracle," said Larry Underwood, director of Global Psychic Connection, GPC, the group that organized the psychic fair held in Vancouver. GPC also acts as the representative for over one hundred psychics, arranging public appearances and maintaining press relations.

"Clearly the psychic Emma Lulak has a gift. It takes tremendous talent to predict and to be able to advise against tragedy. This is one instance where everyone involved is very glad Ms. Lulak was able to make this prediction. I think it is fair to say that this is nothing less than a miracle," stated Mr. Underwood. GPC does not represent the psychic Emma Lulak, and she was unavailable for comment for this story. By all appearances, her presence at the psychic fair was, in itself, destiny, as she was not even listed to appear.

Regardless if people believe it was sheer luck or a genuine display of psychic skill, Emma Lulak's chance meeting in the hallway with Ms. Hammond will ensure that the Hammond family will keep Ms. Lulak in their prayers for years to come, and will be sure to put regular smoke detector maintenance on their calendars.

Fifteen

I can't believe it. I'm in the paper. Of course, no one knows it's me. Well, except for Jane and Nick. *What am I going to do if people find out it's me?* My mom knows I'm not psychic. If I *were* psychic, I would have known I was going to get caught sneaking out of the house when I was fifteen. I would have known better than to allow my mom to drive me and my prom date to the dance. I can just picture my dad doing that thing where he raises one eyebrow and just stares at me. His largest concern will be how it might reflect on him and the new family. High-level insurance managers do not have a psychic for a daughter.

What would Doug think of the whole thing? He might point out that if I *were* psychic, I should have seen the whole thing coming, with him leaving me and all. Why did I tell them I was psychic? I'm going to look like a strange stalker woman if all of this comes out. *Is there any way people could figure out it's me? Will Nick get into trouble with the skeptic crowd for being friends with a fake psychic?* He didn't want to do this. I had to talk him into it. I hate learning these little life lessons just a little bit too late. Maybe if anyone asks I'll act like I don't know what they're talking about; someone must have impersonated me, saying they were a psychic. Denial is my best option. Then the phone rings again.

"Did you read it?" Jane asks without even saying hello.

"Yeah, I read it."

"What are you going to do?"

"I'm not going to *do* anything. No one knows it's me. The whole thing will just go away."

"Are you kidding? This is HUGE! It's on the front page of the newspaper! This is just the kind of thing that gets picked up by the wire services. People love this stuff. You could be famous. Trust me, by this evening Larry King is going to be talking about it on his show. The guy is a psychic junkie. If you get to go on *Larry King Live* I want to meet him, too."

"Larry King, huh?" I start some hot water boiling. As long as I am going to be up this early, I might as well have some tea.

"How did you know about the smoke detector?"

"What do you mean? I just figured it was a good guess. I mean, when was the last time you checked the battery in your smoke detector? I said a whole bunch of things."

"Don't you think it's weird, though? That you would guess that and then the fire happened that evening? Don't you wonder if, I don't know, that maybe you had some kind of insight?" The tea burned my lips and I put the cup down. I hadn't really thought about it. When I read the article I was mostly concerned about anyone figuring out it was me. I was getting a sick, heavy feeling in my stomach. I hung up with Jane so I could think.

I waited for a decent amount of time to pass before I called Nick—at least ten or fifteen minutes. He sounded like he'd been asleep when I called. *Does he plan to sleep the day away?*

"Nick, you need to wake up. Do you get the paper?"

"What are you talking about? Do you know it's only six in the morning?"

"You need to get a copy of the paper. There's an article in there about one of the predictions I made yesterday. It came true." It was quiet on his end. I can't tell if he thinks this is significant or if he's fallen back to sleep. "I told Melanie's friend to check her smoke-detector batteries and then there was a fire last night. What do you think?"

"I think she's lucky she ran into you."

"Just lucky?"

"Why, do you think you had a *real* psychic moment?" As soon as he says it, I feel like a moron. I wonder if I hang up if he'll go back to sleep and forget I called.

"No. It just seemed strange. I thought you would want to know, for your article."

"You're a pretty amazing person, even without the ability to foretell the future. I appreciate you letting me know, for the article. I'll see you later for dinner."

"You bet." I hang up. I bet he's fallen asleep already. I feel entirely too keyed-up to sleep. I feel another premonition coming on: This article is going to cause trouble.

Sixteen

Granville Island is a shopping paradise. In the early 1970s it had been a dying industrial park. How someone came up with the idea to turn it into a craft and fresh-food market I will never know. Now the renovated factory site hosts stores selling handmade sweaters made with chunky wool that look like a live poodle was knitted up, and strange kidney-shaped pottery that seems to serve no earthly purpose. It's the perfect place to buy Christmas gifts for the person who has everything. My favorite part is the fresh-food market, with stall after stall of towering fruits and veggies; stalls of fresh homemade pasta stuffed with tomatoes and cheese; butchers; fishmongers; a chocolatier, and several bakeries pumping out steaming clouds of fresh-bread smells. I never manage to leave without bags of food I have no idea how to prepare; the place always convinces me that I should learn how to cook. The resolution never manages to last until I get home, but it feels great to be there.

The market at Granville Island has what could loosely be called a food court, but there are no fast-food joints. The Stock Pot makes the most divine soups; Pie A'la Mode sells every pie possible; and an assortment of exotic Asian restaurants prepare dishes I can't pronounce but cause my mouth to water the instant I smell them. It's the perfect place to meet friends for a meal.

I arrived for my meeting with Nick almost two hours early. It gave me time to work my way down several of the aisles. I am now the proud owner of bags of goodies: homemade Thai curry sauce, a selection of cheeses made from goat, sheep, and other non-cow-related animal milk, fresh pasta, enough asparagus to feed a small African nation, handmade soap that smells like vanilla, and some kind of purple potato that the stall clerk promises is to-die-for creamy. All this shopping for food has resulted in making me hungry, so I decide to purchase a cookie (Nick might be late and I don't want to take the chance of wasting away) when I hear Doug call my name.

"What are you doing here?" he asks, touching my elbow. I consider telling him I was in line to buy bread, but I figure he knows me too well for that lie to work.

"I'm meeting a friend down here and I thought I would get a cookie while I waited."

"You and your chocolate mania," he says, pushing his hair from his face. *Damn, but he's cute.*

"Are you meeting that guy Nick?"

"Yep, as a matter of fact, I am." I smile, trying to look casual, but at the same time ready and willing to take Doug back.

"Maybe we should double up for dinner? That will give

you and Melanie a chance to meet." The desire for the cookie crumbles as my stomach heaves at the thought.

"We should do that sometime." *Like when hell freezes over.*

"She's just over there. How about when Nick arrives we head over to A'la Mode?" Doug points a finger toward a couple of aisles over and I see Melanie looking at a stall of painted silk scarves, the very same Melanie who knows me as Emma Lulak. A strange gurgle comes out of my throat, and before I can say anything, Doug takes a couple of steps forward and calls out her name. In slow motion I see her toss her hair and turn to face us. There is no time to run away.

I fall flat to the concrete floor and roll under a display table of honey and jam made from strange fruit like Saskatoon berry, and I pull my bags in after me with a quick yank. I peek out from under the tablecloth and see Doug's shoes joined by a pair of hot pink heels. Hot pink shoes to shop in? I mean, how impractical can you get? What is *really* annoying is that even her ankles are skinny and somehow sexy. It would be difficult to see me as sexy, given that I'm lying under a table, now coated in dust and what appears to be jam boogers.

"She was just here a second ago." I hear Doug say with some confusion. In case Jane is right and I have some semblance of psychic ability, I concentrate on sending thought waves into Doug's brain that he should leave. "Maybe she ran off to the bathroom. We should wait here." *So much for a mind meld between the two of us.*

"Do you think this is a good idea, Douglas? I suspect she isn't going to want to meet me. She must hate me for stealing you away." Melanie's pink shoes cuddle up to Doug's loafers.

I will her to step into the blob of gum that is inches from her right foot, but she misses it.

"Don't be silly. Sophie is the most practical woman you'll ever meet. She's down to earth. She knows no one 'stole' me."

"I'm sure she's great. It's just that I've been looking forward to spending the day with you. Then I want to take you home and make you dinner. And you can have me for dessert." She laughs and I concentrate on not vomiting or snorting any of the jam clots up my nose.

"We could go over to the A'la Mode shop—I mentioned meeting there for a drink. Maybe she went there."

The set of shoes moves away and once again I send a silent prayer of thanks to the gods for not making Doug the sharpest crayon in the box. I figure I can make a break for the bathroom and call Nick's cell phone from there, far from Doug and Melanie, the melon-breasted "don't-hate-me-for-stealing-you" bimbo. I scurry out from under the table, stand up, and brush lint off my pants.

"Emma?!" I turn slowly. Melanie is staring at me with open-mouthed amazement as she walks toward the table. She left her purse on the jam table and returned for it. I should add absent-minded to her list of faults. At least she didn't see me crawl out from under the table. "Oh my god, it *is* you!"

"Uh, yes. Melanie, isn't it?" I notice that there is a jam clot stuck in my hair, swinging slowly like a pendulum in front of my eyes. I tuck it behind one ear as if it is some kind of special fruit hair accessory, all the while keeping an eye out for Doug.

"I tried to contact you, but I couldn't find you in the phone book or anything. Did you see the article in the paper?

You know my friend Holly, the one you told about the smoke detector? There was a fire at her house! Just as you predicted."

"Yes, well, I knew that. That's why I told her. I really should be going." I take a step back and Melanie grabs my hand. Her fingernails are painted to match her shoes. I wonder if she has coordinated nail polish for all of her shoes. How does she find the time?

"You have to meet my boyfriend, Douglas! He's just around the corner."

"No, I don't think that's a good idea." I try to back away, but she's got her Barbie-pink hooks into me.

"Oh, but you have to, I told him all about the reading you gave me. How our relationship is doomed, but he didn't believe a word of it. He says he *is* the kind of guy who can commit." *Oh really? He's the kind who can commit, can he?*

"Melanie, the reading I gave you was meant for you alone. You shouldn't be sharing it." I look into her eyes. "His old girlfriend is nearby, isn't she? You're going to meet her?" Melanie's eyes open wide.

"That's right. How did you know?"

"I can feel the energy in the air. Trust me when I tell you this, you cannot meet her. I sense disaster, a really bad feeling about that meeting. You should get Doug and just go. Tell him you never want to meet this girlfriend. Never ever." This isn't even technically a lie. I'm fairly certain that any meeting with the three of us *would* be a true calamity.

"Okay. I mean, it's important to him, but if you're sure it's a bad idea." I nod enthusiastically, the clot in my hair swinging wildly. "Can you tell if I stay away from his girlfriend that we'll be able to work our relationship out?"

"I'm sorry Melanie, but I really have to go."

"Wait, I need your number."

"Sorry, I generally don't do readings for the public. I'm a sort of recluse kind of psychic. I told you everything I sensed. I really think you should break up with Doug. Your future with him won't be happy."

"He's still in love with his ex-girlfriend, isn't he?" She looks sad as she says this. Maybe he talks about me all the time, about what a mistake he made leaving me.

"What makes you think that? Does he still talk about her? What does he say?" She takes a step back at my questioning, and it occurs to me that I might seem a bit too interested in the topic. "I mean, are you listening to what he's really saying, what the underlying message is? If you're asking that question, it makes me think you already know the answer."

"I don't know. One minute I'm sure he loves me—lord knows he tells me all the time—but then the next minute I'm sure he doesn't. I know I should break up with him the way you say, but it's hard."

"Yes, well, the right thing to do isn't always the easiest thing to do." Great, now I sound like my dad giving a lecture.

"I still want your number. My friend Holly works for C-Fun radio, and she wants to have you on her show, a call-in kind of thing. You blew her away. She thinks her listeners would like to hear their readings. She thinks it would be a big hit."

"Well, although that's really flattering, I don't think I should." I glance up and see Doug coming around the corner; he's looking at his watch. I think, *I've got to get out of here now before he spots us.* I'll worry how to get out of the radio show later. "Okay, here's the number of my agent." I rattle off Nick's cell number. When she fishes for a pen to write it down, I take advantage of the moment and head toward the door. "Talk to you later."

The door swings shut behind me, and I allow myself to take a deep breath. I'm pretty certain Doug didn't see me talking to her. Disaster avoided, with the small exception of figuring out how I'm going to get out of doing a radio show.

Seventeen

GEMINI

Relationships play a strong role in your life—look for support to help get you through a difficult time. There is nothing more valuable than a good friend.

I remember playing with a Ouija board at Julie Hubbel's seventh grade slumber party. We had already engaged in all other required slumber party activities:

- teasing her little brother until he cried,

- eating our combined weights in sugar-laden food products,

- dancing to her Duran Duran album collection, and

- painting our chewed fingernails with her mother's nail polish.

Large groups tend to make me uncomfortable. I do better one-on-one. I always seem to be the one who's hanging around the outside of the circle. The only time I tend to be the center of attention in large groups is when I've done something to draw attention to myself, like trip, spill something, or laugh until soda comes out of my nose. My best friend growing up was Laura. We got along fine, but she came from the school of thought where the more friends, the better. She was trying to integrate herself—with me stuck to her side like a barnacle—to a group of popular girls. This is how we ended up at Julie's slumber party. Technically, Laura had been invited and then she had talked to Julie, who invited me a few days later. I was trying hard not to feel like I wasn't wanted. However, considering that Julie had called me Sara at least four times, I didn't really feel like I'd really bonded to the group.

Stacey had brought her older sister's Ouija board. Stacey was one of those girls who peaked in high school. She was a cheerleader, ran on the track team, and served on every committee and club the school operated. You couldn't turn a yearbook page without seeing a picture of her smiling with that big, blonde hair. Despite the fact that I'm certain that Stacey had little, if any, experience in contacting the great beyond, she acted as if she were a professional. She felt perfectly comfortable bossing the rest of us around. We had to turn off all the lights and light candles. The only candles we could find were in a box of Christmas decorations that smelled of cranberries and sticky pine. Stacey insisted that we all be quiet and concentrate on the flames so that the spirits would feel welcome. Amy started crying. She was pretty certain that using the Ouija board put us at high risk for going to hell. She kept saying that talking to dead people was a really bad idea. She warned everyone that the devil would use the Ouija board to possess us. However, when we had to choose

between our immortal souls and the opportunity to find out
which boys harbored a secret passion for our twelve-year-old
bodies, we chose the boys. Amy flounced off and sat in the bathroom by herself while the séance lasted.

We took turns gently placing our fingers on the plastic triangle while Stacey intoned in a singsong voice for the spirits
to answer our most pressing questions, like who would get
asked to dance at the Snowball Fling. When it was my turn, I
tried to keep my mind open so as not to pressure the spirit
world to feel that it had to come up with a specific answer. Although I don't mind admitting that if the name of Ryan Reilly
had come up, I would have been open to the idea.

Stacey smiled as I sat down. The triangle slowly started to
spell D-A-N. Everyone started giggling. The only Dan in our
class was Dan MacTavish. Dan had some kind of unfortunate
erupting skin condition combined with a body that seemed to
consist only of long limbs that didn't seem well connected at
the joints. He was the kind of kid who always seemed to be
falling down and spilling his books or his lunch tray. He stut-
tered when called on in class and his clothes always looked
like he had slept in them. Looking back with the wisdom of
age, I suspect that Dan went on to graduate from college at
the top of his class, owned a software firm that went public
during the dot-com days, and that he currently designs rockets
for NASA. I'm certain he's a lovely man who is now capable
of dressing himself. However, at that time I would rather have
leapt in front of a train than have anyone consider Dan and I
as a couple.

I pressed down on the triangle to slow its progress to the
letter M. I could feel Stacey pulling on the triangle. I knew

then that there was no spiritual connection, just her chance to be queen of the slumber party. We locked eyes over the board, a battle of wills and finger strength. Unbeknownst to her, I had been playing hours of video games. Ms. Pacman had honed me into a virtual muscle-beach finger diva. The triangle started to move away from the M. Shuddering from the pressure of our combined fingers, it shot across the room. Everyone was shocked into silence for a minute. We all agreed that clearly the spirit world had strong feelings on the issue and that perhaps Amy was right—there are some things you shouldn't mess with. The group determined that some mysterious "Dan" was in my future and we moved on to trying to watch an R-rated movie on cable without Julie's parents figuring out what we were doing.

I'm not giving this as example of proof that there isn't real psychic energy out there, just that I haven't seen it myself. I'm not trying to suck all the magic out of the world. I just figure that life is complicated enough without magic. That was my last attempt to contact the afterlife for answers.

Besides, what are the dead doing spending all this time worrying about what the living are doing? One would hope that the afterlife would have better entertainment. And if they make all this effort to get through to us, then why don't they have anything useful to say? For the record, if I come back from the dead, I promise to deliver the following useful information:

- winning lotto numbers

- where missing items like car keys, watches, and earrings can be found

- the answers to key test and exam questions

- who really is going to ask you to the Snowball Fling

Of course, I'll be dead, so it will be hard to punish me if I don't deliver. But what the heck, it's worth a shot.

Eighteen

CANCER

It's a chance to get out and let yourself go—fun is the name of the game today. Let loose and be willing to try something new. You can't find a new favorite unless you try more than the old standbys.

We couldn't eat at Granville Island, as I had to hide my dual identity in case Melanie and Doug were still lurking about the place. Nick decided he would pick a place for dinner. I had never been to La Gavoroche, because the restaurant clearly doesn't want anyone from the general public to find them. There didn't seem to be any signs or menus posted outside. The door looked like a private residence. It was a two-story Victorian home with painted gables. Maybe this keeps out the riff-raff so only serious foodies are allowed in. The hostess knew Nick by name, and the manager came out to shake his hand and to tell him about some wine from France that had just arrived. We were seated at a table toward the back and they brought out crusty bread with basil butter. The bread was still warm. It oozed costly, I hoped Nick meant it when he said he didn't expect me to buy dinner.

"You must bring all your dates here."

"I come a fair bit. I love good food, but I dislike cooking. This way, I don't even have to do the dishes. I grew up eating Scottish oatmeal, so imagine my delight to discover there were other food options available, other than haggis, that is."

"You come by yourself?" I exclaimed. I thought of my foray into single dining. Nick didn't look like the type to crawl out. "Do you ever feel uncomfortable? I mean, eating alone."

"No. I usually just bring a book. I'm not averse to coming with someone, it just usually works out that way. Most of my colleagues are married. When I was a student, I had my head down. I was more interested in theories than people." He picks up the menu and looks through the list of specials. His eyebrows crunch together as he concentrates on his options. Nick is one of those guys you can tell is smart just by looking at him and not just because he carries around books with titles like *Nuclear Proliferation in Eastern Nations* and a biography of Charlie Chaplin.

"What got you interested in the whole skeptic thing?"

"I think I've always been interested in how things work. When I was a kid I was fascinated by magicians. I knew it was a trick, but I couldn't figure out how they did it. I started spending all my paper-route money at the magic store, learning different things. When I was in high school, I bought my first car with money I made from doing magic at kid's parties." He looks bashful as if he had just admitted to a secret life as a Chippendale stripper.

"Get out." I give his shoulder a gentle push. Nick leans over, close enough that I can smell the soap on his skin. I have the sudden feeling he's going to kiss me. I can feel the heat from his hand and my hair stands up as if to meet his hand part way. He reaches up and touches the side of my face. He pulls his hand away and is holding a quarter. I touch it, and then touch my ear. "How did you do that?" I fish around to see if there is any more money lurking in there.

"Magicians never give up their secrets. You have to take them to the grave." He smiles, handing me the quarter. He turns back to the menu. "You should try the pear and blue cheese salad. It's great."

We order dinner and when it arrives, dig in. Nick was right. The food is a perfect balance of flavors. We talk over our various favorite books. I love anyone who's a reader. It also turns out that Nick's a classic film nut. He owns approximately six billion DVDs and his favorite director is Hitchcock. He's the kind of person who discusses camera angles with all the passion of a religious zealot. He's appalled that I've never seen the movie *Rear Window*, so we ask for our desserts to go, and head over to his place to watch it immediately, before my lack of cultural knowledge goes on any longer.

I have to admit an interest in what Nick's place looks like. I can imagine it either having the sloppy, single-guy dorm room décor, or the English country home style, heavy on the antiques. Turns out, it's neither, which blows my theory that I have the psychic ability to guess a guy's furniture style.

Nick's apartment look is sort of an eclectic mix of all kinds of things that defy any type of defined style. He has this funky cabinet for his TV that's some kind of Japanese antique; the couch is leather and a bit worn. The pictures on the wall are framed vintage movie and travel posters. The desk is an old table with a high-tech computer on top. There are books everywhere, mystery novels, biographies, nonfiction science texts, and travel guides. They're stacked in the corners on every table and shelf. It's the kind of place where you feel instantly comfortable taking off your shoes and tucking your feet underneath you on the couch.

Nick makes coffee for himself and vanilla tea for me, and we sit on the couch to watch the movie. For the record, if you haven't seen *Rear Window*, you really should. It's about a fellow who sits in his apartment and watches his neighbors, a guy who doesn't focus on his own life, but who instead lives vicariously through others. I can relate to that a bit. Sometimes I think I would rather read about something than do it. When the movie ends I can't believe it's eleven p.m. Mac must be crawling up the walls by now. Hell hath no fury like a dog that hasn't gotten his walk. I lean against Nick's desk to put my shoes on. He has a photo tucked in the corner, and I peek to determine if there's a lady professor in his life he has failed to mention so far. But it's clearly an old family shot. Mom, Dad, an attractive bent-eared mutt, a younger version of Nick in a graduation gown, and someone who has to be a close relative, his own version of a mini-me. Nick looks over my shoulder.

"You asked me earlier what got me interested in the skeptic thing? There's another reason right there." He taps the photo. "That was my brother Simon. He was killed in a car accident about three weeks after my graduation."

"I'm so sorry." I'm not sure what to say.

"Losing my brother was terrible; watching what it did to my family was horrific. My parents just couldn't cope. My dad decided that he just never wanted to think about it again. He would change the topic whenever Simon was mentioned. He was the kind who wanted to box up my brother's room, shut the door, and sell the house. My mom went the opposite direction. All she wanted to talk about was Simon. She just couldn't accept that he was gone. She found every reason she could think of to bring him up, to cook his favorite foods, you name it. She wanted more time to do it right, to be the mom she knew she could be. She and my dad were like magnets that repelled each other." Nick put the picture back down on the desk. "My mom went to a psychic for a year or so after Simon died. That finally did it for my dad. He didn't want to hear any messages from the beyond. My mom took it as a rejection of her and Simon. She left him. They ended up getting a divorce about two years later." He shrugs.

"I had no idea. I feel bad that I dragged you into all of this."

"You didn't drag me into anything. I wanted to do it. When all this is done, I'll write it up and expose the whole rotten industry. It will be a cathartic experience. I spend too much time burying myself with science. It's good to feel like I'm doing something."

"Are you sure?"

"Of course. Sure, you've got a winsome personality, but you haven't talked me into anything I didn't want to be involved in."

"I'm sorry about giving Melanie your number. I didn't know what else to do."

"I understand. I'm assuming when she calls I'm telling her

you won't be doing the show?" He's looking at me, waiting for an answer. I know doing the radio show would be a mistake, but I have to admit it sounds like fun. I've never been asked to be on the radio before. It's like being discovered.

"I was thinking it could be an interesting addition to your article," I venture.

"You're too kind to be thinking of me." I can't tell if he's making fun of me. "Doing a reading for Melanie was one thing, but doing it on the radio would be going too far. With our luck we would be found out anyway. Can you imagine how hard it would be to explain?"

"You're right; Melanie would most likely claw my eyes out if she found out." I give a sigh. My media career is over before it even began. "The point of the whole exercise was to get Melanie and Doug to break up. As far as I can tell from today, Doug seems as crazy about her as ever."

Nick gives me a hug. "I'm certain she wouldn't claw your eyes out. She wouldn't want to ruin her manicure. As for Doug, if he chooses her over you, then he's a fool and you're better off without him."

I give him a hug back. "You are so sweet."

"Curse of the nice guy syndrome—I can't help myself. I long to be surly and sultry but I can't seem to pull it off. Not brooding enough."

"A nice guy with a passion for horror movies, eh? Most likely hiding a secret psychotic side," I call over my shoulder as I head out the door. I can hear him laughing as the elevator door slides shut. There is no way I would consider doing the radio show. It's entirely too risky. I would most likely end up making an ass of myself and have very little to gain from the whole thing. If anything, it would just make the situation worse. I would have to be an idiot to consider it a minute longer.

Nineteen

You get news you've been waiting to hear. Now is the time to
move forward with a project you've been considering.

BEEP—"*Sophie, are you there? If so, pick up—it's me,
Jane. . . . Damn. Okay, you need to give me a call when you
have a chance. Doug called me today. Big news. Call me.*"

BEEP—"*Where are you? It's Jane again. Is it that you're not
speaking to me anymore? Seriously, you need to give me a
call. Doug is having second thoughts about Melanie I think.
Call me when you get home.*"

BEEP—"*I've decided you must have moved and failed to give
me your number. I'll be up for another hour or so, if you get
home before ten-thirty give me a call—otherwise I'll call you
at work tomorrow.*"

It took forever to get home after leaving Nick's place. Traffic over Lions Gate Bridge was backed up because someone's
car had stalled. I didn't get home until past midnight. I had to

take Mac for an immediate walk to make up for the fact I'd
been gone all night before he'd even "speak" to me. It was
quarter to one in the morning when I realized that there was a
message on my voicemail. After I listened to Jane's messages, I
had to ask myself some hard questions:

- Could I wait until morning to find out what Doug had said
  to her without my brain self-combusting?

- When Jane suggested that if it was after ten-thirty she
  would call me tomorrow, was that because she was the
  tired mother of two who needed her rest and didn't want
  late night calls, or was she just being thoughtful of not
  wanting me to feel like I had to call right away?

- Would Jane, my best friend in the whole world, want me to
  be unhappy, lying awake wondering what she had to say
  when I could simply call and answer all my questions?

I decide to call. I can hear the baby crying when she picks
up. I tell myself the phone hadn't woken Ethan up, but that instead I was giving Jane an opportunity to have someone to chat
with since she was already up. At any rate, it was well worth it
to hear her news. Doug called Jane to talk. Apparently, he's
convinced that I'm head over heels in love with Nick, which is
driving him crazy. Now he's starting to wonder if he was taking me for granted and that maybe he overlooked my many at-
tributes. Plus, Melanie is perhaps not as wonderful as he had
first thought. This is no surprise because when I performed
Melanie's reading I gave her a big list of things to do that I
know drive him nuts.

- Have lots of potpourri around. I told her it would bring in positive energy from Mother Earth, but the truth of the matter is that Doug has allergies.

- Unplug the TV so they can have more "together time," especially during sporting events.

- I told her that if she wanted to get closer to Doug, she should try to interest him in things besides work and hockey. Talk to him all the time about her feelings and interests.

- Make the toilet paper pull from the top of the roll instead of from underneath.

- Cook broccoli.

- Bring her parents around for weekly dinners.

- Talk about her interest in having a baby with him.

- Sleep with socks on, big, thick socks.

I made a list of everything that I knew Doug couldn't stand and tried to find some way to advise Melanie to do more of it. If I could have come up with some way of suggesting she give up sex altogether I would have tried. But it seemed like that might have been pushing my luck.

At any rate, she must have taken *some* of my advice, as Doug told Jane that perhaps he was more in love with the *idea* of Melanie than the reality of her. He asked Jane how serious she thought I was with Nick. Jane thought he sounded quite sad. She told him that she knew I missed him, but that I wasn't the type to pine away. She suggested that he give me a call so we could talk. I make Jane recreate the conversation over and over until I am sure that she has remembered exactly what he'd said as well as the tone of his voice. She's a pretty good sport about the whole thing, considering it's the middle of the night, or early in the morning, depending on how you want to look at it.

After I hang up the phone, I dance around the house with Mac nipping at my ankles. Doug loves me. I love Doug. The whole thing is going to resolve itself and we'll go back to being a couple. I was right to hang on. We *are* meant to work out. Maybe this will be the time he'll propose instead of just talking about it. We'll get married and live happily ever after.

That's the prediction I make for myself.

Twenty

Take a trip down memory lane. The answers you seek may be found in your past.

I met Doug in Vancouver. I had only lived here a few weeks. It was a Halloween party; Jane and Jeremy had talked me into going. I had to come up with a costume at the last minute so I'd worn a black dress I'd been saving for a fancy occasion, with bloodred lipstick and a pair of fangs. I told anyone who asked that I was a high-society vampire or a character from an Anne Rice novel.

Doug had dressed up as pirate. His friend Brian had come as a pirate, too, and bent his leg at the knee, duct-taping a plunger stick-side down to his kneecap as a peg leg. It looked great but it wasn't very functional, and he kept falling over. This increased with his beer intake. Doug didn't have as fancy of a costume. It consisted of a puffy white shirt, which I would later discover belonged to a girl he'd been dating, and an eye patch. A poor excuse for a costume, but he had this rouguish look in his eye that perfectly befitted a pirate. Somebody at the party was a huge Barenaked Ladies fan and continued to play their music over and over with brief interludes of The Cars. Whenever I hear the song "Be My Yoko Ono," I think of Doug.

Jane said she thought I was attracted to Doug partly because he was the kind of guy who hadn't paid attention to me in high school. She may have been right. Doug was handsome, broad in the shoulders, and solid looking, definitely the captain of the football team/prom king type. The kind of kid who had his whole life mapped out for him, as opposed to myself, who always felt like I was making it up as I went along.

Doug was born to be popular. He didn't think attention was anything special because he was used to it. If you live in an area where it's always sunny and warm, I don't think you notice the heat. I doubt that people who live in California are aware of the weather. Every day is a nice day. I think being popular would be like that. You're used to sunlight and warmth, and so that seems normal. Not having it would be strange. If Doug is sunshine and heat, I am partly cloudy and cool. I wasn't unpopular. No one made fun of me or teased me. They just didn't notice me.

I had gotten up to get a drink from the cooler, holding my fang teeth in my hand. When some guy bent down to fish out a beer, Doug nudged him aside, saying that he "must have been raised in a barn; you should always get a lady a drink before serving yourself." He twisted off the beer cap and handed the wet bottle to me with a gallant bow. I had wanted a wine cooler, but it seemed ungrateful not to take it, so I drank the beer with a smile and tried to ignore the bitter taste. He asked me out that night and that was the beginning of our relationship.

I used to ask Doug what made him notice me that night, but

he always said he couldn't remember. That drove me nuts, because I could tell you everything about that night. What we were wearing, what we talked about, and even what time he kissed me—11:48 p.m., while leaning against a bookcase. Maybe it's a girl thing, keeping track of milestones and special events. I always remember birthdays and always mentally thought of Halloween as our "anniversary," even though it wasn't anything near that official.

I know everyone thinks I'm crazy for doing all this to get Doug back, breaking in to his apartment and pretending to be a psychic to get rid of his girlfriend, but I would do anything to be with him. Isn't that what you do for the person you love? I mean listen to love songs about climbing the highest mountain, swimming the ocean, blah, blah, blah. I can't imagine my life without him. I can't bear the idea of starting all over again. I have shared history with Doug; knowledge of where he came from, what he likes, what he dislikes. I know what to expect.

Nick told me that one of the reasons so many people believe in psychics is because psychics tell people what they want to hear. They fulfill their expectations. *God* is such a huge concept that it's hard to imagine a divine presence really looking out for you, what with having to watch every sparrow that falls and all. It's much easier to believe that someone who actually knows you, who is dearly departed, is using their time in the hereafter to take care of you.

I believe people go to psychics because they want an answer to all the things for which there is no answer. I can understand that; I'm a researcher by trade. It's not that I'm not willing to work to get the answers, I just want there to *be* one. I don't think that's asking too much. Doug is the perfect answer for me. He's exactly the kind of guy I imagined spending my life with, except for the small fact that he doesn't always seem to feel the same way.

Twenty-one

LIBRA

When problems seem insurmountable today, don't despair—
look at what resources and support you have that can help you
reach that lofty goal. Don't overlook family—they can provide
the bridge to the next level. Take it one step at a time.

It's been two days since I spoke to Jane, and no word from
Doug. I've called Jane approximately six thousand times, to repeat the discussion to try to determine if there was some key
fact that she left out that would have resulted in Doug deciding
to leave the country and cut all ties with his loved ones, namely
me. I spent an entire evening watching the phone, willing it to
ring, but no luck. During the day I keep calling my machine to
see if there are any messages, and then curse myself in case
Doug has picked that exact moment to call but gives up when
he gets the busy signal.

The fact that Doug hasn't called could mean a couple of different things:

1. He could be spending the time to give our relationship a lot

of careful consideration, trying to figure out exactly what to say that will win my heart back,

or

2. His whole call to Jane was a lark, a passing fancy, and he's now having crazy bunny sex with Melanie and couldn't recall my name if I were standing in front of him with a "Hi my name is" nametag on my chest.

I got the idea when I turned the page on my calendar. Today is Doug's mom's birthday. Doug isn't the kind of guy who's good at remembering dates and pivotal events. I was the one officially in charge of making sure that cards and presents were allotted out. I considered using it as an excuse to call him and remind him. Remind him of both his mom's birthday as well as how useful I can be. I'm afraid if I call I'll look like I'm chasing him. It seems what's most interesting to him is when he thinks *I'm* not interested. Playing hard-to-get is difficult when you really want to be caught.

Doug introduced me to his mom, Ann, for the first time when we had been dating for about five months. She stopped by to drop off an Easter basket full of chocolate for him. I don't think he planned for me to meet her, but it would have been rude for him not to introduce me when I was sitting right there. Meeting the parents was definitely a commitment step, and it made him nervous. Personally, I was thrilled to meet her and was determined to make her love me.

Doug's mom had been a fashion model when she was younger. She still had the look, like there was a camera on her somewhere, every hair in place, the perfect smile. She stopped working after she married and turned into a master social planner. My mom was more of the khaki pants, floral blouse, and sensible shoes kind of mom, the type who looks like she has a minivan parked around the corner and a pot roast in the oven at home. Doug's mom looked like she stepped out of a high-fashion spread and fully expected a limo and driver to be waiting. My mom made you feel comfortable enough to put your feet up and take a nap; his mom always made me feel like I had something stuck in my teeth.

To be honest, Doug's mom scared the pants off of me for a really long time. She was the kind of person who, when you came over for dinner, had about twelve pieces of silverware at each place setting. I tended to find out only after I started eating that I was using a shrimp fork to eat my salad or some other gauche maneuver. Everyone at the table would be staring as if I had started gnawing on the family dog. The whole thing made me so nervous I had a hard time eating at all. I suspect that for years she thought I was anorexic. She may sound stuck-up, but she isn't like that at all. She's a classy lady from stem to stern. I was terrified that she would discover that I was from the "wrong side of the tracks." She and her set are so far from the tracks they can't even hear the train whistle. After a while, though, I started to discover things I had in common with his mom, and began to feel more comfortable. The main thing we had in common was a desire for Doug to settle down and start a family. I suspect she figured that I might not know how to use proper silverware, but I knew that I didn't have any major deformities, had a university degree, and had learned to dress myself. The other thing we had in common was a fierce love of Doug. We both thought he was the cat's meow. It was enough to bring us together. We weren't close friends, but we had a bond.

I haven't talked to her since Doug and I broke up. Is it reasonable to ask for visitation rights to your ex's family? It's not like I've broken up with the family just because Doug and I aren't dating. It would be rude to ignore her birthday. If I were to make a homemade cake and bring her a gift out of the goodness of my heart, she might mention it to Doug. Maybe a friendly word from his mother would tip the balance. She would see me looking great, confident, and happy. She'll tell Doug he's a fool to let a prize like me go. She sees in me the perfect daughter-in-law. Okay, maybe not perfect, but far more her type compared with Melanie. Those large breasts are definitely not her style. She'll tell Doug how sophisticated I am, how much she values me as a person. A wise word from a mother can make a huge difference. It's certainly worth the time to bake a cake.

Or buy a cake. I tried to make one, but it turned out all misshapen and flat on one side. When I attempted to apply frosting, the cake developed some kind of structural weakness, resulting in a major crumb breakdown. It didn't look like the kind of baked good you would want to give as a present to a loved one. It looked cursed, like I was hinting that she was getting older and falling apart. You have to be careful of the message you may be sending. I went to the bakery and bought a cake. I took it home and dragged a knife around the top in an effort to create a faux homemade-frosting effect. It still looked too good, so I stuck my finger into the side and messed it up. I slid the cake onto a cookie sheet and covered it with tinfoil. The perfect blend of quality store-bought cake combined with the appearance of homemade care. I picked up a bouquet of flowers on the way over.

Doug's parents live in West Vancouver in a home that looks like a set from The Home and Garden Network. It is a large house trying to look small and unassuming, like a tall woman who slouches to try to underplay her natural assets. It has a gate across the drive, and once you pull up to the house you notice the view—the house sits up on the bluff overlooking the ocean. You can see the cruise ships passing under Lions Gate Bridge. I always thought that when Doug and I got married, one option would be to do a small wedding in his parents' backyard. A reception for us and about one hundred of his family's present-buying friends and family.

Ann is clearly surprised to see me. I suspect Miss Manners does not cover situations wherein the ex-girlfriend stops over unannounced. I hold out the flowers and cake with a cheery, "Happy Birthday!" She invites me in for tea and a piece of cake as I knew she would. You can count on manners.

"So, how are you doing?" She folds like an elegant origami swan onto the leather couch, tucking her silver-blonde hair behind her ears. She is wearing diamond earrings the size of walnuts. Despite the fact that she didn't know I would stop over, she isn't wearing sweatpants. Instead she has on a powder blue pantsuit with a flowered, coordinated scarf tied around her neck. I had bought a new outfit for this meeting, and yet she still looks more pulled together. I try to copy her graceful descent to the couch but end up sitting down hard, tea sloshing into the saucer of my cup and the leather couch making a whoopee-cushion sound.

"I'm fine, Mrs. Chase, and you? Any plans for your birthday?"

"I keep telling you, call me Ann. I'm doing well. At my age I don't make a big deal about birthdays." She brushes her silver-blonde hair off her face. "It's very kind of you to think of me."

"Yes, well, after all this time, I feel like we're family." I smile conspiratorially, reminding her that if her son hadn't been so slow to cough up a ring we really *would* have been family.

"I was sorry to hear that you and Doug decided to break off your relationship. You two made a nice couple."

"It was a bit more of Doug's decision than mine. He felt the need to test the waters, I guess." I pause. I have to know if she knows about the Melon. "Have you met Melanie, his new girlfriend?"

"Doug brought her by the house last weekend." I choke down a large gulp of hot tea, working to keep the smile on my face. *I can't believe he's brought her home to his parents already*. I feel a blister forming on my tongue. It makes my voice come out with a lisp.

"Oh, that's super. I haven't met her yet, myself. It's a bit unfair. Doug's already had a chance to meet Nicholas, my new beau. Did he mention that I'm seeing someone?"

"No, he didn't mention a thing. You know Doug, he's not one to talk about feelings and relationships. I'm glad to hear you've found someone." She shifts on the couch and takes another long sip of tea. Bigsey, their Yorkshire terrier, comes running in, the bell on her collar heralding her arrival. Even the dog is well dressed, with a pink silk bow in her hair. The dog has better breeding than I do. She can trace her family tree to dogs owned by the French royal family in the 1800s.

I sense I'm running out of time. Ann's going to finish her tea and then it'll be time for me to go. I won't see her again. It's not like she's going to invite me over for dinner anymore. I look around the room desperately. I love this house, with its color-coordinated cushions and knickknacks that cost more than I earn in a year. I love this tiny little yappy dog descended from inbred royalty. I love these people. Don't they love me? Can they really just wish me the best and send me off into the sunset? I feel a hot flood of tears coming to my eyes.

"Well, maybe I should be going," I squeak out. *I need to get out of here before I fall apart and blow my cover as a confident woman.* My hands are shaking and tea is sloshing around in the cup like I'm on the deck of a ship.

"Are you all right?" Ann leans forward. She looks concerned about me, like I have some fatal illness. My lower lip starts shaking. I stand up in a rush, totally forgetting the tea cup in my lap. The cup seems to fall in slow motion and shatters on impact with the floor, the fine china scattering everywhere. Tea stains the cream-colored carpet in a giant blot—the carpet they custom ordered, handwoven by some Turkish woman and imported. Bigsey starts barking madly and running in circles. I fall to my knees and start gathering up the china pieces.

"I am so sorry." I use the sleeve of my sweater to blot the tea. "I don't know what I was thinking. I'll pay to have the carpet cleaned. I'll send someone over today." I am really crying now and my nose is blowing snot bubbles.

"Sophie, please, leave the cup, get up. It's not important." She pulls on my sleeve, urging me up. I can't look her in the eyes.

"The Safeway on Marine Drive rents Rug Doctor cleaners. I can run down there and pick one up before this even dries. It won't take me a minute." My nose is bubbling now like a witch's caldron and the tears are falling onto the carpet. This is not going at all as I had planned. She takes the cup shards from my hand. One of them cut my thumb and it's bleeding. *Great, as if the tea weren't bad enough, now I'm bleeding on to the rug.* Maybe later I can go out to the yard and drag some grass in, and rub *that* onto the carpet, toss on some red wine, open up a couple of fountain pens, make a modern art project out of the whole thing. Ann presses her linen napkin to my thumb and eases me back to the couch.

"Take a deep breath." She looks at my face and hands me some tissues. I can just imagine how I look. "It will be all right." She pats my knee. I am having difficulty not throwing myself into her arms and really letting go. If she thinks I'm upset now, she hasn't seen a thing yet.

"I miss him so much. I love him, I really do." I let out a wail and Bigsey joins me in a sympathy howl.

"I know you do. But you'll find someone else that you love just as much. I'm sure you will." She hands me another handful of Kleenex. Her nose wrinkles a bit as she takes the damp, snot-covered tissues from me. I think it speaks volumes to how much she must really like me. That's not the kind of thing you do for just anyone. I'm pretty sure I'm not projecting an image of a confident and self-assured woman. I suspect I'm coming across like someone who should be on *The Jerry Springer Show* or taking large amounts of medication.

"I should go. I'm so sorry about all this. I don't know what's come over me." Great, now I sound unstable, too. If "overly emotional" weren't appealing enough, now I can add "unbalanced" to the package.

"It's all right. Just sit there and I'll get you another cup of tea."

"No, I should leave. I just wanted to wish you a happy birthday. Honestly. I hope you enjoy the cake." I stand up and back up, bumping into the bookshelf. One of her ceramic collectible birds totters for a moment and then falls. I watch it spiraling down and whacking Bigsey right on her kiwi-sized head. She lets out a surprised yelp and runs off. The bird breaks into two pieces. I close my eyes and will the bird to heal itself. I open one eye to peek. Nope, still there. This patch of carpet must be a black hole; gravity is much stronger here. I should consider myself lucky not to have fallen to the floor. I open my mouth to apologize again, but it seems a bit much. I just look at Ann, the rug, the dead bird, and make a run for the door. I can't face the brain-damaged dog.

Twenty-two

SCORPIO

Nothing happens overnight—so remain patient. The things you deeply desire require good timing. Try not to get too involved in the problems of others or you won't be objective enough to help solve them.

Operation Mother Support did not go as planned. All I can hope for now is that she doesn't mention the whole sordid thing to Doug and that the dog survives. Bigsey will most likely require in-depth therapy to get over post-traumatic stress disorder. Maybe she and I can get a group rate. Perhaps Ann will feel some kind of woman solidarity and not embarrass me any further. It can be one of those things just between the two of us. I called a carpet-cleaning company and gave them my Visa card number and her address.

Nick phoned to say that there were four more messages from Melanie on his cell phone. She keeps trying to book a date for me to come in and do psychic readings on the radio. He left her number on my machine, telling me that "the ball's in my court." I pick up the phone and then put it back down. I can't even imagine what I would say to her.

I call Jane. I tell her the whole disgusting thing—the carpet, the howling dog, the faux homemade cake, and the headless, overpriced collectible bird. She's a good friend. She doesn't tell me that she told me so. She just brings over some Baskin Robbins mint chocolate-chip ice cream and lets me have another good cry. She takes Mac for a walk while I take a hot shower and put on clean jammies. Times like this is when you really appreciate girlfriends. She tucks me into the couch with a fleece blanket that she's warmed up in the dryer. She tells me not to think too much about it, that she'll get a sitter tomorrow and come over to help me out. She's a planner. If there's anyone who can actually create a plan to get my life together it will be her. I pull Mac up onto the couch. He snuffles around, digging at the blankets until he's lying pressed up against the back of my knees under the blanket. Only his stubbly muzzle is sticking out. He starts snoring after about two minutes. The sound relaxes me and I fall asleep.

Twenty-three

CAPRICORN

It is time to make a fresh start. A clean house will make for a clean break. Throw out what you don't need and make room for the new. You'll be surprised at how good you'll feel once the project is done.

Jane has a university degree in business administration. She hasn't worked since she had Amanda, but if the country was ever invaded, the prime minister should select Jane to lead the nation to safety. She gets this look in her eye when she's got a project, like a religious zealot. You can see her itching to make color-coded lists, prioritized and organized alphabetically.

Jane comes over in the morning before I've even woken up. This comes as no shock. People who have children have a totally skewed version of what time people should get up. It's like they all become farmers who want to start the day before the sun rises. Mac jumps off the couch and barks at her standing in the door. I would have barked, too, if I could have come up with the energy. She shuffles me into the shower. I can hear her banging around in the kitchen. By the time I come out of the bathroom she is setting out plates. Jane makes the most amazing French toast. She makes sandwiches with cream cheese in the middle and adds orange juice to the egg mixture. Then she soaks the bread/cream cheese sandwiches in the mixture and fries them up in real butter. It tastes divine and is worth every one of the six billion calories. She makes a pot of Earl Grey tea and watches me shovel it in with a self-satisfied look. When I push the plate away, she pulls out her lists. Nations have gone to war with less detailed lists.

Jane is not the kind of person who does things in a small way. She's brought over a trunkload full of boxes. We go through every room and closet and box up every item of Doug's—clothing, pots and pans, and magazines. We have a moment of silence in the backyard when I place Doug's sock on top of the grill and then light it on fire. It burns slowly and gives off a rather nasty smell, but it still feels like an important ritual. Jane also makes me box up all the clothing I own that no longer fits, and stuff that I bought fully planning to find something to match with it someday. She washes my kitchen cupboards, refolds the towels in my closet, and wipes out my fridge. She has me cleaning the bathroom and making the bed with the new sheets she's bought. She makes me toss every set of sheets that I shared with Doug into another box. Jane makes stacks of paper, and everything has to be sorted into "keep," "file," or "toss" piles. She's brought her label maker and made up file folders and photo boxes. In another life she could have been a librarian. I collapse onto the couch. I can't believe how good the place looks. It smells like pine cleaner and fresh laundry. Jane's just getting started.

After lunch Jane goes back to her car and pulls out cans of paint. Doug had always been a big fan of white walls. He liked a "blank canvas" for his paintings, which had been modern swipes of bold color. He'd taken the paintings when he left, leaving me with white walls that had a vague dingy outline of where the paintings had been hanging. Jane pops the lids of the paint cans. She's picked a soft, buttery yellow. She must have gone to some all-night hardware store. She came equipped with brushes, tarps, and rollers, and we spend the rest of the afternoon painting. Mac manages to step into the paint tray and track yellow pawprints across the hardwood floors. I decide I like the look and leave them. We order Indian food for dinner and then pack her car with the clothing for the Salvation Army.

"Are you sure you don't want me to call Doug and arrange for him to pick up his stuff?" Jane asks, leaning against her car. She has yellow paint flecks in her hair. We'd dragged all the boxes and his recliner out into the garage. He had already taken the overstuffed couch. It wasn't until now that I realized that he had taken everything that was in good shape, and left me with the rest. I was surprised at how much was still in the house. When he first left it seemed like he'd taken everything.

"Nah. I can call him. I feel like I should. Besides, you've done enough. How can I ever thank you?"

"It's all in the best friend job description. No thanks needed."

"The place is amazing. I can't believe how different it looks." I give her a hug.

"It's your place now." She smiles and gets into her car. She rolls down the window. "Besides, an orderly house makes for an orderly mind. Give me a call tomorrow."

I wave to her and go back into the house. The yellow walls look warm and inviting. I light a couple of candles. One of them has a vanilla scent. I go downstairs to the basement and pull out the black-and-white photographs I had taken in a continuing education photography course a few years ago. I had them blown up into 8×10s and framed, but never put them anywhere. I drag them upstairs and dust them off. I lean them against various walls trying to decide where they would look best.

In the end I open up a bottle of wine and leave the photographs on the floor. The walls look too fragile to hammer nails into quite yet. With the bookcases cleaned out everything stands out more. I keep wandering around, picking up various things and remembering where I had gotten them. Mac roams from room to room smelling the corners. He has never seen the place this clean. He probably wonders if he's still in the same house. I debate going to bed and calling it a day, but know it will be easier if I finish the whole thing in one swipe.

I get Doug's machine when I call.

BEEP—"*Hi Doug, It's Sophie. I cleaned the house out a bit today and boxed up some more of your stuff. It's in the garage when you want to pick it up. Your old recliner is out there, too. I don't know if you want it anymore. If you don't, let me know and I'll arrange to have it picked up. I swung by the house the other day to wish your mom a happy birthday. She told me that you had brought Melanie over to meet her. It sounds like you guys are getting serious. I just wanted you to know that I wish you both all the best.*"

BEEP—*"This is a message for Melanie. Melanie, this is Emma Lulak. Sorry I haven't returned your messages, it's been a bit hectic. I've consulted with my spirit guides, and determined that doing the radio show just isn't the right thing for me. I appreciate you offering me the opportunity. Take care."*

BEEP—*"Melanie, this is Emma again, sorry to bother you. I've been thinking about that potpourri issue. On further thought I think I got that part of the reading wrong. I think you should avoid it. Oh, and having your parents over every weekend might be a bit too much, too. Okay, take care."*

BEEP—*"Hi, Nick, it's Sophie. I wanted to let you know I've decided against doing that radio show. I still want to help you out with the article, though. I'll make you dinner tomorrow if you're free. Give me a call."*

I brush my teeth and crawl between the sheets. They have that crisp, new sheet feeling. I can still smell a hint of vanilla from the candle downstairs. I have a good cry, but then I sleep.

Twenty-four

AQUARIUS

Cooking provides a chance to show your creativity. Food feeds
the soul as well as the stomach. Dive into the kitchen and let
your creativity flow. Invite friends and share the bounty.

I am a kitchen goddess. I made lunch for Jane, her husband,
and both of their kids. This means that there were technically
two menus. For the adults I made an Asian chicken salad with
toasted almonds, for the kids, hot dogs with Spaghetti O's, ice
cream for dessert for all. Jane's husband, Jeremy, hung the pictures for me, and we all sat in the living room and discussed
how amazing it looked. To let Jane know just how grateful I
was, I promised to baby-sit for her and Jeremy this weekend.
They could have a nice dinner out and the night to themselves
while I watched Ethan and Amanda. Jane was overcome, but as
I told her, it's all in the best friend's job description.

Flush with my lunch success, I had pulled out cookbooks to
find the perfect thing to make Nick for dinner. This is complicated, as he is a bit of a foodie. I ended up deciding on rare tuna
steaks with a citrus salsa and a green salad. It had the extra

bonus of being mostly prepared before he shows up. People watching me cook makes me nervous.

Nick arrived on time with flowers for me and dog cookies for Mac. Dinner turned out, it didn't look as picturesque as the cookbook photo, but it tasted okay.

"This meal was fantastic. I had no idea you knew how to cook." I'm trying to take that as a compliment and not focus too closely on the idea that he doesn't think I looked remotely domestic. "You're a woman of many talents."

"I've got a present for you. For all your patience, all the help you gave me, for everything." I go to the other room and bring him a binder, placing it down in front of him. I'd considered wrapping it up with a bow, but it seemed like overkill. He opens it up to the first page and reads through the table of contents. Nick looks up, his eyes wide, and then he starts flipping the pages.

"I can't believe you did all of this. When did you ever have the time?"

"Research is what I do for living, you know. It's everything you could ever want to know about Alfred Hitchcock and his movies." I lean in over his shoulder. "Here, check this out. I've divided it into his early British period and the movies he made in the US. For each movie I've got a cast list, running time, and a short summary of the plot. I printed off original film reviews, too. I was able to get a full script of *North by Northwest*. I wanted to get them all, but they're expensive. Then, if you flip to this tab, you'll see I made a list of what modern movies have been an homage to his work. Then under this tab, here, I made a list of what video stores locally carry his things and under this one a list of books about him and his movies. The last tab has personal information. He was a dog lover. I like that in a man."

"This is the Hitchcock bible. I can't believe you found all of this stuff." He keeps flipping back and forth. "How can I ever repay you for this? It's amazing."

"This one's on the house. I wanted to do it for you." I love doing nice things for people. It makes me feel all "angel of mercy"-like.

"Are you serious? There's no way I can accept this as a present. It must have taken so much time."

"I want you to have it. Think how much time you spent training me to be a psychic. You didn't have to do that."

"I wanted to. I'm sorry it didn't work out for you and Doug."

"Yeah, well, you win some, you lose some. Maybe it's for the best in the end." I pick up my wine and hold it up for a toast. I've decided that when in doubt, I will practice repeating positive things until I start to believe them. "I predict for myself a new life and new adventures." We clink glasses and drink.

"Are you sure you're not thinking the radio show would be a good adventure?" Nick raises an eyebrow.

"I'm certain it would be an adventure, but you were right. It's one I should take a pass on."

"You're not disappointed, are you?"

"No, not really." I take a large gulp of the wine. "Can I be honest?" He nods. "I had a ton of fun being a psychic. I can understand why people do it. Everyone believes you've got all the answers. You feel special."

"I can understand that." Nick puts down his wine and pulls his chair close to mine. "Can I be honest with you?"

"Sure."

"When I said I was sorry things didn't work out for you and Doug, I didn't mean it." My stomach took a freefall to the floor.

"No?"

"No. Not at all, actually."

"Oh." I wasn't sure what to say. He is looking at me with this intense stare, like I am a statistical problem to be unraveled. He starts to lean closer, but then the phone rings. *Damn.* He sits back in a hurry and fiddles with his napkin. It is Jane on the phone making plans for me to baby-sit for her. Once I get off the phone, Nick is standing, ready to leave. I linger at the door, but the moment is gone. He gives Mac an ear rub and heads off. I wonder how he would kiss. The brief kiss I had given him the night Doug was over went by too quickly. I hadn't paid enough attention. I suspect it wouldn't be at all like Doug. Not that he was going to kiss me. The effects of the wine and new paint smell must be getting to me.

Twenty-five

PISCES

After some reflection you may end up changing your mind about a key decision. We can learn from our past if we take the time.

The first person I ever kissed, except family members of course, was Joel Metcalf. We were both in drama class together. We were doing the play *Grease* and I was playing Rizzo and he was Danny. We had to kiss in one of the scenes. I was more nervous about that than I was about singing in front of the whole school.

The drama crowd was a strange mixing of high school society. The first few rehearsals everyone stuck with their own peer group. By the time the play opened we would all be hugging and promising to all hang out together, friends forever. You could bet that after the closing-night party, it was as if the fairy tale were over. Cinderella's coach turned back into a pumpkin and we returned to passing each other in the halls like total strangers.

Joel was a transfer student. His parents had moved from Chicago. He actually had a walk-on part in a Shakespearean play in Chicago. A play with paid actors, costumes not made by someone's mom, and sets that actually looked like what they were supposed to represent. Sure he had only been "spear carrier #2," but it was still a real acting role. He talked about moving to New York when he was finished with school. Everyone else talked about being a star, but he was interested in being an actor. It made you think he would make it. He had a Flock of Seagulls hairstyle that flopped in his face all the time. He liked bands that were only played on the alternative college radio station. He was tall, lanky, and he had this amazing laugh. I was smitten.

I worried that my limited kissing experience would show and I would suffer from excessive saliva or tongue spasms. I spent several nights practicing by kissing Mr. Winky, my childhood teddy bear. Let's be honest, I knew Mr. Winky was no match for Joel. The first kiss was a bit of a dud. I thought he would go left, but he went right, so there was that awkward nose hockey moment but then we managed it. After practicing daily for a few weeks we got pretty good. Good enough that we started kissing outside of rehearsal.

Our relationship was odd, like one of those doomed wartorn romances. I knew that we didn't really belong together as a couple. We would be together only as long as the play and its magic lasted. He wasn't the kind of person who would stay with me.

I baby-sat for Jane last night. That's when it hit me: This is my future. With any luck she and Jeremy will let me move in to the room above their garage, where I will become strange Auntie Sophie. Jane will have to force her kids to kiss me on the cheek for the holidays. They'll complain that I smell funny. I'll develop a high-pitched, desperate laugh, the laugh of the socially eclipsed. I'll become one of those strange spinster old ladies who are too friendly, like a Muppet gone bad. I will only be let out of the garage on special occasions.

Why is it that unmarried men are called "bachelors," but unmarried women are "spinsters"? Sure, we can try to call ourselves "bachelorettes," but it's not fooling anyone. I believe it is time to take the term back. In the same way other oppressed groups have taken back other derogatory names. I plan to found a group called SPINSTER, it will stand for Single, Pretty, Independent, Normal, Sexy, Terrific, Energetic, but Romantically challenged. This group will only be open to single women over the age of thirty. We will have a manifesto that all new members will have to sign.

The Official SPINSTER Manifesto

- We will no longer attend dinner parties hosted by coupled and married friends unless they promise NOT to invite the sympathy fix-up who will be so repulsive that we have no choice but to believe that our friends think we are desperate.

- At family functions, when surrounded by younger cousins or siblings, we will not wince when an elderly aunt asks, ignoring all other accomplishments in our lives, "So you're the unmarried one, right?"

- We will register for nice china and towels and force loved ones to buy us gifts we really want instead of books on cooking for one.

- When attending other people's weddings, we will not compete with teenage girls and the flower girl to catch the bouquet as if they were throwing food supplies to starving people.

- When we meet a man we will no longer wonder if he could be Mr. Right, and will instead settle for Mr. Right Now.

- If no man appears on the scene, we will consider it acceptable to begin a relationship with BOB (Battery-Operated Boyfriend).

- We will no longer wait to meet the right person to do things with; we will proudly eat on our own, travel on our own, and take on new adventures whenever possible.

The only way my life is going to be interesting is if I make it that way. When Joel and I broke up after the play, I never fought to get him back. I rolled over and accepted it. I may not be in control of what Doug chooses to do, but I do control my own destiny. That's why I called Melanie's friend Holly. I'll do the radio show once and only once. It's a way for me to end my psychic career and take a chance, live a little. If you don't take some chances in life, then what's the point? I know it's risky, but this isn't the kind of opportunity that comes up all that often. I realize not everyone will think this is a good idea, but being on a radio show is just the kind of kick-start adventure my life needs. I've got to stop living through books, stop being just a reader and start being a doer. As the first official member of SPINSTER it is my responsibility to be a role model for others.

Twenty-six

I'm twenty minutes late for my meeting at the radio station. I was home calling agents. When Melanie's friend Holly called me to ask me if I had an agent, I felt like I had to say something. Apparently all the big talents have their own agent—who knew? I told her I had one, which in the technical sense would be a lie. I've *thought* about getting an agent, but it's been busy, what with cleaning out the house and trying to move on with my life.

When I hung up with Holly, I knew I should call someone. The time got away from me. When I started calling this morning, there were several agents who would consider taking me on, but I needed to find one who was free this afternoon. As it turns out, most agents had a full schedule. You would think a few of them would get in the habit of keeping an open slot for these kinds of emergencies. I gave a few of them that advice. I wanted to cancel the meeting then and there, but I know I can't or I will never get up the guts to do it again. Holly said there were some papers to be signed before I could go on the air, and that I should bring my agent to look them over. I decided to take it as a suggestion instead of a firm plan. I figure at this point I've got two choices: I can either try to bluff my way through it, or I have to cancel. No way am I canceling. This is my shot. If I don't do the show, I might as well admit my life is destined for boredom.

The radio station office is in a downtown high rise on Georgia Street. The elevator ride makes me a bit sick. It feels like my stomach is still on the ground floor while the rest of me rushes up the eighteenth. The receptionist is sitting behind a giant wooden desk that fills the room. Above her head, a neon sign with the radio station logo hums. The desk looks as if it is a giant redwood tree on its side. I wouldn't be surprised to see a hippy environmentalist latched to the side with hemp rope. She must be sitting on some kind of raised platform. I feel like an elementary school kid called to the principal's office. I fight the urge to pull a chair up to the desk and stand on that to talk to her. Find out how she feels to have to look up at someone.

"Myron, our station director, and Holly Hammond are already in the conference room. Would you like to wait here for your agent or would you like to go in now?" she asks. Now would be the time to admit that I don't have an agent, but instead I look at my watch like I'm wondering where my agent is. Pesky late agents, it's getting harder and harder for psychics to get good help.

"Yes, well, why don't I go ahead and join them?" I follow her to the conference room. She is wearing these high heels that could double as a deadly kung fu weapon if thrown. They must be at least three or four inches high. If I wore those shoes I would pitch forward onto my face before taking two steps. Who cares if she can type? This woman has talent. We stop outside a wood paneled door and I can hear voices inside.

"Here you go," she says, opening the door. The far wall is composed of floor-to-ceiling windows with a view of downtown and the mountains. The table looks as if it is floating in the center of the room. Myron and Holly are huddled at one end looking at some documents. They both look up at the same time and I wish I had taken the time to stop in the bathroom to freshen my lipstick, comb my hair, and make sure there aren't giant food particles stuck in my teeth.

"I'll have your agent join you as soon as he arrives. There is coffee, tea, and water on the table." She gives a winning smile to Myron. *Look*, it says, *I'm polite, efficient, and doing it all while wearing stilts*. Myron stands up and walks over to shake my hand. Holly is a step behind and envelopes me in a hug. She sits next to me at the table. I see we've become friends since I saw her last. I pour both of us some water.

Myron doesn't look anything like the corporate cut-out I imagined him to be. To tell the truth, he is pretty cute. He looks around forty with dark hair and thick, full eyebrows. He seems exotic, like someone in his family tree was Spanish. He's got an expensive suit on, but he's not wearing a tie. His hands are rough, like he spends his weekends sailing or riding horses, some kind of manly callus-building activity. I wonder if I should say anything or if as the official talent I should act like a prima donna. Maybe this radio opportunity will allow me to meet interesting single men.

"I appreciate you joining us, Ms. Lulak." I nod and look out the window. *How long before they guess I don't have an agent coming?* I make circles of water on the table with my glass. They should have coasters. This is going to leave a cloudy water mark. "My name is Myron Brackenridge, but I imagine with your keen psychic skills you already knew that." Myron gives a half smile. "I have to admit I am a bit more skeptical about this than Holly. I am not interested in our radio station becoming a format for poorly performed magic tricks. However, our programming staff and Holly are really interested in the idea and assure me it's all the rage."

Splendid, he hates me already and he's not the kind of guy to hide his feelings. I don't think he's the man for me. I guess this is how he ended up in radio, as opposed to a more people-oriented profession. Of course if the whole radio thing doesn't pan out at some point, he would be a brilliant collections agent. He strikes me as the kind of guy who would love to foreclose on a home and kick a family with disabled kids out into the street. He gives me a wan smile and writes something on his pad of crisp lemon yellow legal paper. I didn't think to bring paper. I wonder if I should ask him for some so I can write things down. I'm guessing that if I had an agent they would have brought paper. I bet they cover that kind of thing in agent school, always bring paper and writing implements.

"You're amazing. I can't even begin to think how to say thank you." Holly gushes, leaning in to touch my arm. If she were any closer it would constitute an intimate relationship.

"Yes, well. I'm glad I was able to help." I shrug noncommittally, trying to act like paranormal activities were all in a day's work.

"You literally saved my life." Holly shakes her head as if in disbelief.

"What we were thinking of is having you appear on Holly's show. It's a chat format. Have you listened to it before?" Myron breaks in, already tired of the lovefest. I nod enthusiastically like I've been tuning in for years instead of just this past week. "So you know the format. The two of you will discuss the reading you gave her and psychic issues in general. Then we'll have you take calls. Have you done this kind of format before?"

"Uh, no, not exactly this kind of format."

"You've been on radio before, though?"

I laugh and toss my hair in what I hope is a confident manner without exactly answering the question.

"Maybe we should call your agent and see if something has delayed him. I'm hoping we can sign an agreement quickly so we can get you on the show today," Myron says, tapping the tip of his pencil on the pad of paper.

"If you'll excuse me, I'll just step out and give him a quick call," I say, standing up. It feels like there is an oxygen shortage, like we're up too high and the air is thinner. I find the women's restroom, lock myself in the stall and sit down. The walls are covered with some kind of granite or marble. I sit, pressing my hot face against its cool side. This isn't going well. Not only am I lying about being a psychic, a psychic with an *agent* no less, I am now also lying about having radio experience. It could be that this SPINSTER Manifesto was going a bit too far. I concentrate on deep breathing. I hear the door open. It's the receptionist; I recognize her voice and the sound of her stilts on the floor as she talks to another woman.

They are chatting about someone the receptionist is having an affair with and if anyone else at work knows. They're worried his wife is going to find out. The place is a den of immoral living. I'm wondering how long I can stay in the bathroom before Holly and Myron come looking for me. I like the idea of sitting here until everyone else goes home for the night. I consider just getting up and leaving altogether. What are the odds the receptionist would try to stop me? I sit for a few more minutes before I get up. I can't keep trying to crawl out of places. Sometimes you've got to stand up. This was a mistake. I'm going home. I stop to check my teeth in the mirror on the way out and put on some lipstick.

Myron and Holly stop talking when I enter the room. I hate when that happens. "I think we're going to have to reschedule. My agent has had an emergency and won't be able to come." I give a shrug like I'm personally really disappointed and wanted nothing more than to have this meeting. I stand by the door. I feel like I'm waiting for permission to leave.

Myron gives an annoyed sigh. You'd think he could be a bit more understanding here. My imaginary agent is having a real emergency. It could be a death in the family or an accident. "I'm sorry to hear about your agent, however, the agreement is standard. We could have you sign it now and we'll fax it over to your agent to sign off on later. That way we won't have to miss today's show."

"I'm not sure I should. I mean, not without my agent present."

"Of course the agreement won't be binding until he signs, but I can promise you it's standard. I can't imagine there would be any difficulties." He pushes a piece of paper across the table. I start reading it but it's full of legal contract language, blah, blah, blah, "the artist hereforeafter known as Emma Lulak" blah, blah, blah, "wherefor, default, first rights for replays in North America," blah blah, blah. The words start to link and dance across the page. I need time to make sense of this. I can't tell what I am agreeing to, and for all I know there's a paragraph here on giving away my firstborn. Not that there's a chance of *having* a firstborn, or any children for that matter, with Doug firmly planted in Melanie's bed and my newly confirmed spinster status. Myron hands me a pen. I know I should leave, but if I refuse to sign the form he's not going to let me on the air. If I don't get on the air now then this whole thing is over and I'll go back to my day-to-day life. I take a deep breath and take the leap. I smile at Myron and sign the form.

No guts, no glory, as they say.

Myron grabs the form with alarmingly quick reflexes. He takes my arm and leads me down the hall. We pass large glossy photos of the various radio personalities and I have a strong urge to slow down and take a closer look. Some of these guys are scary, take Chuck Goodine, the guy who does the morning show. He has a voice that sounds like warm honey. A voice that makes you want to invite him over, skip the dinner and movie formalities, and go right to bed. However, he looks like the high school yearbook photo of the kid voted most likely to need extensive plastic surgery. Surely being on the radio pays well enough that he could do something about those teeth. They all but spray fanlike over his lower lip. He looks like a rabid beaver, or a spokesperson for British dentistry. I can't wait to tell Jane. Myron pulls me along until we get into what looks like the business end of the hallway. Door after door is marked with various studio numbers.

Myron sits me down in a room that isn't much larger than a walk-in closet. It has a table, microphone stand, and a pair of headphones. There is a window into what looks like a NASA control room. Holly and Myron go into the other room and I can see them through the glass. I give them a confident wave. I have to admit to being a bit disappointed with the setup. I'm not sure what I expected, something a bit more old glamour Hollywood. Instead the room has seventies tweed wallpaper that's torn in a few places, and the desk looks like it was salvaged from a Dumpster. There's a Styrofoam cup sitting on the desk with cold coffee in it and a wad of dried-out gum stuck to the edge. I push it to the far side of the desk. I slowly sit down in the chair. I'm starting to think my original idea of making a run for it from the bathroom might have been the better plan. Who knew adventures could be so stressful? I put the headphones on my head knowing they will ruin my hair. They are giant black foam earpieces. I suspect I look like a robotic version of Princess Leia. I can't hear a thing. Myron is waving at me so I wave back. We do this back and forth for a minute, and then Holly comes into the room. She gives me a smile.

"You didn't turn on the intercom. You can't hear us without that." I nod and turn to the desk. There is a metal box about the size of a shoe box covered with dials and buttons. None of them are helpfully marked INTERCOM. There is a strong need for Jane's label maker here. I push a large button and a shrill feedback sound erupts. In the other room Myron yanks the headphones off his head. Holly leans in and pushes a small, non-descript lever up. I can now hear Myron cursing.

"Oh, *that* intercom button," I say. She gives me a pat on the shoulder and then joins Myron.

"Ms. Lulak, you're certain you've done this before?"

"It's been awhile." I'm holding my purse like a life vest. I feel like I'm going down. It would feel good to close my eyes and just slide under the table.

"What is your agent's name, Ms. Lulak?" Myron's forehead is all wrinkled up. Great, now even he feels sorry for me. He thinks I am incapable of getting a competent agent on my own. He's going to rat out my poor imaginary agent to the professional association or something. Poor guy has a family emergency and is on the verge of being thrown out of his profession. I would feel bad for him if my own life wasn't so screwed up.

"I really think I should wait to do any of this until I've talked to my agent." Or at least until I've had a chance to learn a bit more about this radio thing. There must be books on this subject. I stand up and turn toward the door. The headphones I've forgotten I was wearing are connected by a cord to the table. It draws taught for a second, and then yanks me back like a bungee cord. I fall to my knees and then bounce back up. I can hear Myron's tinny laugh through the headphones. I yank the headphones off and try not to look like I'm bolting for the door. Holly dashes after me, catching up to me in the station lobby.

"Are you okay? Is it nerves? Look, a lot of people get nervous about being on the radio. It's not a big deal, Myron is just one of those guys who doesn't have any patience. We'll send him off for some coffee and I'll coach you through it." She's being so nice. I doubt she would be if she knew I'd lied to her. I feel tears starting to well up in my eyes. Great, now I have no human dignity left. Myron's standing next to the receptionist and another secretary. Geez, why don't we make some popcorn and they can pull up their seats.

"I'm sorry about taking up your time," I mumble.

"Ms. Lulak, this is a serious radio station. I was not amused with the idea of doing a psychic call-in to start with, and your behavior today has not been a confidence booster." Great. Now that I'm being lectured to, I've changed my mind and decide he's not remotely attractive. More dark and sinister. The kind of guy who looks like he should be tying innocent girls to railroad tracks. "This whole thing is ridiculous," he huffs.

"Psychic phenomena is complicated and I don't need to defend myself to you." I'm wiping my tears away with the sleeve of my shirt, making long streaks of mascara. The cheap stuff is never waterproof. Holly is looking frantically between me and Myron.

"I have no idea of what you are trying to do. I doubt you have a psychic bone in your body," Myron says.

"Yes, I do."

"No, you don't."

"Do too." Our conversation has sunk to junior high lows. It's a stand-off. Then it comes to me. I turn and face the receptionist. I point a finger at her. I detest pointers, but you have to admit it is dramatic, "You!"

The receptionist looks stapled to the floor by her stilettos.

We've gathered a nice crowd in the lobby now. Everyone is standing around in a half moon facing me and the elevators. It's a mini–theater-in-the-round.

"You!" I point at her again. "You are in love with someone, I can sense it." She points to herself with one perfectly manicured hand. Myron rolls his eyes.

"That's your psychic skill? Guessing that a young woman is in love—very impressive." I ignore him.

"You are in love with someone who already loves another. Wait, he's married." The receptionist gasps and her face goes pale. *Take that.* "I can feel his presence nearby. He has been to this office, hasn't he?" I turn around like I am sniffing the air, sucking in those psychic vibrations. She nods her head in agreement. "He works here, doesn't he?!" I can hear the other staff starting to whisper. "You are afraid, afraid that the relationship will end badly. You are tired of being alone. You want to meet someone and have a permanent relationship. I'm telling you, it will not be with this man." I nod wisely. The receptionist is crying now. Myron looks very uncomfortable. Suddenly, I've got a hunch who the married guy in the office might be. I fix Myron with a look, and his eyes widen. I nod. I'm tempted to point at him, too, but instead I settle for a knowing smile. He looks like he might vomit. Holly is doing her open-mouthed fish routine again. That girl is very easily entertained. Not bad for my first public reading. The elevator bell bings and I turn and walk inside.

"Wait! What should I do?" the receptionist cries out.

As the doors slide shut I yell out, "You should dump him the way he's dumping his wife!"

Holly must have taken the next elevator as she catches me

on the street as I walk out the front door. She's full of apologies from Myron. Apparently the radio station wants me more than ever. They are even willing to up my fee. I consider telling her to stick it, but instead I allow her to lead me back. I have a hunch things are going to work out just fine.

Turns out, I was wrong.

Twenty-seven

You have found your groove and are on top of your game.
Things seem to fall into your lap today.

When I predicted that things would go fine, I was unbelievably
wrong. It didn't go fine—it went amazingly brilliant! I think
there are few things more boring than people who go on and
on about how clever they are, but I really can't help myself. I
let Holly lead me back to the station. The receptionist clicked
around me in her stilettos like she was my personal fairy godmother. She brought me water and when I casually mentioned
that I preferred Perrier, she ran to the corner convenience store
and bought some—perfectly chilled, I might add. Holly took
me back into the studio and gave me a tour of all the knobs
and switches. The receptionist thoughtfully brought in some
neon colored Post-it Notes and marked down what everything
was for me. They were like Hindu prayer flags, fluttering on
all the gears whenever the air clicked on in the tiny room. Myron personally came down to apologize.

The radio show itself was a breeze. Holly talked about her

experiences. Turns out she is the kind of girl who can't turn around without some type of bizarre paranormal thing happening to her. In addition to the smoke detector prediction I made for her, she's also seen her grandmother appear at the end of her bed only to get a call an hour later that her grandmother had actually passed away. Sometimes, she knows when the phone rings who will be on the other line. For a few years she suspected a malevolent spirit had it out for her due to a series of mishaps including broken shoe heels and a nasty allergic reaction to sunscreen. The girl is a ghost magnet.

I paused for a moment when she asked me when I became aware of my psychic skills. I was semishocked by the fact that she had stopped talking and actually asked me a question. She had been blathering along about her own personal experiences for so long that I was distracting myself by imagining myself in charge of the NASA space launch, what with the headphones and knobs. I hadn't expected Holly to ask me any questions about myself. I thought we would focus on taking calls. I could see Holly through the glass and I knew she was getting worried that I had frozen and wouldn't be able to do it. That's when I discovered that I was born to be a liar, or I was channeling some spirit guide who is way more comfortable with doing radio.

"Well, Holly, when I look back on it I realize that I always 'knew' things, even as a small child. I didn't know that it was anything special. I thought it was something that anyone could do. As I grew older I understood that it was a unique gift but I still didn't think of it as extraordinary in any way. Although it's strange, I sensed at some level that it was something that others would not understand and that I should keep it to myself."

"Did your parents understand or were they disbelievers?" She makes the word *disbelievers* sound like my parents trafficked in kiddie porn.

"My parents split up when I was quite young. To be honest, I didn't see my dad often. My mom was pretty busy trying to support us, so I don't think she had a lot of time to worry about the 'hunches' I used to have. I believe that being psychic is like any other skill, it takes practice. For a long time I simply didn't practice."

"What changed for you?"

"Recently I suffered a personal setback. Someone that I cared for very much hurt me. I realized then that I had known in some way that it was going to happen. I needed to start listening to that inner voice instead of hiding from it. I needed to try to save myself from the hurt and also to assist others. I certainly don't consider myself a professional in any way, but if my ability can help others in some form, then maybe that's why I'm here, to do just that."

Holly gushed about how she couldn't agree more. How we often don't know that we touch other people's lives. How my prediction of how she needed to check her smoke detector might have seemed like a small thing, but was a true lifesaver. Then she opened up the phone lines. I was nervous at first, but it was easier than I had expected. A lot of people called simply to tell their own stories of how they had a strange feeling about something and lo and behold, it had come true. *Coincidence* is not a term these people are familiar with. They honestly think everything has some deep meaning. They all seemed rather keen on the idea that they might be psychic themselves. I think there could be a major industry in training others to be in touch with their psychic skills—provided you don't let on that you're faking it. Everyone seems convinced that they have some huge well of undeveloped talent in this area. Even if they didn't think they had any skill, they were certain that I did. After the first couple of calls I actually relaxed and had a good time.

"Can you tell me anything about my dad?" the caller asks, sounding like she is already crying.

"I can try. I'm getting an image of a man and a little girl. You were quite the daddy's girl, I think." Sobs come through the headphone, which lead me to believe I am on the right track. "You are feeling badly about things you said when you were a teenager. Your dad is telling me that he knew that you didn't mean it, that you were just doing your job of growing up, which means growing apart."

"I've felt so bad since he died. Sometimes I was just awful to him."

"He's smiling now. I get the sense that the only thing he's angry about is you being unhappy. He says he raised you better than for you to spend too much time worrying over these things. He had a special name for you, a name only he called you. . . ."

"How did you know that? Oh my god, I can't believe it." She gasps. It wasn't a hard guess—how many parents give their kids a pet name? I keep that thought to myself. "My dad used to call me his poppet."

"Well, Poppet, your dad is telling you to take care of yourself. He watches over you." The woman cries some more and thanks me. This psychic stuff is easy, but I feel a bit bad about the girl wanting information on her dad. It makes me think of what happened to Nick's mom, but honestly, this woman sounds so much happier after we talk. Thankfully most people are calling with questions about their love life.

"Am I going to meet anyone?"

"Yes, I can see a figure. I see the two of you sitting at an outdoor café, and you're laughing."

"Wow, that's great, can you tell me anything else?"

"It's hard to get a good picture of him, more of a sense. He's dark haired, with sort of floppy bangs that he keeps pushing out of his eyes. He's got a great smile, sort of crooked." I'm getting a bit carried away picturing my perfect guy, when I notice the caller is getting quieter. Somehow I've gone wrong. Maybe she's really into blonds.

"A dark-haired guy?" she asked. Uh-oh. I suspect I know the problem. This woman is not looking for the man of her dreams. She is, as they say, playing for the other team.

"Yep, it's a guy. I see the two of you at the table. Wait a minute, he's waving to someone to join you. I get the sense it's his sister. He kisses her on the cheek. I see this woman, who looks like the female version of him, same hair, same smile, is now kissing you. I think it is the woman who is your partner." There is silence that greets this before the caller begins to gush. She's thinks I'm brilliant. Holly thinks I'm brilliant. The sound guy looks like he thinks I'm brilliant.

When the show ends, Holly rushes in while I'm still trying to get myself untangled from the wires, cords, and headphones.

"You were amazing! I can't believe you knew that woman was gay." I think about pointing out that I hadn't known until she all but spelled it out for me, but decide against it.

"I appreciate you giving me the chance to do the show. I'm glad you think it went well." I feel like I've won a beauty pageant. Everyone is coming into the studio to shake my hand or pat my back. I feel like breaking into a rendition of "I Feel Pretty" from *West Side Story*. I wouldn't be completely surprised if someone pinned a tiara to my head and handed me a large bouquet of roses. I do my best to suppress the urge I have to wave to everyone.

Nick may be wrong about this psychic thing. I'm not saying I have any actual skill, but is it really that wrong? I do have an unerring ability to guess well, that must be some kind of special gift. Everyone who called had a problem and I offered them some advice or comfort, like a call-in psychologist. I think the problem is that there isn't enough hope in the world. All I did was offer people a reason to hang on. In a lot of ways you could look at it as similar to doing them a favor. Holly made me promise that I would come again next week and do another show. I hesitated for a moment, but it really wouldn't be right for me to hide my light under a bushel. It would be like driving away from the scene of an accident instead of stopping to help.

Twenty-eight

CANCER
Your star is burning bright. Others may find it difficult to adjust
to the new you. You may need to be alone; don't let their negative
energy dim your light.

"Okay, you have to tell me how you guessed the one woman was gay." Jane and I are sitting in my living room sharing a pint of Häagen-Dazs cookie-dough ice cream reliving my media debut.

"I didn't at first. She just sounded so disappointed when I was describing her future date that it occurred to me that she was looking for something completely different." I shrug waving my spoon about.

"Do you think she'll be keeping her eyes out now for a dark-haired, crooked-smile lesbian?"

"Got me. At the very least she'll have something nice to daydream about while she waits for Mr., I mean, *Ms.* Right to come along."

"What if she doesn't connect with her real Ms. Right because she's too busy looking for the one you described?"

"I don't know. There must be some kind of lesbian destiny. I suspect if it's meant to be, it will be."

"But it's not really destiny, is it? I mean, you told her something that isn't true."

"I told her what she wanted to hear, that there is someone out there for her. Does it really matter if the person is dark haired, blonde or dyes her hair green? Look, if it really bothers you, the next time I'm on Holly's show I'll make an announcement that I may have been wrong about the dark hair part. The caller should keep her mind open to all possibilities." Jane put her spoon back in the container.

"What do you mean, 'next time'? You're not going to do the show again, are you?"

"I hadn't been planning on it, but Holly and Myron all but begged me. I'm telling you, it was almost embarrassing."

"I thought you were going to do it one time to get this Holly person off your back."

"What does it matter? I'm telling you it was a ton of fun. Did I mention how they brought me Perrier water? You know when I was in junior high I used to pretend to be a radio DJ. I would make mixed tapes for my friends, complete with commentary between all the songs. Maybe this radio thing was meant to be." Jane wasn't eating any of her ice cream. She was getting that look. The perfected mother "I'm so disappointed in you" look that is designed to shame you into a particular behavior.

"This isn't the same thing as being a DJ, though, is it? You're not introducing songs, you're giving people predications. It's not like you're really psychic."

"The point is, no one is psychic. It's not like I'm putting a highly talented psychic out of work by giving fake predictions. All of them are fake." Jane chewed on the inside of her cheek; it looks like she has a dimple vortex.

"I know *you* don't believe in psychics," Jane says.

"Don't tell me *you* do." I can't believe this. Jane believes this hokey stuff? Jane, the master of detail and organization? Jane, Ms. Grounded in Reality, believes?

"I don't know. I don't automatically assume it's fake. I think there are a lot of things that we don't understand, that we can't understand. I don't think you should be playing around with it. I mean, it was one thing to try to get Doug back, but to keep doing it seems wrong."

"You have to be kidding. C'mon Jane, use your brain here."

"Are you saying to believe in this stuff is stupid? That anyone who believes differently from you is stupid?"

"No. I'm just saying the whole thing is ridiculous. Honestly, Jane, I can show you how it's done. It's just a game."

"You can show me how you do it. That's all you know. You don't know how other people do it. I've heard a lot of stories I don't know how to explain. I think acting like you know everything is more ridiculous than me saying that I don't know how everything works. What happened to believing in a little magic once in a while?" Suddenly I don't feel like eating ice cream anymore, either.

"Let's agree to disagree on this one, okay?" Who says I'm not a peacemaker?

"Okay, I'll agree to drop it, but I think you should agree to stop with the radio show."

"Regardless of being psychic, I'm giving people good advice.

Did you hear everyone that I talked to? They were all so thankful. They liked what they were hearing. I was helping people."

"So you're saying that you want to do this to help others? You want to go back on the radio strictly for humanitarian reasons. You're like the Mother Theresa of psychic Healing now? This wouldn't have anything to do with wanting to be the center of attention?"

I stand up and march into the kitchen, tossing the ice-cream container back in the freezer. It had been a great day. I was feeling on top of the world. All I wanted to do was top off the day with some ice cream, and my supposedly best friend, who I would think would want to help me enjoy my success instead of trying to make me feel like I had run over someone's puppy and then backed the car up and spit on its fuzzy little carcass.

"I didn't mean to upset you," Jane says, leaning against the kitchen doorjamb. "It's just that I think if you do this radio show again you're asking for trouble. What if someone recognizes your voice? It sounds like you. What if Doug figures it out? I have this feeling it will turn out badly. You had a good time. It was a lark, but you should quit while you're ahead."

"So now *you're* making predictions?" I know that sounds snotty, but I couldn't resist.

"I'm trying to give you some advice."

"Consider it taken." I cross my arms and wait for Jane to say she's sorry so we can go back into the living room and return to talking about my media success.

"Well then, I guess I better get going." We look at each other for a minute. We both know that Jeremy promised to get the kids dinner and she doesn't need to be going anywhere.

"Sure. I'll see you around." I don't walk her to the door. I give the fridge a small kick when I hear the front door latch shut.

After a few rum and Diet Cokes, I've decided that I shouldn't be surprised that Jane felt the way she did. In every friendship there is one leader and one follower. Jane was the Lone Ranger, I was her Tonto. She was Sherlock Holmes, I was her Watson. She was Batman, I was her Robin. You get the idea. When I met her in college she was beyond cool. She had perfected the black eyeliner, red lipstick, and thin clove cigarette thing. She had been popular in high school and rode that wave of confidence right into college. As opposed to me, who sort of tried to scuttle in under the radar. She never worried about what she was wearing. She had this sense of confidence that she looked good no matter what she threw together. If someone didn't like her, Jane didn't spend hours agonizing over it, she just figured it was their problem and moved on.

I met Jane in a modern literature class. It was taught by Professor Limtick. He was this crusty old guy who had more hair growing out of his ears than on his head. He would chew on the earpiece of his thick black-rimmed glasses while lecturing. It really grossed me out. He gave off the vibe of a teacher who saw students as an inconvenience. We were reading Margaret Atwood's *A Handmaid's Tale*. Professor Limtick was going on, and on, about women's persecution of each other. How women kept each other down, but didn't blame each other, but instead blamed men. I was slowly getting steamed, but it never occurred to me to actually say something. I wasn't that kind of student. Jane raised one perfectly manicured hand.

"Yes?" Professor Limtick asked, as if he was already bored with her question before she even asked it. The best part was she didn't even ask a question. She didn't doubt her opinion, she just stated it.

"I think you're wrong."

"I beg your pardon?"

"I think you're wrong. I mean, women are mean to each other, but that pales in comparison to the role men have played in keeping women in a weaker role. To imply that women are limited to having catfights is simplifying the issue too much."

I don't think Professor Limtick knew what to say. He bit completely through his ear-piece. You could hear the plastic crack. He mumbled something and moved on to another topic. I ran up to Jane after class to tell her how much I appreciated her comments. I thought she was brave. What struck me is that she didn't think it was being brave at all. She just assumed that her opinion was as valid as his. She invited me to go with her to get a cup of coffee and we were friends from that day forward.

The point is, Jane was the leader in our relationship. She introduced me to her social circle. She set me up with friends of the guys she was dating. She picked the movies we went to see. She moved to Canada first. I'm not trying to make it sound as if she was on a power trip or anything, she's just the kind of person who always seems to know where she's going. You know how when you're in a group and are trying to decide where to go for dinner and everyone's saying, "I don't know, where do *you* think we should go?" Jane never says she doesn't know. She always knows where she wants to be and what she wants to be doing. It isn't that she isn't willing to listen to my opinion; it's just that I often don't have one. I'm the one always asking for advice, not the one giving it.

I can see now how hard it must be for Jane to see me having this sudden success. She's always been the one who had the spotlight on her. I imagine seeing the focus turning on me, the "media glare," so to speak, must be very hard. I realize that I'm going to have to be the bigger person in this instance. I'll give her a couple of days to recognize that she's being silly, and then give her another chance. It might be asking too much to ask her to be happy for me at this moment. I decide to celebrate this mature insight by adding ice cream to my rum and Diet Coke, thereby making a tasty, boozy ice-cream soda.

Twenty-nine

LEO
Be willing to look inside and question yourself. Others will challenge your decisions in the days to come, but now is not the time to back down from your dreams.

Today is the fourth time I've appeared on Holly's show. I have my own swipe card for the bathroom and under my picture it says "Media Talent." Granted, the name on the card, Emma Lulak, isn't really mine, but the point is that it still looks pretty cool. When I come in the receptionist always has a cold bottle of Perrier waiting for me in the studio. She gave me a thank-you card today. Turns out she broke up with her married lover, it *was* Myron, by the way, and as I predicted, she met someone else. This was also not a hard prediction to make. She's stunning and is able to walk in shoes that force her breasts in one direction and her bum in the other in a desperate bid by her body to find a balance point. She's not the kind of woman who would be stuck sitting at home alone for too long. The UPS delivery driver who drops off packages at the station asked her out. She thinks he's dreamy, looks amazing in tiny brown shorts, and is single. She's in heaven. She thinks I am responsible for this turn in her love life. Maybe in some way I am, since if I hadn't shaken up her view of life, she would still be sneaking around with Myron to seedy motels. I don't know if he actually took her to seedy motels. It's possible he took her to upscale places like the Four Seasons, but the point is she's no longer forced to live out a lie where her love is something shady and shameful. Now she can ride around with pride in the UPS truck with her new man, assuming, of course, that UPS allows this kind of hanky-panky.

I have the radio thing down. I know which buttons to push, and I call the sound guy by his first name, Brandon. I've perfected the ability to hold the headphones up to one ear while the sound check runs. I've even decided that I was wrong about Holly. I had assumed that since she was friends with Melanie, she was an empty-headed bimbo, but that simply isn't true. She's very spiritual and interested in self-exploration. She takes all kinds of classes on "discovering yourself" and has stacks of notebooks filled with her introspections. She feels that keeping a journal is an important part of charting your own path. How do you know who you are if you don't know where you're coming from? Something like that, it made more sense when we were talking about it over coffee. It's inspired me to go out and buy a notebook so I can chart my own introspections. I've decided, however, that a plain notebook isn't what I need. I want a nice leather journal, maybe embossed with some kind of design. After all, I plan to have some pretty serious thoughts and I should make the effort to store them in something fitting.

I walk out of the radio station, giving the security guard a cheery wave. I love walking in downtown Vancouver, provided it's not pouring rain. The last time there was so much rain in one place at one time, it was a time for ark-building and gathering animals two by two. Today, however, is dry, which makes it a perfect day to wander from the radio station to Robson Street. Robson Street is Vancouver's version of New York City's Fifth Avenue, Paris's *Champs Élysée's*, or London's Kensington High Street. Haute couture shops sitting next to trendy boutiques, next to kitschy tourist T-shirt shops. Everyone looks like they just stepped out of a photo shoot. Even the street people look sort of chic. It is a shopping paradise. There are several shops that could be harboring my future journal. Although it is a rough job, I plan to go into each and every shop until I locate it. It's a quest—*Indiana Jones and the Lost Ark of the Journal* kind of thing. Once discovered, possibly along with a sweater, or some new makeup, I will go to one of the many Starbucks that litter the street like confetti after a New Year's parade. I will order a chai tea latte, because it sounds exotic, and sit outside at one of the wrought-iron tables and write my deep thoughts in my new journal.

"Sophie!" I look up. Nick is across the street, waiting to cross. Suddenly it feels like my saliva is thickening up and it's getting harder to swallow. I wouldn't say that I have been avoiding Nick. I mean, if you want to be technical, he's only called three or four times, six tops. I've been a very busy woman. This radio thing has kept me busy. I've had to memorize the various astrological signs. People are very fussy if you aren't able to immediately know their sign based on their birthdate. I've had to keep notes about what kinds of predictions I've made. I've checked out my local library's entire collection of psychic self-help books so that I can be sure that I've got the lingo down and can use the term *chakra* in a sentence. I've rewatched the video that Nick lent me about a million times. I have now officially watched it more than I have seen my DVD of *Pretty Woman* or *Pirates of the Caribbean*. On top of all of this, I had to keep up my hours at Stacks of Books and take Mac to the park on a regular basis to avoid dog vengeance demonstrated by shoe-chewing. Mac is not a dog who will be ignored. The point is, although I haven't gotten back in touch with Nick, it hasn't been an avoidance thing.

I paste a wide smile on my face and wave at him as if I am sitting on top of a parade float. I manage to get a swallow down while I wait for the light to change. Even though there is no traffic coming, Nick waits obediently at the corner until the light changes and the flashing walking guy gives him the okay. He walks across with one hand stuffed deep in his pocket, his pants bagging at the knees. His leather briefcase is clutched in the other hand. It looks like he normally drags it behind his car at high speeds.

"Nick! It's so good to see you." I lean in and give him a brief one handed hug. "I am so sorry that I haven't called you back. It's been crazy."

"Crazy?"

"Listen, how about we grab a cup of coffee and catch up? If now isn't a good time for you, I mean if you're on your way to something, we could make plans to meet another time."

"I came down here to try to catch you leaving the station." I'm not really sure what to say to that. In one way, I feel guilty. In another way, I think it's not like it's been months and that he had no choice but to turn to stalking me. I mean, I would have called.

"Well, we found each other now." I give him another smile

but it feels like my lips are stuck to my teeth. First it felt like there was too much saliva in my mouth and now it feels like there isn't anywhere near enough.

"About these radio shows . . ." He pauses, looking away and down the street for a moment as if fascinated by the squeegee kids. They darted out into traffic between lights.

"You're wondering how much longer I plan to do them." He looks relieved that I've said it and saved him the trouble of having to confront it. "I can imagine you're disappointed."

"I thought you'd decided against doing the show. You can imagine the situation that this puts me in. I work for CSICOP. It's our job to investigate psychics and now the psychic with the fastest-growing popularity is one I trained. You're like some Frankenstein monster out of control." He runs his hand through his curly hair and it juts out here and there like he just crawled out of bed.

"Am I really like the fastest-growing in popularity?"

"I think you're missing the key point here."

"I had no idea. I mean, I knew the show was gaining popularity here and the show is available for download online. Do they have some kind of tracking system for these things? Like a bestseller list?"

"Bestseller list? Are you planning a book?" he asks.

Well, I haven't thought about it in any serious way. I've only done four shows, but they've gone extremely well. Holly thinks that I'm a natural at handling callers. I'm a good writer. I could write a book, how hard can it be? Just one sentence at a time really. Not that I'm thinking of writing a book, mind you, it's just interesting to think about. I'm trying to imagine what I would wear for those snappy author photos that they have on the back of the book when I notice that Nick is giving me a strange look.

"Of course I'm not thinking of doing a book! I was just sort of intrigued when you said I was growing in popularity. I guess that's what I get for being trained by the best. I'm serious, I couldn't do this without you." I put my hand on his arm and he pulls back.

"I appreciate your vote of confidence, but I would rather you weren't doing it at all. If my colleagues found out I was involved in this, it would be very embarrassing for me."

"I certainly don't plan to tell anyone."

"That's not the point," he says, his voice rising in volume. "The point is that you asked me to do this as a favor to you. You misled me. You indicated that this was about your relationship. Now you're on the radio giving readings to every person who places a call."

"I know how you feel about this."

"No, you don't you don't know a thing about it!"

"I know you don't believe. I don't believe. But you know a lot of people do. What's wrong with that? So they believe in something that isn't true. Who does it hurt, if they're getting something from the experience? Heck, who knows? Maybe there's something to it. Regardless, if they feel better, then what's the big deal? Do you tell little kids at Christmastime that there is no Santa Claus?"

"I can't believe you. You're saying it's okay to con people, to lie to them. You're selling something that doesn't even exist. I didn't think you were the kind of person who would do this."

"I'm not doing anything wrong. It's entertainment, that's

all. Maybe what's bothering you is that you can't investigate me without it reflecting poorly on you."

"So that's it. You refuse to see reason." He shook his head. "You're right, I'm worried about looking bad. I have a reputation that I'm proud of. What you're doing goes against everything that I believe in. To be involved in it, even against my will, makes me ashamed, and I feel ashamed for you, too." Nick turns on his heel and starts walking away.

"Nick!" I grab his shoulder. He turns to face me. His eyes look full, as if he's close to yelling or choking me. He seems to be taking this whole thing a bit too far. "Please don't be mad."

"You don't want me to be mad? Then just stop. Stop the whole thing and admit what you're doing." We stand on Georgia Street looking at each other for a moment, and then he turns again and walks away.

Thirty

VIRGO
Things seem unsettled and out of your control. Try to see challenges as a chance to learn something new instead of as obstacles.

I knew I was upset because it sapped my desire to shop. Normally, I could have a limb lopped off and I would just tie a silk scarf to close off the artery and keep dragging myself through the mall. Now I just want to go home and curl up on the couch with my fleece blanket and Mac. Liberal doses of chocolate may be required. It seems like everyone around me has turned against me. They're acting as if instead of pretending to be a psychic, I'm conning elderly people out of their pensions.

Instead of a fancy leather embossed journal, I end up writing on the back of some wrapping paper that I found in the closet.

Reasons to keep doing the radio psychic show:

- I love it.

- It makes money, which, to be honest, comes in handy when your profession is working in a bookstore.

- Despite what everyone thinks, I am helping people.

- No one is getting hurt. I'm not taking money for doing the readings. The radio station pays and they aren't paying me that much. I am certain they are not in any financial danger.

- This gives me something to be excited about, the first thing that feels good since Doug left. I think I deserve my fair share of happiness.

Reasons to stop doing the show:

- I might get caught.

- Jane.

- Nick.

I put the pen down. I pick Mac up and look him in the eyes. When all else fails, you have to turn to the one who knows you best. Mac has deep, chocolate-colored eyes, buried underneath his bushy old-man eyebrows. I can see the serious set of his mouth through his beard. He knows I have something important to say.

"You don't think I'm a bad person, do you?" Mac licks the end of my nose. I can tell that he's using his interspecies communication to tell me that of course he knows I'm not a bad person. I'm the giver of cookies, the provider of squeaky toys, willing to walk him even in the rain, that if there should be some type of natural disaster and we were down to our last kibble—I would share with him.

"If the two of them asked me about *why* I was doing it instead of jumping all over me for the reasons that I shouldn't be doing it, then maybe they would have understood." Mac fixes me with a look. He loves me, but he's not afraid to tackle the hard issues.

"Okay, maybe I could have bit a more understanding myself. I'll admit that, but I really love this." Mac continues his stare, no blinking, no looking away. Damn, he can be hard.

"Of course I don't love it more than my friends. Give me a break, here." Mac gives a low woof, not really a growl, more of a doggy sound of disgust. I look at him, but in the end I am the one who looks away. He's amazing, a dog of so few words and yet so convincing. He would give the Harvard debate team a run for their money.

"Okay, you win. You're right." I put him down on the couch, where he winds around in circles until he finds just the right spot and lies down. Now that his work is done, he's ready for a nap. It looks tempting to join him, but I think I should spend the time preparing for tomorrow's radio show. After all, if it's going to be my last, I should make sure it's memorable.

Thirty-one

LIBRA

Being connected to the right person makes all the difference, even though you say you would prefer to be independent. A curious whim will lead you to a new, exciting place. You will regain something you thought you had lost.

The show has been really busy today. The phones are ringing off the hook. Myron met me at the door this morning with flowers, not cheap flowers, either, from some checkout counter at the 7-Eleven but fancy florist flowers. Apparently the station's ratings have shot sky-high since I joined the team. He wants to talk with me after the show about becoming a regular. It seemed like it would be ungrateful to take the flowers and then quit on the guy. It will be easier to go with my original plan that I dreamed up after Mac and I had our discussion. I thought it would be sort of dramatic to have a sudden "vision."

My vision is simple. As Jane would say, and I'm sure she will when I tell her about this, simple is classy. Not to mention that simple is easier to remember. I have to admit that I spent a fair bit of time coming up with a vision that even a skeptic would love. My plan is to wait until the end of the show and then announce it: Giving psychic predictions is wrong, and people should stop going to psychics. The magic of the future is that it is unknown. Seeking answers about what you don't know denies you the chance to find it out for yourself. The point of belief is not asking for proof. My advice to all the people out there that have been listening to me is to have a little faith. Then I will wish everyone all the best and retire from my short, but glorious career as a media psychic. I'll call both Jane and Nick tonight to let them know what I've done and apologize to both of them for being such a jerk. I'll end the day by giving Mac an extra cookie to thank him for his wisdom.

Holly was late for our show. Normally we hang out in the break room and have a cup of tea before the show, but not today. She came rushing into the studio only a few minutes before we started and sat down without saying anything. Brandon, the sound guy, waved at us through the window and counted down on his fingers: three, two, one. He pointed to Holly, who gave a cheery hello to our listeners and welcomed me back to the show. She won't meet my eyes. I think I know the problem. She probably heard about the ratings and the flowers and is feeling threatened. I can understand, this has been her show for years. Now I'm here and she's most likely wondering where she fits in. As one who has been the supporting cast for years, I know how she feels. Once today's show is over she'll feel differently. I had planned to clue her in before we started taking calls but there just wasn't enough time. I guess it will be a pleasant surprise for her, too. She just has to have a little faith.

We came back from a commercial break and I took a few deep breaths. It was time for a vision.

"Holly, before we take any more calls today there is something I want to say. Something that may shock a few people."

"Well, this is a coincidence; I have something that may be a bit of a shock for you, too." She's smiling, but her eyes look chilly. My heart starts to do a slow tilt. The Perrier water I had been drinking starts to boil in my stomach. "As many of our listeners know, I met Emma for the first time at the psychic fair. She gave me a prediction that literally saved my life. However, she also gave a good friend of mine some predictions—let's hear how those turned out."

I heard the studio door open. There stood Melanie, her arms crossed over chest, one hip thrown out to the side. She doesn't look like she wants to thank me for much of anything. She steps past me, sits next to Holly, and pulls on the headphones.

"Thanks so much for having me on the show, Holly. My name is Melanie Feehan. Like many people I was interested in talking to a psychic about my relationship. I know that a love relationship isn't as important as some of the other reasons people seek out help, but it sure was important to me. That interest is how I came to meet Emma Lulak."

There is silence where I think I am supposed to say something but the only sound that comes out is *urgh*. It is the same sound that Mac makes when he horks up a half-chewed kibble or a piece of one of my shoes.

"Melanie, what can you tell us about the prediction Emma gave you?" Holly says sweetly, her voice like melting cotton candy.

"She advised me that the relationship I was in was bad for me, that I should break up with the man I was seeing. She said that we were all wrong for each other. You can imagine my disappointment. I had only recently started seeing this fellow and I was really falling for him." Holly makes a sympathetic sound. I feel pinned to the seat, my face heating up. Brandon keeps flicking his eyes back and forth between Holly, Melanie, and myself, like it's some kind of evil emotional tennis match.

"Why, Melanie, I can't even imagine. To have finally met the love of your life, only to be told that destiny is against you. You must have been devastated." Holly clucks her tongue. She could win an Oscar for this performance. I take back the nice things I said about her. She's a crystal-rubbing troll. "But just when you must have thought everything was over, you learned something that changed everything for you. Can you tell our listeners about it?"

"I found out Emma Lulak's real name is Sophie Kintock," Melanie says looking over at me.

If I open my mouth to say anything, I am at risk of throwing up. With the way my luck's going, the vomit will short out the control board and I will be electrocuted. Technically, at this moment, I wouldn't completely mind being electrocuted. In fact, it may be worth it to end this. I'm beginning to suspect that being electrocuted would be the only positive ending to this situation.

"Finding out her name was one thing, but then I discovered that Sophie was actually the name of my boyfriend's ex-girlfriend." Brandon's mouth falls open. I keep hoping that he'll cut them off and put on another commercial, but he looks like he'd like to pull up a chair, pop open a beer, and stay for awhile.

"You're kidding!" Holly says, looking not at all surprised to hear this news.

"No, Holly, I'm afraid to say it's no joke. The very person

I was trusting with my life wasn't interested in giving me advice. She was trying to destroy my life."

"It wasn't like that," I manage to get out. I'm trying to decide if it sounds better to admit the truth. I wasn't interested in destroying her life; I wanted to save my own.

"What were you trying to accomplish?"

"I wanted to, I had hoped that . . ." My voice trails off. I'm not sure how to start.

"Don't you feel that using your powers like that is unethical?" Holly demands. Good lord, she still thinks I'm a psychic, although an unethical one. One who is willing to stoop to new lows to try to destroy the life of her ex's new girlfriend. "By giving her that reading you were messing with her future! That has to be bad karma. Let's see what our callers think." The call board is lit up like a Christmas tree.

Do you ever see those nature shows where a pack of predators turn on some slow-moving injured animal and drag it down? It was like that. There was blood in the water and this group of hippy-dippy crystal rubbers were hungry. I wonder if there is still some way for me to have my vision without sounding desperate. Call after call, people wondering just who I think I am and how disappointed they are in me. I feel like crawling under the desk. I haven't felt this ashamed since my mom caught me sneaking money out of her purse to buy Calvin Klein jeans. Brandon starts waving frantically at Holly, holding up three fingers; clearly whoever is on line three is a live wire. Perhaps it's someone else who would like to describe exactly what kind of torture I deserve. The caller's voice clicks on.

"Has anyone ever considered that even though she misled

you about her name, that her prediction about how your relationship was not meant to be could still be right?" The voice carries through my headphones. I know that voice. I put my hands over the headphones to lock in the sound, to keep every bit of that voice going into my ears instead of slipping away. "Sometimes you don't recognize what's right in front of you. You need something magical, to realize that what seems ordinary, truly is extraordinary." Holly looks confused but when I look over at Melanie I realize she knows who it is, too. She isn't happy. Melanie draws her finger over her throat. She wants the call cut off. Brandon looks to Holly for direction. I stand up shaking my head furiously. If Brandon attempts to cut off this call I will launch myself through this window.

"Thanks for your call, let's hear from someone else. . . ." Holly starts.

"Wait!" The caller yells out. "Don't you want to hear about destiny? Sophie told the truth. I don't belong with Melanie. I belong with her." Melanie starts crying. Holly has returned to her open-mouthed trout imitation. "If Sophie still believes in our future, in me, in us, then I'm downstairs outside the studio. Can you hear me, Sophie?"

"I hear you. I'm on my way." I yank the headphones off. Holly is rubbing Melanie's back. I want to say I'm sorry, but it feels like there aren't enough words to really represent the feeling behind the statement. I settle for a halfhearted shrug, grab my purse, and run out the door. The receptionist starts clapping as I jog past. I want to stop in the bathroom and make sure that I look good, but I'm afraid if I do then Doug won't still be waiting downstairs, that he'll have left. The elevator seems to be going too slowly. It feels like it's stopped and I have this awful moment where I imagine I'll be stuck between floors. My life stuck in limbo between psychic destiny and Doug.

I burst out the front entrance the building. It's pouring rain and everywhere I look there is sea of umbrellas. Then I see him, standing at the corner. Doug has the cell phone still held to his head. He folds it up and sticks it in his pocket. He's wearing his leather jacket but has no umbrella. His blond hair is soaked. It looks dark brown slicked to his head. We stand there in the rain just looking at each other for a while. He walks up slowly and gazes down at me.

"Please let me come home," he finally says, so quietly that I almost can't hear him over the rain, cars, and passing people. I step forward and Doug wraps his arms around me. I feel like I'm already home.

Thirty-two

SCORPIO

Acting like things haven't changed may work on the outside, but those who care for you can see the truth. Look inside to learn the problem. Only by awareness will you be able to solve it.

Doug moved back home. In many ways, it feels like he never left. Seeing his stuff next to mine makes me realize how empty the place has been. I'd tried to convince myself that I liked having it to myself, that it was as good, or better, than before. The truth was, it was just like when you glue back together a piece of broken china. It may look okay, but it's still shattered. I like getting up in the morning, opening the closet, and seeing his shirts snuggled next to mine. When he's not around I lie down on his side of the bed and stick my face into his pillow and just wallow in the smell of him. The refrigerator is full of his favorite things. I don't even mind having to deal with putting the toilet seat down or facing the danger of butt-splashdown in the middle of the night.

The only one who didn't seem convinced that Doug's return was a good thing was Mac. He was having some "adjustment difficulties" to his banishment from the bed. He had chewed

Doug's Italian loafers into confetti-sized leather pieces, which in case Doug missed the point, he then peed on. He moped from room to room looking wistfully at the furniture he was no longer able to sit upon. He sighed deeply whenever he laid down. With every change there are "transition" challenges, and I'm certain once Mac has a chance to get used to the changes he'll be fine. He used to be quite fond of Doug. Doug has taken to buying expensive organic dog treats as a bribe, but Mac continues to act as if he's being handed a vile, repulsive piece of dog snot.

Doug has been amazing. He's brought flowers home almost daily and instead of going out we've been having a lot of romantic dinners in. He says he doesn't want to share me with anyone right now. This is fine by me, after the whole Melanie incident I'm not much interested in sharing, either. He hasn't talked to her since he moved out of the apartment downtown. She's called here a couple of times, but Doug just deletes the voicemails. He says there isn't anything left to say. He thinks that what she and Holly did by dragging everything into the public was wrong. He says there's no excuse for making our private lives public.

The only thing that has been a bit uncomfortable is the fact that Doug believes the whole psychic thing to be a fact.

"Why didn't you ever tell me that you had that ability? I used to wonder how you knew some things, but I never would have guessed." *How do you respond to that?* I'm pretty sure if I told him the truth, that the whole thing was a lie, he wouldn't be amused. I settle for vague nonanswers. Doug requested copies of the tapes from the radio shows I was on. I came home from work one night and he was listening to them on our stereo.

"Do you ever think that the fact that we broke up really brought your skills into focus?"

"What?" I put down my bag while Mac did his happy welcome-home dog dance around my feet.

"Well, I was listening to you tell Holly how you felt so hurt when I left. I just wonder if the shock of that somehow shook something free."

"I don't know. Does it matter?" Doug stands up and comes over to give me a hug, pushing Mac out of his way with his foot. Mac gives a low growl and stomps away, undoubtedly plotting further revenge on Doug's shoes.

"Of course it doesn't matter. I just find it interesting to discover more about my secret witchy woman," he says, kissing my neck. He's developed this habit of calling me Witchy Woman, which I suspect he thinks sounds somehow sexy but in reality has become annoying. I haven't said anything because it seems a bit petty and small to argue that I am not fond of the love name he's given me. It's not like he's calling me Lover Blubber or something like that.

I almost told him the whole story the first night he was home. As we were lying in bed he told me when he heard me on the radio and realized I had this special power and how amazing that was. He realized that I was special, and that he would be a fool to let me get away. That someone doesn't have to be new to be exciting. He asks me constantly if I have any predictions for him, if I could see into the future. I keep trying to come up with interesting things to say, but I suspect it doesn't really matter what I say; he just likes the idea of me doing it. For him I had mastered a neat trick like being able to lift my leg above my head. All the women's magazines will tell you that you have to find some way to keep your man interested. If you let your relationship become routine you might as well package him up with a bow and hand him over to another woman. If Doug found the fact that I was a "psychic" interesting, then I was willing to be a psychic. I was willing to bark like a dog if it would work. The important thing was that Doug was home. I had gotten exactly what I wanted and I couldn't be happier. Honest.

Thirty-three

CAPRICORN
The well-designed life you've created seems a bit stale this week.
Only you have the power to reinvent yourself. Don't be afraid to
ask for encouragement from those you love if you need it.

"Have you talked to Nick?" Jane asks, rocking Ethan in his
stroller back and forth. Making up with Jane was the second-
best thing that happened this week, right after Doug coming
home. I showed up at her place with a package of Pepperidge
Farm Orange Milano cookies and an apology. We both had a
good cry and then everything went back to normal. I find
good friendships are like that, humility and chocolate are the
glue that holds them together. Today Jane swung by Stack of
Books to bring me lunch. I had given mine to Doug. As I was
leaving the house this morning he thanked me for packing a
lunch for him and how he had forgotten how thoughtful I
was. It seemed petty and small to admit that the lunch in the
fridge had been mine, so I just gave him a kiss and let him
take it. I tried to convince myself that I could get by on the tea
and stale graham crackers that we keep at the store. By eleven

a.m. I knew it wasn't going to work, and phoned in Jane as my emergency plan B.

"I called Nick after the radio show, but he seemed kind of weird. I told him that things had worked out between Doug and me and that I wouldn't be doing the radio show anymore. I thought that would make him happy but he still seemed ticked off. You know in that quiet, unspoken, 'everything is fine' kind of way." I took a huge bite of the bologna sandwich Jane made for me. She had packed me the perfect kid lunch: bologna and mustard sandwich, corn chips, and an apple. It tasted wonderful.

"Maybe he still wants you to admit that the whole thing had been faked. He is a skeptic, after all. As it turned out, everyone who heard the radio show thinks you're not only the world's best psychic, but also some kind of romantic hero."

"I guess that could be it." I shuffle my feet against the floor. "I told him how I'd planned to tell everyone not to believe in psychics, but I'm not sure he believed me."

"You told him you're sorry. You're not doing the radio show. If he's still mad then that's his problem. Maybe he just ran out of things to say. After all, you guys became friends because of the psychic project." She shrugged. "It's not like you two had a lot in common."

"That's not true. We actually had a ton of fun together. He's got a wicked sense of humor and he got me interested in Hitchcock movies." I wave my hand to show the vast amounts of things we shared. "All kinds of things."

"Okay, clearly you were close. He deeply impacted your life, or at least your movie-viewing habits. I stand corrected."

Jane cocks her head and watches me stuffing corn chips in my mouth. "Do you like him?"

"Nick? Of course not. I mean, of course I like him, but not *like* him, like him." Jane nods in slow motion. She's like an enemy spy who won't stop with the X-ray eye of death until she hears the truth. "He's not my type. It's possible that when Doug and I were having problems Nick was someone who listened to me and who was very kind. I was lonely. It's possible—and I am not convinced of this—but it's possible that I started to confuse feelings of friendship with something more."

"Uh huh." Jane seems to be moving ever so slightly closer. Soon she's going to be sitting on my lap while we have this discussion. I'm certain this is the reason why it feels like the temperature is rising.

"The point is, I am very fond of him and I wish that we could get past the whole radio thing." I sweep the crumbs of my lunch off the counter.

"I think you should tell him you like him."

"What would be the point of that? Have you been paying attention? Doug's home; we're back together. We're starting all over again. After everything I went through to get him back, why would I do anything to put that at risk?" Jane leans back and bends down to pull Ethan's shoe out of his mouth. "Besides, you make it sound like I would be better off with Nick instead of Doug, and that's absurd."

"You're right. Forget I said a thing," she says. "I should get going; I've got to get to the grocery store. I'll catch up with you later." The bell on the door rings as she steps out and for some reason I'm feeling disappointed that she didn't try to convince me to say something to Nick, which is utterly ridiculous. I suspect it's simply a case of my feelings waiting to catch up to all the changes I've been through in the past week. It's emotional whiplash.

Thirty-four

A Q U A R I U S

The stars are aligning in exactly your favor. Something you've been waiting for is on the verge of arriving. A trip down memory lane will help you remember just how far you've come. Enjoy this special time.

Doug has arranged for us to have dinner out with his parents. He used to think it was odd that I wanted to spend time with his family. I told him that since my family was so far away it was nice to see his. He replied that if I was missing my family I should go home and visit them. He never actually told me to leave his family alone, but that was the message. There was our relationship, and then his relationship with his parents. He wasn't a person who wanted a lot of overlap in those areas. Spending time with family felt to him like we were trapped in an episode of *Leave It to Beaver*, the perfect family.

Suddenly he's made plans for us to have dinner with his parents and has turned into the fashion Nazi. Nothing I have picked out is right. A pile of clothing is heaped on the bed. Finally he takes over and goes through my closet to choose something for me to wear. Despite the fact that we're simply going to their house, he's got me decked out in an outfit I bought to wear to a Christmas party two years ago. Based on the way it fits, either the heat in the closet is too high, resulting in shrinkage or, more likely, the post-breakup ice-cream infusions have caught up to me. My bottom seems to have expanded out in some new and unappealing directions. In the end, I have to use a safety pin to close the pants, as I can't get them done up without the threat of the top button popping off in the middle of dinner, putting someone's eye out. With my luck, it would hit the dog.

On the drive over I wonder if I should tell Doug everything that happened on my last trip to see his mom. He hasn't mentioned a thing, which makes me suspect that she hasn't told him. This would be fine if she doesn't plan to ever talk, but if she spills her guts over dinner or drinks, that could cause trouble. What if the dog sustains some kind of brain injury? (Although, how you could ever tell on a dog that dumb is beyond me.) This leaves me with the tricky situation of determining if I should do a preemptive telling. It's just the kind of thing that normally really annoys Doug, and we've been getting along so well. He looks amazing. He's wearing these impossibly soft black pants and a gray cashmere sweater. He catches me watching him and reaches over, taking my hand and kissing it. He never used to hold my hand. I'm going to take it as an omen that tonight is going to go perfectly.

I was afraid we would be overdressed, but Doug's parents also went the extra mile. There's a lot of cheek-kissing and red-carpet-type hugs at the door. It feels like a celebration. Doug's dad, Theodore, has mixed us some cocktails. After three of his pink frothy martinis, I'm feeling in the festive spirit and am almost able to block out the fact that my pants are tighter than a sausage casing. We have drinks and appetizers in their living room. I notice that the broken ceramic bird is gone. I wonder if Ann might have tried gluing it back together or buying another one, but instead, the entire shelf is simply rearranged as if the bird had never existed. For some reason this made me sad, like the rest of birds should have waited a decent amount of time before moving on with the rest of their lives.

The dining room was set with their china and crystal, all reflecting the candlelight. I have never seen these people eat on anything other than fancy dishes. I wonder if somewhere, buried deep in the basement, they own a set of chipped nonbreakable, dishwasher-safe Corningware. I doubt it. Ann made a scallops and risotto dish with saffron and cream. If I had to guess I would estimate that the approximate caloric intake of the dish approaches a number close to the amount of the national deficit. The only thing that keeps me from licking the plate is the fact that I don't want to fill up too much, as there's the promise of dessert. The wine that accompanies the dinner is divine, and I suspect that this single bottle costs as much as I make in a year. Theodore tells a funny story of how he and Ann picked out a case of this wine when they were traveling through Burgundy, France, and of their efforts to lug it around for the rest of their trip. I laugh along as if I were familiar with these kind of problems when jet-setting through foreign lands. My biggest problem when I was traveling as a student was a container of tuna fish that exploded in my backpack. No matter how often I washed everything, I smelled like a fish hatchery. Wherever I traveled, the town's stray cats would follow me around like I was the Pied Piper, which was nice, as no one else wanted to be near me, particularly on warm days.

I help Ann clear the dishes. I offer to help wash, but she shoos me out. I suspect that she doesn't trust me around all these breakables. Theodore takes the towel from my hand and suggests I relax by the fire in the living room with Doug. When I walk into the room Doug pulls me down next to him on the couch. I curl into his side, tucking my head into the crook of his neck. I had dreamed of this, though of course in my dream, my pants weren't cutting me into two, but you can't have everything. I shouldn't have had that second helping of risotto. I wonder if there is a casual way I can unhook the safety pin without him noticing.

"I can't believe how close I came to losing you," Doug murmurs into my hair. "I know how lucky I am that you were willing to give me a second chance."

"I feel lucky, too."

"Really? I thought you must have known that things would work out. I still can't believe that you had this ability and never let me know." I fidget a bit. Doug's interest in my psychic abilities makes me nervous. I'm afraid he is going to start asking me for stock tips or winning lotto numbers. He seems fascinated that I had this secret that he knew nothing about. It makes him wonder what else he doesn't know. Suddenly I am a woman of mystery. I'm hoping that he will drop the whole topic, sort of in the way he has dropped the topic of Melanie. Both of us have perfected the art of not mentioning her.

"I have something I want to say—do you know what it

is?" Suddenly I thought I might know. It made sense, the dressing up, the formal dinner with his parents. My stomach burrowed down toward my feet. Was this it? I had imagined being a bit more sober and less overstuffed. What if I'm wrong? What if what he wants to ask me is nothing more than to hand him the remote so he can watch the game?

"I think so. I have the feeling you want to ask me a question, a rather important question," I say, hedging my bets. Doug laughs and reaches into his pocket.

"How am I ever going to surprise you?" He pulls a ring out, a brilliant-cut diamond in a platinum setting. It is huge. It looks like something Elizabeth Taylor would wear on her *thumb*. It wasn't exactly what I had imagined for myself, but it *is* a diamond ring, a real diamond engagement ring. I make a squealing sound and Doug slides the ring onto my finger. "I'm taking that sound as a yes."

"Yes, of course, yes." I pull my hand around and stare at it. If I had really been psychic I would have gotten a manicure. My nails are chipped and in desperate need of some polish. No matter; it is a ring on my finger. It fills my ring finger up to the knuckle. It looks like something you would find on the Home Shopping Network, only it's a real diamond and it flashes in the light of the fire like a flashbulb.

"Is it time to celebrate?" Theodore asks, leaning in the room. He is holding a chilled bottle of Dom Perignon. Ann is right behind him holding four tall champagne flutes.

"She said she would have me!" Doug announces and we stand to take the air kisses from each parent.

"Welcome to the family," Ann says, the smell of her Chanel No. 5 in my nose competing with the bubbles from the champagne. This is what I have always wanted, but it doesn't feel the way I expected. I had imagined that I would feel like I was walking on air. Instead the situation seems unreal, and it might be all the drinks, but I feel like I'm standing outside the situation watching it happen to someone else. The champagne makes my stomach roll over. It isn't mixing well with the saffron cream sauce. I am not in the mood for dessert anymore; I'm focusing all my attention on not throwing up on the living room rug in my future in-laws' home. I wonder if can manage to vomit on the stained spot where I dropped the tea.

"We'll have to sit down and chat about wedding plans once you two set a date. Do you already have a date in mind?" Ann asks.

"Gosh, I'm not sure." I look at Doug, who is busy doing the manly half handshake, half hug with his dad. "I always imagined a summer wedding, maybe something outside."

"What about your religion? Should we check the calendar to find out when the solstice falls?"

"My *religion*?" I ask. Doug has moved closer, and puts his arm around me. The safety pin finally gives up the effort and pops open, stabbing into me. I wouldn't be surprised to see cream sauce and champagne slowly leak from the tiny hole. I try to shift to dislodge it.

"Yes. I've been reading up on it. Theodore and I would like to be very open-minded about the whole thing. I'll admit I'm hoping you'll be willing to consider several traditional elements, as well, not take the whole thing too far." She looks nervously at Theodore.

"Mom!" Doug says. I have no idea what she is talking about it. My mom is Methodist in a hobby type of way; she doesn't take it very seriously. We went to church on Christmas, Easter, and when my grandparents were in town. I wouldn't describe it as a radical religion or anything.

"I'm saying that we know it's your special day, but we would still really like to have our minister there. After all, he's been involved with our family for a long time; he's the one who baptized Doug, you know. I don't know much about Wicker, but I'm sure we can find a way to blend everything." *Wicker?* She's worried about furniture made from reeds? Does she think I am going to do a Pier One–themed wedding? Then it occurs to me what she means.

"*Wiccan?* You think I'm a witch?"

"Oh, yes, sorry, Wiccan, what did I call it?" She's looking at Theodore for help, but he's too busy drinking down what looks to be a liter of Scotch out of a cut crystal tumbler and is staring out into the yard. He must have already finished his champagne. His liver must be the size of a Labrador retriever.

"I'm not a witch." I cannot believe I am having this conversation. No wonder the poor woman looks so nervous. She is probably imagining a society wedding with guests dressed up like druids sacrificing a goat on the tee-off green of her country club. On the positive side, they are being quite open-minded about the whole thing. At least they haven't tied me to a stake in the backyard and threatened to burn me alive.

"I'm sorry. I thought that's what you explained." She's now looking to Doug for some answers. I join her.

"Sophie is a psychic. She's able to predict the future, talk with those who have passed over, that kind of thing," Doug says. Ann doesn't look relieved with this piece of news. Now she's imagining a wedding where the bride lurches out of a coffin instead of coming down the aisle.

"It's not really a big deal at all," I try to clarify. "Sometimes I have hunches about things, that's all." I shrug off the topic and try to steer the conversation back toward safer areas. "I would love a traditional wedding."

"You can speak to the dead?" Theodore asks, breaking in just as I was about to bond with Ann over discussion of tulips, silk, tulle, and floral arrangements.

"Well, in a way, I guess."

"Could you contact Hazel?" he asks. I have no idea who Hazel is; Doug didn't talk much about his family, so it's possible that this is Theodore's mother, or some well-loved distant cousin. The name is vaguely familiar, as if I've heard it before but I can't place it. The three cocktails, wine, and champagne I've ingested is not helping. Not to mention the constant poking of the safety pin, which is further distracting. Theodore is staring at me with intense concentration as if we were discussing the possible expansion of his company to the Far East in a high-powered board room meeting. Whoever Hazel is, she was clearly important.

"I can't know for sure if I could reach Hazel until I try."

"I had no idea you could communicate with dogs," Doug says and even Ann looks quite impressed with this development. Hazel was a dog. Suddenly, I remember—Hazel was the name of their family dog when Doug was young, some kind of prizewinning Yorkshire terrier, if I remember correctly. Great, now I'm going to have to do a reading for a dead dog. What in the world am I supposed to say? "Things are great here in the kennel in the sky?" "I always remember fondly the squeaky toys you gave me?" Somehow when I imagined planning my wedding, a wedding I feared would never happen, I didn't picture discussing a dead dog instead of dress designs. I suspect Mac will be disgusted with me.

Thirty-five

Although a past love wound seemed to be healed, there may still be work to do. An idea you've been tossing around should be investigated if you still feel passionate about it.

I've been thinking about my SPINSTER group lately. I feel badly about abandoning them.

Why is being an unmarried woman something that we should be ashamed of, as if we've failed? Men don't feel this way. When they haven't married, they make it sound like they've gotten away with something. They don't have an air of desperation—if anything, their single status makes them even more appealing to the other sex.

I've been thinking about this since I've graduated from spinsterhood to the status of "newly engaged." I feel like one of those kids who had a horrible birth deformity, as if a giant, softball-sized cyst on the side of my head was suddenly removed. Now I realize that many people were avoiding the topic of my spinsterhood in the same way they would have avoided mentioning toilet paper clinging to my shoe, embarrassed for me but unwilling to drag the unappealing topic into the light of day. I guess I should consider myself lucky that people didn't think I should be locked up in my parents' attic.

Despite the fact that I now feel a compelling urge to defend my former spinster status, I am glad to be engaged. I feel relieved that Doug's asked me to marry him. This change in our relationship means:

- Doug is really serious about being back together. Now that his mother is involved, there is no turning back.

- I get to wear a great dress that will make me look like a princess. Prior to selecting the perfect dress, I get to buy bridal magazines the size of a New York phone book and will then spend days trying on different types while the salesclerk calls me "The Bride."

- I get to select a fancy hairstyle that requires professional construction and at least half a day to create and an entire case of hairspray to hold in place. It will have more structural support than a high-rise building.

- I can force my friends to buy overpriced candy-colored bridesmaid dresses that make them look like Little Bo Peep on crack, a fitting revenge for all the dresses they've forced me to wear over the years. They will need to buy shoes that are dyed to match and that will leak dye all over their feet, staining them for weeks to come. The dye may or may not be toxic, depending on how much I feel they are supporting me during this difficult time.

- I can register for all kinds of things that I never needed before, like fondue pots, croquet and badminton sets, designer drink coasters, shrimp forks, and glasswear that can only be used during the holidays.

- My friends will throw me a bachelorette party, complete with a tacky stripper dressed up as a police officer who will call himself "Officer Love"; overly sweet drinks with fruit cocktail in them; and expensive lingerie that looks to be made of string and silk handkerchiefs.

- Any mood swings will be completely understood as I am The Bride, who is under a lot of stress planning her "Special Day." Signs of unhappiness or crankiness will be addressed with trips to the spa and liberal doses of therapeutic chocolate instead of being told to get over it.

- I no longer have to refer to Doug as "my boyfriend," which makes us sound like we are still in high school and I was hoping that he would ask me to the prom. I also no longer have to call him "my partner," which always made people wonder if I was a lesbian. I can now officially call him "my fiancé," which is far more respectable.

I have always wanted to be married. When I was growing up I used to buy bridal magazines and cut out various pictures and keep them in a shoe box under my bed. I blame Princess Diana, as that event is the first time I can remember being so obsessed. I knew every detail of her wedding. I got up at approximately four in the morning to watch the wedding live. My mom and dad had split up right around that time, which may have accounted for my sudden fascination with Happily Ever After. I sat in the living room about six inches from our

TV so that I could be a bit closer to all the action. I was still in my pajamas and I held my shoe box of clippings close to my chest. I had fixed myself a breakfast of Frosted Flakes and cried while the unnoticed cereal slowly turned from crisp, appealing flakes to soggy ones, and finally into just beige paste. My mom wandered in after the wedding was over and the *Today* show crew was replaying the highlights.

"It'll never last," she said as she made her coffee, spilling creamer on her bathrobe. I was livid. How could she say such an awful thing on Diana's special day? It was like she had showed up at the church and spit on her beautiful long train in front of the whole royal family. Of course, this was before we knew anything about Camilla; maybe my mom was psychic. She certainly was a cynic. Her experience with my dad left her doubting in the concept of Prince Charming and the benefits of married life. All she got out of marriage was a used fondue pot, me, stretch marks, and a bitter opinion of men. She went from a married mother in a color-coordinated house to divorced, working in a variety of dead-end jobs and living in spackle-colored rental apartments.

My dad wasn't the kind of guy to take divorce partway. When he split up with my mom he pretty much split up with me, as well. Maybe he figured that since he took the TV, the car, and half of the towels, dishes, and linens, he should leave her something. My mom used to tell me that my dad found it to be too hard to only see me part time. Even as a dumb kid, I knew this wasn't the whole story.

The rest of the story had to do with Sharon, who was my dad's new underage wife. Sharon was everything that my mom wasn't: younger, firmer, and totally enamored with my dad.

She was also a corporate powerhouse when they met, all lipstick, red suits, and shoulder pads. She worked in the Chicago branch of his company. My dad's business trips to Chicago increased, until one day he came home and announced he was moving there. I was quite excited at the time because I thought the whole family would be moving. It was my mom who broke it to me a week or so later that we wouldn't be joining him. He hadn't moved out, he had moved on.

A few weeks later I flew to Chicago for the first of many horrific visits. Sharon treated me like I was a rowdy college buddy of my dad's whose presence is tolerated, but she had clearly established plans to phase me out of his life. When they got married, she didn't ask me to be a bridesmaid because she said she didn't want to put me "in an awkward position." I was a preteen at the time and everything about me was awkward, but that didn't mean I didn't want to wear a frilly dress. The reality was that Sharon didn't want me in any of the official photos; she was already airbrushing Dad's past out.

Right after they got married we discovered that Sharon was more fertile than the Egyptian delta lands. She would have four kids with my dad in six years. My step-siblings popped out already brandishing day planners, finance sheets, and briefcases. They became perfect Stepford kids from the moment they were born. We never really bonded. My dad got more and more busy with his new family and obligations to them. Finally we stopped pretending it was a case of the dates and details needing to be worked out, and I stopped visiting. He called on occasion and kept up the pretense, but it was clear after a year or two that he had officially resigned as my dad.

I blame my unhappy childhood for my fascination with

getting married. What I don't understand is that now that I am on the verge of getting what I always wanted, why I am obsessing about being single and feeling the need to defend how it wasn't that bad? I am still tempted, at least for the months leading up to the wedding, to get a T-shirt made that says "Spinster" in a loopy script across my breasts. It could be fun.

Thirty-six

To: <u>nickmckenna@ubc.ca.edu</u>

From: <u>sophie@hotmail.com</u>

Subject: Hitchcock film festival

Date: April 11, 2006

I wondered if you noticed that CBC is running a Hitchcock film tribute on Saturday. It runs all day with his movies back-to-back, along with some commentary. It struck me as the kind of thing you would be interested in. Haven't talked to you in a while, hope you are well. Sophie

To: <u>sophie@hotmail.com</u>

From: <u>nickmckenna@ubc.ca.edu</u>

Subject: Re: Hitchcock film festival
Date: April 11, 2006

I had seen that CBC was running the tribute. I am hoping to catch some of it, but will miss most of it Saturday night as I will be at the opera. Thank you for thinking of me. I am doing well, but with the semester coming to a close have been quite busy. I trust you are well.

To: nickmckenna@ubc.ca.edu
From: sophie@hotmail.com
Subject: Re: Hitchcock film festival
Date: April 11, 2006

All those fat people screaming in Italian at each other? You've got to be kidding. Who actually goes to the opera? I thought it was only for old people.

To: sophie@hotmail.com
From: nickmckenna@ubc.ca.edu
Subject: Re: Hitchcock film festival
Date: April 11, 2006

And people who enjoy culture. You should try it sometime.

To: nickmckenna@ubc.ca.edu
From: sophie@hotmail.com
Subject: Re: Hitchcock film festival
Date: April, 11 2006

I tried culture once, found it too chewy.

To: sophie@hotmail.com
From: nickmckenna@ubc.ca.edu
Subject: Re: Hitchcock film festival
Date: April 11, 2006

You are truly one of a kind, Kintock. Take care of yourself.

Thirty-seven

I am willing to admit that part of me was hoping that Nick would invite me over to watch movies at his place. However, the important thing is that we had a civilized e-mail discussion, which is clearly the first step in rebuilding our friendship. E-mail will lead to phone conversations, which will lead to meeting for coffee, which will eventually lead to us being friends again. I am putting Operation Friendship into the second step of action now by taping the film festival for Nick. Since he is at the opera and missing it, I will demonstrate that I am the kind of friend who is thoughtful and considerate.

I figured that as long as I was going to tape the movies for Nick, I might as well watch them. Truth is, I'm getting to like them. The movie *The Birds* is beyond creepy. You get the sense that the whole world has turned upside down. Once nature turns on you, you know you're in trouble. Mac and I are curled up on the couch under my fleece blanket. I had no idea small, innocent sparrows could be so scary, but now that I think about it, I notice how they have those really creepy-looking feet, not to mention tiny little birdy eyes that make them look untrustworthy. Even Mac seems a bit unsettled; whenever there's a whole bunch of bird cries on the TV, like when they chase Tippi Hedren down the street for example, he barks low *woof*s at the TV as if to warn them not to come any closer.

"I'm home!" Doug switches on the light in the living room as he walks in, and both Mac and I sit up, surprised at the sudden glare. He scoops Mac up with one hand and puts him down on the floor, taking his spot and curling up behind me. I can feel the chill from the outside still clinging to him. "Sorry I was late, I stayed to have a few beers with the guys after the game." In our old relationship I would have been annoyed that he stayed out late with his friends and didn't call. The new, confident, engaged me understands that boys will be boys and that he needs time with his friends. Besides, he's convinced I'm psychic, so I only have to look at him with the "eye" and he'll tell the truth, so there's almost no risk that he will cheat on me.

"No problem." I give him a kiss, cuddle in, and turn my attention back to the movie. The birds are hammering away at the side of the house when suddenly the TV clicks over to Spike TV and a *Dirty Harry* movie. "Hey!" I spin around to see Doug holding the remote.

"What? Were you watching that?" I swallow the urge to ask him what he thought I was doing sitting in front of the TV.

"It's really good. Have you ever seen any Hitchcock movies?"

"I hate old movies; they're hokey and fake."

"As opposed to *Dirty Harry*, which you would classify as more of a documentary?"

"C'mon, *Dirty Harry* is a classic."

"So is *The Birds*."

"So if they're both classics it shouldn't matter which one we watch, should it?" He kisses my neck.

"But you've seen this movie a million times. You know how it ends," I point out. Doug gives a deep sigh.

"You win. We'll watch your movie this time." He turns the channel back. The birds are still attacking the house. A minute later Doug starts kissing my neck. It's not that it doesn't feel nice, but it's hard to concentrate on psychotic birds when someone is salivating on parts of your body. Doug's hand snakes around and slides into my shirt. His hands are cold and I shiver. He's taking it as some kind of orgasmic shudder and is now munching away on my neck like it's an ear of corn and his hands are attacking my breasts like he's milking a cow. It's getting considerably harder to focus on the movie.

"Doug?"

"Mmm-hmm."

"Aren't you interested in watching the movie?"

"Not really." He keeps kissing away. It's silly for me to be annoyed. After all, I'm taping it. I could watch it later. The important point is that Doug is feeling affectionate, well, perhaps more than a bit affectionate; the correct term might be "randy as a goat." "I've got a surprise for you; can you guess what it is?" he asks. I wonder if this is his idea of dirty talk because if it's what I'm thinking, it's not really a surprise at this point.

"Why don't you tell me?"

"What? You don't know? Don't you even want to try to

guess? My mom was sure you would guess." I find it hard to believe that his mom would be involved in his sex life. She loves being involved in his life, but there are boundaries. If she's involved it means he's talking about something else. I love surprises. I wonder if it's a different ring, maybe something less *Dynasty*-looking. I turn over on the couch so I can see him. Doug's got a look in his eye. He's up to something, but a good kind of something as opposed to a Melanie melon-breasted kind of thing.

"Tell me. I'm too tired to guess."

"Well, if you're too tired it can wait till morning," he teases. I poke him in the ribs until he starts laughing. "Resorting to torture? You play dirty."

"Tell me!" I poke a few more times into the ticklish spot under his ribs.

"Okay, okay, I've decided to take you away from all this." He waves his hand grandly.

"Away from our living room? You've got an exciting trip to the kitchen planned?"

"No, how about a romantic weekend on the Island instead?"

"Seriously?" I was always trying to plan romantic weekend getaways before but Doug was always too busy. I can't believe he's actually taken the time to plan all of this—ferry reservations, hotel plans. It takes a lot of work.

"It wouldn't be very nice of me to lie to you about that kind of thing, would it?" I give a little squeal and snuggle back in. I can't believe I wanted to watch a movie instead of spend time with this guy. "My mom planned the whole thing." I sit back up.

"Your *mom* planned our romantic weekend?"

"You bet, she and my dad got a room right next to ours." Suddenly I'm starting to wonder just what kind of weirdness his family is into. Come to think of it, his *dad* has sort of small birdy eyes.

"They're coming with us?"

"My parents have planned an engagement party for us. It's going to be at the Empress Hotel, and they've invited a bunch of our family friends. It's a great way to announce the engagement and for you to meet everybody."

"Wow." For some reason I feel let down. It feels like we're rushing into a party, or at least that I should have been involved in the planning of the whole thing.

"It's going to be great. She e-mailed the menu over to me, and the food looks amazing. I made sure they put strawberry shortcake on the list for you. She invited your parents."

"My parents? As in my mom and dad?"

"Do you have other parents?"

"No. It's just that I doubt they'll come. It's a long way, and the flights are expensive. They hate even being in the same room together. I'll be shocked if we get them out here for the wedding, to be honest."

"They already said they would come."

"They did? Your mom must be some kind of miracle worker," I say. What I think is if she's so interested in brokering peace, perhaps she should fly to the Middle East and see if she can work something out over there and leave my family alone. It's not that I don't want them to come, it's just that whenever they're together things tend to turn tense.

"My mom is a party animal. She's been planning this wedding since I was eleven years old. You should see the decorations she's got planned for the engagement party. It makes me wonder what she's going to come up with for the wedding."

"I'll admit, I'm wondering, too. Think she'll run any of it past me, since it's my wedding, too?"

"Whoa. Are you mad?" *He wants to know if I'm mad?* My wedding, the one *I've* been planning since I was eleven is being hijacked. She had her wedding, why does she feel the need to do mine, too? "Look, if you want we can talk to my mom. She doesn't mean anything by it. She just wants to do this for us because she's so happy. Trust me, it's going to be a great party. You can invite whoever you want." *Well, that's nice, I can invite whoever I want to my very own engagement party that I didn't even know I was having.*

"When is this party?"

"End of the month. I thought we would take Friday off and leave on an early ferry over to Victoria. We'll have Friday night all to ourselves. My mom booked a carriage tour for us. The party is on Saturday evening."

It's stupid to be annoyed. His mom has planned a beautiful party for us, a party that will be a fancy, society kind of event. The kind of thing where local newspapers come and take pictures of all the beautiful people—of which I will now be one. I'm only being snotty because I didn't think of it first. If I had, it would be more of a barbeque-type event where people drank beer and ate hot dogs. Besides, my parents are coming.

I can't believe Ann talked my dad into coming. My dad, who has never been to Vancouver, because he is convinced that since it's Canada it will be buried under snow and he'll be forced to take a dogsled as a form of transportation. The party will be perfect. I'll buy a perfect thank-you gift for his mom and while we sip champagne, I'll talk with her about the wedding and casually ask that she find the time to discuss any future plans with me. Everything will turn out fine. I'm sure of it. The sinking feeling in my stomach is most likely due to an overconsumption of popcorn and not a prediction of horrible events to come.

Thirty-eight

GEMINI

Preparing a stunning feast or putting together a fabulous look
for a gathering of loved ones gives you plenty to do. An annoying person should be ignored, not engaged. Relax and let events
happen.

Jane and I have been in the mall for approximately seven hours.
If we are here much longer we are at risk for being mistakenly
identified as shoplifters by the security guards, who are starting
to look at us with shifty eyes as we circle around again. We've
been wandering from store to store looking for the ideal dress
for my engagement party. The decision on what to wear has
taken on the importance of negotiating world peace. The dress
must look demure and sophisticated, while still at the same time
make me look sexy and irresistible. I don't think I'm asking too
much. I also don't think it's asking too much for my best friend
in the whole world to support me in this quest. I'm discovering
that Jane is a bit of a fair-weather friend. She was all for this
shopping trip this morning, but sometime around hour five she
started to lag. I sense her enthusiasm is dropping off.

I'm trying on a navy sheath dress at Talbots. It's made
from a shiny taffeta and has a bit of 1960s Jackie O. style.

The mere fact that it's from Talbots screams class and timeless style, but I worry it's somewhat lacking in the sexy department. I turn to look at the rear view in the mirror.

"I like it. What do you think?"

"I told you I liked it the first two times you tried it on." Jane is sitting in a chair next to the three-way mirror sipping a smoothie. I bought it for her hoping that the energy powder they put in would pick her up a bit, but so far it doesn't seem to be working any magic.

"I know you like it, but do you *love* it?"

"I love it." I glance at Jane out of the corner of my eye. She isn't even looking at me.

"I know it's been a long day. Maybe we should get some dinner and think it over."

"Sophie, less time and consideration has been spent designing nuclear facilities. You've tried on every dress in the greater Vancouver area. This is the dress, trust me. Let's buy it and call it a day."

"This party is important; I need to have the right look. I'll be looking at these pictures for the rest of my life. I'm only going to get one chance at this. I don't want to look back and wonder what the heck I was thinking when I picked out my outfit. What if it sets up the marriage on a bad note?" I turn to scrutinize the front of the dress again, trying to imagine it was the first time I was seeing myself. "The red one at The Bay was a bit more dramatic, maybe I should try it on again."

"No more. My feet can't take it. I don't think I have it in me to walk another step in this mall. You've tried the red one on a million times. It's just a dress. What are you going to be like when you have to pick out a wedding gown?"

"You don't want to know, but I'm thinking you should invest in better footwear if you plan to keep up with me." I look at the dress again. It's beautiful, simple, elegant. "Are you sure I should get this one? You're not just saying that to get out of more shopping?"

"Yes, I said it was the one the first time you tried it on. It's possible you don't remember, seeing that it was so long ago." Her smoothie makes a slurping sound as she drains the cup. "What's the problem with making the decision? This isn't like you." She's right. I'm usually not a shopper, more of a buyer. I go into the dressing room and change back into my clothes. I stand there looking at myself in the mirror. I should lose some weight, nothing like bright lights and a full-length mirror to highlight the fact that it looks like I'm storing grapefruit in my thighs.

"I don't know. I just want everything to be perfect," I mumble.

"You know what my mom told me when I was planning the wedding with Jeremy? She said that I should remember that the wedding was just a day, less than twenty-four hours. I should save all that energy and effort I was spending on the wedding on the marriage instead. No matter what happened, or what went wrong on the wedding day, it wouldn't matter as long as at the end of the day you were happy to be married to the guy who was waiting at the end of the aisle." I think that over. Jane's parents have been married since approximately the Stone Age. They have turned into one of those married couples who have matching sweaters and look a bit like each other. It's cheesy, but they're happy. There could be worse people you listen to in the marriage advice department.

The sales clerk rings the dress up and places it in a garment bag, layering the hanger with tissue paper as if she is tucking it in. It feels like trumpets should sound to mark this moment, but all in all it's rather anticlimactic. Jane drives me home and takes a pass on coming in for a drink. She says she's ready to go home and put her feet up. She's worried that if she does it at my place she'll lack the ability to leave. I hang the garment bag up on the closet door, lie down on the bed, and look up at it. My engagement party dress. The dress that will officially change me from spinster to respectable, about-to-be-married person. Never has so much rested on one dress.

Thirty-nine

CANCER

Remain in control of your emotions at all costs. This may be more difficult than usual, especially when it involves love and romance.

I love taking the ferry to the Island. It feels like an adventure, and I can almost talk myself into the idea that I'm on some kind of mini–cruise ship. I'll admit it's a poorly equipped cruise ship, and instead of shuffleboard courts, casinos, and a club, it's got a White Spot burger cafeteria and a bank of video games. On the positive side, the gift shop sells every tacky women's magazine available on the open market. This means I have the opportunity to read to my hearts content articles like:

- Nibble on Places He Doesn't Know He Has—and Drive Him Wild!

- I Was in Love with My Teenage Daughter's Boyfriend!

- Six Dozen Things to Make with Chicken Leftovers!

- Are You Sexually Repressed? A Ten-Step Program!

All the headlines have an exclamation point. It's life on speed with better-than-average-looking people. I'm somewhat annoyed with an article in *Cosmo*, "Is He the Man for You?!" I took the test and Doug and I only scored in the midrange. The article called this level "warmed-over leftovers." I really should stop reading this trash.

I always manage to "forget" my book in the car parked below in the bowels of the ferry, so I'm "forced" to buy a stack of glossy magazines to pass the time. I buy one, sometimes two, of the chocolate-chip cookies from the cafeteria and sit by the window watching the ocean slip past. If the view outside gets dull, the people-watching opportunities on the ferry are second to none. It's the cable TV of people-watching. You can always count on a strange mix. Hippies wearing clothing made from scratchy-looking natural fibers. Kids run and scream down the aisles while parents try to pretend they don't know them. Some office escapees who are still tethered to work by a laptop computer. On a good day you can eavesdrop on people having an argument or discussing the future of their relationship.

Jane and Jeremy have decided to take the day off, too, and have come over on the same ferry. They're two of the few people I invited to the party. I'm enjoying the pile of magazines Jane and I bought and the men have gone off to get some fresh air. This is man-speak for taking a walk on the deck, gawking at the girls who have stripped down to their bikini tops in the hope of catching some rays during the crossing. Jane has wandered off to the bathroom. She's left the kids home with a sitter for the weekend and says she still isn't over the thrill of being able to go the bathroom completely alone. She's been gone so long that I'm starting to suspect she is just sitting in there enjoying the quiet. It's possible she's asleep.

I'm completely excited about the party. My earlier misgivings were undoubtedly based on my own insecurities. Ann has planned a party with a Cinderella theme. The hotel will be decorated with glass and crystal with curly willow branches spraypainted silver. The table clothes are an icy blue and the flowers are a pale shell pink or white. The cake will have a tiny crystal shoe on top. The only thing missing is a giant pumpkin coach. Doug is going to wear his gray suit, which has a very thin blue pinstripe. Jane found a deep purple dress that she promises is beautiful, but slightly less beautiful than my blue dress.

Jane and I will spend Saturday afternoon before the party at the spa getting a massage and pedicure. I will be buffed, shined, and relaxed, a picture-perfect bride-to-be. My parents are flying in tomorrow and promised to behave themselves. It's going to be perfect. Despite the fact that this party is grander than anything I have ever attended, it's nothing compared to the ideas Ann is throwing around regarding the wedding. She's been interviewing wedding coordinators, seeking the perfect balance between creative and traditional. I've decided that instead of being upset that she's involved, I should be reveling in the fact that she wants to help. Not to mention that she and Theodore are pretty much planning on paying for the whole thing. As Ann pointed out, it wouldn't really be fair for my folks to be responsible, when their family has so many people they need to invite. This comes as a huge relief. My dad is not likely to donate much toward the wedding, as he is undoubtedly saving up for my two wicked step-sisters' weddings. My mom's budget would be more Holiday Inn and cocktail weenies than wedding planner and china. I'm happily thinking about my own dress when a voice interrupts my train of thought.

"Sophie?" My eyes pop open and there stands Nick. He's wearing his casual professor look, which means that his shirt is still buttoned up to the neck complete with tweedy sport coat, but he's left the tie at home. I sit up fast and my stack of magazines slide to the floor. Their glossy pictures wink up in the fluorescent lights of the ferry. I feel like a kid whose been caught with pornography. Why couldn't I have been caught with a stack of magazines like *Discover*, *Scientific America*, and *The Smithsonian*? Nick is holding a book under his arm; I can just read the title: *The Velocity of Honey and Everyday Physics. Damn; just once I would like to catch him with a Stephen King novel.*

"It's so good to see you." I stand up and give him a hug. "Did you get the tape I sent over?"

"I did. I wanted to thank you, it was kind of you. Did you get the CD I sent?" About two days after I delivered the tape of the Hitchcock movies, a CD entitled Opera's Greatest Hits showed up in my mail. There was no card, but of course I knew who it was from. There was only one person I knew who thought the opera had any great hits. I'll admit to playing it a few times. Some of it's quite nice, but it's lacking any catchy, sing-along songs and the beat isn't exactly something that you dance to.

"It's good. I particularly liked one song." My brain mentally raced through the filing cabinet of my mind trying to remember the name of any song listed on the CD. "You know the one, the first one."

"Do you mean 'La donna è mobile'?" he asks. I slap my forehead as if trying to knock something free in there.

"Of course! I can't believe it slipped my mind. I love it. I've been playing it in my car pretty much nonstop."

"You really like it?" He raises one eyebrow.

"Of course I do!" I get the sense he doubts I'm cultured enough to enjoy opera, which is utterly ridiculous. I could enjoy opera, I just don't. I like a lot of cultural activities—take ballet, for example. I've seen the *Nutcracker* on TV at least ten times. I've also seen that movie about Mozart, the one where he has that really annoying hyena laugh.

"I'm pleased to hear it. I've got season tickets if you would like to join me sometime."

"That would be great!" *I'll have to bring earplugs, but it will be worth it.* It's the first time that Nick has indicated any interest in seeing me. Operation Friendship is working its magic. I give him a big smile. "Why are you going over to the Island?" I ask.

"There's a CSICOP conference in Victoria this weekend."

"A skeptics conference? Who says you don't know how to have fun! Are you guys planning to go after Bigfoot or Nessie this go-round?"

"The topic this year is teaching critical thinking. We've already done a conference on Bigfoot and the Loch Ness Monster." He's actually able to say this with a straight face. "It should be quite interesting. We'll get a turnout from most of the west coast. Ray Hyman is one of the keynote speakers." He looks as excited as if he was announcing that U2 had agreed to play during the conference dinner. He fascinates me; his interests are encyclopedic.

"Sounds fascinating."

"If you want fascinating you should meet Cathie," he said with a wink.

"Cathie?" Her name caught in my throat.

"Cathie's not . . ." He glanced over at me. "Ah never mind. Why are you heading over?" he asks.

The thing is, I haven't told Nick that I've gotten engaged yet. I had planned on telling him sooner, but it was one of those things where the topic just didn't come up. We've hardly talked, to be honest, and it seemed strange to tell him by e-mail. It's the kind of news you want to share face-to-face, except now that we *are* face-to-face, I'm not interested in saying anything. After all, we've just started talking; it seems completely unnatural to just blurt out that Doug and I are thinking of getting married. Well, I guess we're doing more than thinking about it. I'll tell Nick after we've had more time to get used to each other again.

"Oh you know, heading over to see some friends." This is technically not a lie. I *will* be seeing friends. It's not as if I have to say I'm having an engagement party. In fact, since I didn't invite him, it would be rude to mention it. In many ways I'm just being thoughtful. I had considered inviting him, but I honestly couldn't see him fitting in with any of Doug or his parents' friends. My mom would love him, but it didn't seem fair to saddle him with her, so I just left him off the guest list. Not to mention I wasn't sure how Doug would have felt about the whole thing. After all, Doug is under the impression that Nick and I had some kind of relationship. "Maybe I'll swing by the conference, where is it being held?"

"I'm not sure you should." Nick suddenly takes a strong

interest in his own shoes, looking down. What is the matter? Is he embarrassed to be seen with me? Am I not good enough for his skeptical buddies? I thought he was done being mad, but maybe not. Maybe he's the kind of guy who holds a grudge. I mean, honestly, get over it already, I said I was sorry. "What with the whole psychic thing and all," he mumbles.

"Right." I had forgotten, of course as far as his skeptical friends are concerned I'm public enemy number-one, an unrepentant psychic. They would most likely try to burn me alive in order to force me to recant my predictions.

"That is, unless you've given any more thought to 'coming out'?"

"Sorry, I don't think it would be a good idea." Nick nods as if he already knew the answer. We stand there looking at each other for a moment.

"I wish that . . ." Nick gets out before Jane comes rushing up out of nowhere.

"Whales!" she yells. Both Nick and I turn to her. *What does he wish?* I want him to finish his sentence but he's distracted. This is understandable, since Jane is screeching and waving her arms. "Whales!" Jane yells again. "There's a whole pod of them, orcas, off the whatchamacallit side, the right side."

"Starboard?" Nick inquires.

"Right—starboard—come quick!" I look at Nick for a moment and then the three of us turn and run up the stairs to the deck. I lean over the railing and for a moment I don't see anything but large, gray-blue rolling waves and then they break the surface.

It's a pod of about six killer whales, their black dorsal fins oily black as they cut through the waves, chasing the ferry. There are a lot of whales off the coast of Vancouver, but every time I see them it strikes me as more fantasy than reality, like seeing unicorns flying overhead. These huge, beautiful things, lunging and diving, make me want to cheer like I'm starring in my own version of *Free Willy*.

"Look at them!" I yell to no one in particular. Nick takes my hand and squeezes it. I meet his eyes and I can tell he can feel it, too. This is magic, the kind that he believes in. The kind that believes back in you. The whales, as if sensing the audience, start to show off, leaping out the water so that you can see the blur of black and white. I jump up and down, joining them, but I manage to hang on to Nick's hand.

There are a few other people who have noticed the whales. Those who brought cameras are snapping away. I wish I had a camera so I could catch the moment, but I'm glad not to be seeing them through the distance of a viewfinder. I turn and look through the windows of the ferry. Inside I can see people reading the paper, chatting to one another or talking on cell phones. They either don't know the whales are out here, or can't be bothered. After a minute or two, as if growing bored with the game, the whales stop jumping and after a few minutes veer left. I want to scream at the captain to follow them, but after all, it's public transportation, not a whale-watching cruise. I have this urge to jump into the water and swim after them.

"That was amazing," Nick says, finally breaking the silence. I turn to him and have the strongest urge to kiss him. He squeezes my hand and that's when he notices the ring. He looks down at it. It squats on my finger like a giant diamond toad. He pulls my hand closer to his face, as if he can't believe what he's seeing. "Are you engaged?" he sputters.

"No." I swear it jumped out from my lips. Jane spins around and looks at me as if I was speaking in tongues. "I mean, technically I guess I am." Nothing seems like the right thing to say.

"Technically?" Nick asks.

"Well, I mean, it's complicated. I mean, Doug asked me." That's when I see Doug and Jeremy approaching. I let go of Nick's hand like it was on fire. I feel the hot rush of blood into my face as if I've been caught doing something sordid. I take a step forward as if to just walk away, but there's no escape.

"There you are," Doug says. "I found your abandoned pile of magazines and wondered if you had been kidnapped. I couldn't think of any other reason you would leave them behind." He gives Jeremy a manly shove on the shoulder and they yuck it up over my silly girly antics.

"Jane spotted a pod of whales." Doug looks out over the water. "They're gone now," I say, pointing out the obvious since there isn't a whale to be seen for a hundred miles. Doug turns to look back at me and notices Nick. His face turns hard, the lines of his jaw growing more angular. *Uh-oh.*

"What are you doing here?" Doug asks Nick, pulling me to his side. He's acting like Nick is some kind of sex offender and he's been caught trying to peek under the stall in the girls' bathroom.

"I spotted Sophie on the ferry. I simply came over to say hello."

"Well, you've said hello." Doug has now managed to

surgically attach himself to my side like some kind of male Siamese twin.

"Doug!" I give him a look that I hope conveys the fact that I think he's being a weiner. I lean away from him a bit, but unless I'm willing to wrench myself free I'm not getting out of Doug's clutches. He's attached to me like gum in my hair. I look back at Nick. He's got his hands shoved deep into his pockets and is leaning slightly forward. I have this sudden image of the two of them going at each other, fists flying. Doug would win; he has at least five inches and fifty pounds on Nick. With my luck, Doug would end up dangling Nick over the side of the boat like a whale snack in a SeaWorld demonstration.

"I just heard your news. I guess congratulations are in order," Nick says between tight lips. Doug relaxes slightly.

"Thank you. It was inevitable; we've been together for five years."

"Six years, actually." I say this as if it matters in some way. Both Doug and Nick stop their eye-fencing long enough to look at me.

"I can see the two of you are made for each other." For some reason, this compliment coming from Nick makes me think he is insulting me. "I'll shove off, then." Nick leans forward and pulls me from Doug, giving me a kiss on the cheek. "Congratulations. I know how much you wanted this," he says softly in my ear before letting me go. The words are warm from his breath and they tickle my ear. Doug pulls me back and I snap to his side like I'm attached with elastic.

"I hope you have a good time at your conference," I mumble. Nick gives me a warm smile and shakes Jane's hand before he wanders off.

"He's got a lot of nerve," Doug says, shaking his head.

"What do you mean?"

"Coming over here trying to put the moves on you. What is it going to take for him to get the picture? Anyone can see that he's crazy about you."

"Really?" I ask. Doug gives me a look.

"You can't tell me that you still have feelings for him. You would choose that bookworm over me?" Jane and Jeremy look like they're trying to slink away before things blow up into a soap-opera situation. These are the very conversations I normally enjoy eavesdropping on, when they aren't happening to me.

"Don't be rude. I just asked a question. There's nothing going on. He's headed to the Island for a conference and came over to say hello. He's a friend of mine."

"Let's drop it; in fact, consider it never picked up. He's probably going to that *skeptical* conference, you know. He looks like the type."

"How did you know about the skeptics conference?"

"The TV station told me. They're trying to get a representative from that group for the show. They felt it was important I know."

"What show?"

"The local station is doing a show on psychics on Saturday. They called me to see if we would be on. They're interested in our experience and how we ended up together. They think it makes a great human-interest story."

"You didn't tell them that we would do it, did you?"

"Of course I did. It will be a great experience. I've always wanted to be on TV."

"I don't want to be on TV."

"Don't be silly. It will be fun. If you don't like it you can let me do a lot of the talking. Besides, you were great on Holly's radio show, just think of it as radio with pictures."

"Were you planning on telling me?"

"Of course, I just got off the phone with the guy when I was out on the deck with Jeremy. I was coming to find you to tell you, when I spotted you with Mr. Doubting Thomas. You should watch out for him. If he *is* a skeptic he could just be trying to chum up with you to attempt to undermine your abilities. He's the type who wouldn't believe in the Earth circling the sun unless he saw it for himself."

"He's actually a really nice guy." Doug shrugs. I shift tactics. "We've got the engagement party on Saturday. I'm not sure we will have time to do the show. Besides, I'm uncomfortable making a big deal out of everything. I associate the whole psychic experience with our breakup, it brings back bad memories."

"Oh, baby." Doug smothers me in a big hug. I can smell the Bounce dryer sheets I use in our laundry mixing with the ocean air. "You're never going to lose me again. You don't need to worry."

I'm extremely tempted to point out to Doug that I didn't lose him. It wasn't like I misplaced our relationship for a while; he left. I knew right where he was the whole time. The way he talks about it now leaves me with the feeling that he thinks I should be glad that he's returned. As if I did something wrong, and he found it in his heart to forgive me. Technically, *I* am the wronged party here. *I* should be the one demanding apologies and telling him that he doesn't have to worry.

Despite Doug's fine advice I'm worried, not about losing him, but about being on the TV show. My last experience on Holly's show has put me off media events. It feels dangerous, like stepping into a lake only to discover there's something swimming next to you—something large.

Forty

CANCER

With the full moon in Gemini on Friday, you might feel ready to spread your wings and fly. The problem is, you're not as ready as you feel. Promises should be limited to what you honestly want.

When I was little I believed that I might have been exchanged with another baby at birth. I was fairly sure that I had somehow ended up with the wrong family. I considered it possible that I was actually a lost member of the royal family, a minor duchess or something. I wasn't so grandiose that I thought I was a princess, certainly a missing princess would have created more press, but a duchess, well, one of those could get lost in shuffle. Destined for royalty, but forced to live an average life—I think that is why I'm obsessed with spas.

For years I never went to a spa. I felt funny about the idea of strange people touching me, and then having to pay for the experience. For my birthday one year, Jane got me a gift certificate for a massage and a pedicure. As it turns out, strange people touching you isn't icky, it's really nice, provided they're trained professionals. It was like a religious experience. The spa has the same cool marble, and everyone speaks with slightly hushed tones, just like in church. The music is usually Enya or some strange flute music combined with rain sounds. You strip off all your clothes and leave them, along with your worries, in a locker. You're wrapped up in a thick bathrobe. No matter if you are the size of a truck, they make the bathrobe oversized so you get to feel tiny. Then they proceed to pamper you until your bones melt into liquid honey and you ooze from one treatment to another. By the end it doesn't even matter how much they charge. I would be willing to sell off an organ if only they would give a sixty-minute massage instead of a forty-minute one.

Doug called the spa and told them I was appearing on TV that day, and had arranged for me to be upgraded from my planned treatments to a full stem-to-stern overhaul. It's costing him somewhere near the amount people are required to put down to purchase a house. It's his way of making a peace offering after the whole ferry fiasco. I spent the rest of yesterday saying I was "fine" in a way meant to communicate that I was anything but. When he stopped asking what was wrong— sometime during our "romantic" dinner—I became enraged. When he told me I was being childish on the way home, I made the driver of our horse-drawn carriage pull over so I could get out. I threatened to walk back to the hotel and then had a good cry standing by the road. We made up while the carriage driver pretended not to listen. I thought being engaged would be like being on cloud nine, but so far it's been like starring in an episode of *Fear Factor*, one stressful event after another.

I may have forgiven Doug, but I'm still not thrilled about the idea of doing the TV show. However, Doug is like a kid on Christmas morning. He can't wait. He spent twenty minutes this morning debating if he should wear a tie or go with a more casual look. He ended up deciding he should get something new to wear. I wish new clothes would make *me* feel better about the whole thing. I roll my head to the side, Jane is in the chair next to me; we are having our toes done. The chairs are giant white La-Z-Boys, complete with massage and vibration modes; our feet are submerged in a mini–hot tub, bubbling away. Her eyes are closed. I would think she was asleep except every so often she gives a low moan of pleasure.

"Do you think I'm making a mistake doing the TV show?"

"Yep." She mumbles without even opening her eyes.

"Thanks a lot. What can I do? You heard Doug, he's over the moon. He's Ed McMahon showing up at the door with a giant cardboard check kind of happy."

"Yep."

"Are you listening to me?"

"Yep."

"Say something else."

"Something else." It's times like this I wonder why Jane is my best friend.

"Seriously, do you think it's a bad idea?" Jane gives a theatrical sigh as if she's been asked to sacrifice her life for her country. She heaves herself into a sitting position and looks over at me.

"Do you want me to tell you something to make you feel better, or the truth?" I think about it for a second.

"Truth."

"I think the show is a mistake—you're not a psychic. Every time you go out and promote yourself as one I think you are inviting bad karma, or luck, or whatever you want to call it." I picture my luck running through an hourglass like sand.

Sometime in the future I'll be standing under a falling piano and I will have wished I hadn't used up all my good karma. "But the fact that you are lying to a whole bunch of people is nothing compared to the fact that you are lying to Doug."

"You can't expect me to tell him that I made up the whole psychic thing. He loves it. He tells everyone how destiny brought us together. He came back when he heard me on the radio."

"Do you want to be with someone who loves you for something that isn't really you?"

"No." I look down at my polished fingernails. I picked a color called "Bridal Pink." It will look great with my engagement dress. "I don't think Doug loves me just because I'm psychic."

"I don't, either, but if that's true then why not tell him the truth? Why start out married life with this thing in the way?"

"I may tell him sometime, I'm just not sure now is the time."

"The time to tell him would be before he shows up on a TV show talking about it. Once he's done that you are never going to be able to tell him. You'll have to keep the lie up for the rest of your life. When you guys have kids he'll be expecting you to predict if it's a boy or girl."

"On the upside, I'll have a fifty-fifty shot on that one."

"It's your life, do what you think is best." Jane closes her eyes again. She has entered a new level of relaxation that is only possible for mothers of small children who have been able to get away for a weekend without them. At home she falls asleep in the dentist's chair. She says it's divine to sit there with no one hanging off of her. If she can sleep during drilling of her own teeth I guess I shouldn't be too surprised that she's drifting off here.

I shift in the chair. I'm doing what I think is best, I think. I open my mouth to say something but the spa technicians come in to do our pedicures. Spa staff is a bit like the priesthood, you can say anything during a treatment and it's like a confessional. They can't tell anyone; it's a place of emotional sanctuary, at least it's supposed to be. I'm half tempted to ask them their views on the issue and take a vote, but perhaps I shouldn't distract them from the task at hand of scraping my feet.

Ideally, I would tell Doug the truth and we would laugh about the situation. However, life is often less than ideal. Jane tells me all the time that I need to stop expecting life to be a dream world where everything turns out rosy. A lot of women keep secrets from their husbands—how much they spend at the mall, what their stretch marks look like in bright lights, and how their last boyfriend really compared to them in bed. Look at Nick. He kept this Cathie a secret. This will simply be one of those things Doug and I don't share. We'll do this TV show and I'll make Doug promise it's the last one. I'll tell him I had a prediction that I should not use my powers any longer. It will become one of those "remember when" stories we'll share as we turn old and gray together. We'll laugh about it as we sit by the fire enjoying a cup of tea. I just need to think of this show as one last hurdle before our engagement party, eventual wedding, and Happily Ever After. Considering all that has gone on before, how bad can it be?

Forty-one

L E O

Balancing professional and home life is draining. Rehashing the disturbances of the past gets you nowhere fast. Look to the future for bold changes that can make a difference. An unexpected surprise will rear its head today.

The television station is on the top floor of a building that sits on the edge of the harbor in the city center of Victoria. When you enter the lobby the back wall is floor-to-ceiling windows. There's a view of the entire inner harbor. You can see the circle of artists that set up tables along the sidewalk, hawking paintings, homemade jewelry, and pottery. There's the usual assortment of street entertainers, dancers, guitar players, violinists, and, my least favorite, clowns. I hate clowns. There's an actual word for it, *coulrophobia*—clown phobia. I blame it on my grandmother, who arranged for a clown to perform on my sixth birthday. The guy scared me, and in every picture I'm screaming. I don't think this is an irrational fear. I don't think you should trust people who wear baggy clothes and cover themselves in makeup. What is it they have to hide? Then there's the strange thing with balloon animals. What does it say about a person if they want to spend that much time stroking latex? You know they have to practice. That squeaky-squeaky sound they make as they create deformed balloon animals is enough to make me grind my teeth. I'm trying hard not to take the sight of the clowns outside as some kind of evil omen.

I look out the windows while Doug paces around the lobby. He keeps checking his teeth in the mirror in case a piece of terrorist spinach has crawled up his carefully pressed Polo linen pants, past his soft blue cotton shirt, and stuck itself in his bleached teeth. If you ask me, he's paranoid about it. I'm saving my worry for making an ass of myself. It's just a case of different priorities.

We're ushered into the back where the makeup artist puts an extra layer onto me and sponges Doug with a tan concealer. He looks like George Hamilton, overly tanned and pressed.

"Do you think they'll let me sit facing the right side?"

"What?"

"I'm hoping that they let me sit on the right side, I think it's my best side, don't you?" Doug turns one way and then spins and shows me his profile from the other side. "Well?"

"I think you look great no matter which side is showing." Doug gives me a kiss on the forehead, when he pulls back I can see the soft shadow of my powder on his lips. If it wouldn't ruin my makeup, and his new shirt, I would throw myself in his arms.

"Okay, you two lovebirds—let's break it up in here." The producer bustles in carrying a clipboard. Her hair is pulled back so tightly I doubt that she is capable of closing her eyes. "We do the show live and there's a small studio audience, so don't let that throw you. We're going to take you in and have you sit on the couch while we get set up. Our host is Ellen Bigham. She's so pleased to have you both here today; she's really looking forward to it. Now, any questions?" The woman speaks so fast that I'm still on her first sentence about the love-birds when she speaks again. "Okay, perfect. Let's go. You both look divine by the way. Simply divine." She gives Doug an arm squeeze. "You're just a little slice of heaven!" Turning to me, "What do I have to do to get one of these for myself?"

"You should have Sophie do a reading for you. Maybe she can tell you when you'll meet your own Mr. Wonderful," Doug says. The producer links arms with Doug and leads us out of the green room toward the set. She looks back at me and winks.

"Not only cute, but clever, too. You couldn't be more right, maybe later I'll talk your darling into giving me that reading."

The first thing I notice about the studio is that it's freezing cold. The kind of cold where your nipples feel like they're going to spring off and scurry under a table. The skin on my arms pricked up with each hair follicle popping its head up like a prairie dog attempting to see better. The room is as large as an airplane hangar. In the center there's the set, a tiny living room surrounded by fake walls on three sides. There seems to be about seven hundred cameras all pointing in our direction. The floor is covered with wires and cables, some of which are taped down and others that snake free. The audience sits in bleachers. There weren't as many as I had feared, maybe thirty at most. They look friendly. They stopped talking to each other while we wandered over to the couch. Once they realize that we aren't anyone famous, they go back to talking to one another.

One of the technical guys rushes over to check the sound mumbling, "check, check, check, can you hear me?" The camera crews pull in closer, and then pull back in a carefully organized ballet. The light guys turn on various spotlights and point them so that they're focused directly into my eyes. My throat is growing tighter. It seems as if there isn't enough air getting in. Doug is sitting at an unusual angle, trying to make sure that his right side is facing the camera. I keep taking deep breaths trying to remember the breathing tips that I learned in my yoga class. The problem is that I took yoga because they have those great outfits and everyone looks so Zen. The class itself was a lot of work. My body lacks several key joints required for some of those positions. Apparently I didn't pay enough attention to the breathing advice, either, because nothing seems to be working.

There's a bustle of activity and the host Ellen Bigham bursts out onto the set. She is surrounded by makeup artists and a cluster of clipboard-carrying support staff. She's small, five feet five and with her additional volume of makeup and hairspray she may weigh a maximum of one hundred pounds. She looks like an elementary school kid who stars in beauty pageants. The suit she is wearing is an eye-blistering hot pink and somehow she has found matching lipstick. The studio audience gives an *ooh* sound and she raises a tiny starfish hand and waves by opening and closing her palm. All she needed was a float and she could be the Rose Bowl princess. She sweeps up toward us and Doug stands to shake her hand. One of the clipboard-carrying assistants throws herself in front of Ellen as if Doug is an assassin.

"Please don't touch Ms. Bigham. You might wrinkle her suit." The assistant looks ready to do hand-to-hand combat if

Doug moves too quickly and threatens the linen. Doug sits back down and for the first time looks a bit uncertain. I would be surprised if Ms. Bigham has a big problem with people touching her. She is wearing enough perfume to act as a chemical weapon. There are actual smell waves coming off of her that are almost visible to the naked eye.

"Sorry about Suze. She's my personal assistant and I think she includes 'guard dog' as part of her duties." Ellen gives a tinkling laugh. She sits down carefully, tucking her skirt underneath her and pulling her jacket down. She swipes at her teeth with one finger checking for hot pink lipstick that has wandered off. It isn't until she sits down that I notice her couch has firm cushions. Doug and I are sunk down in cushions that seem to be made of warm marshmallows.

"Thank you so much for asking us to be on the show," Doug says.

"No, thank *you* for agreeing to do it! Now, just ignore the cameras and talk directly to each other or to me as if we were having a dinner party." She leans over and squeezes my arm. My eyes water from the fresh assault of her perfume waves. I briefly consider telling her not to touch me, that she might wrinkle my shirt but it seems catty. The crew starts yelling out countdowns and before I know it the lights are glaring and we are on.

"We've all heard of star-crossed lovers and relationships that were destined to be, but for today's couple it's not just a fairy tale—it's real life. Let's give a big welcome to Sophie Kintock and Doug Chase!" The crew holds up a sign that says APPLAUSE and the studio audience responds with cheers, like a well-trained pet. "Sophie has become the west coast psychic sweetheart. She's made predictions resulting in lives and relationships being saved. The response to her readings has been overwhelming. I know many people are predicting a lot of future success for this talented woman. Tell us how all this happened." I open my mouth, but Doug has already started talking.

"Ellen, like most men, I've had difficulties making a commitment." Doug gives her one of his boyish smiles. "I dated Sophie for a long time, and while I knew she was something special, I had gotten used to her, to our relationship. We decided to break up, to give each other a chance to explore what other fish were in the sea." I clench my teeth. *We* had decided to break up? Talk about your revisionist history. "It felt like my life was coming apart by the seams. I kept misplacing things, like my car. It seemed like nothing was running as smoothly as it had been when we had been together. I was too nervous to contact Sophie, to see if she would want to get back together." He shakes his head ruefully. "By chance, weeks later I happened to hear a psychic on the radio. Imagine my shock to find out that the psychic was Sophie. She had given a reading to someone telling the person they were not meant to be together. I realized then that she was the one. I was letting pride stand in the way of what was meant to be. That's when I stopped believing in chance and started believing in the two of us." He takes my hand and holds it in front of the camera. The studio audience gives a small sigh of happiness.

"Sophie, prior to your breakup with Doug you had kept your psychic abilities secret. What made you decide to come forward at that time?"

"Well, I never really thought of my psychic abilities as anything special. I just saw myself as the kind of person who had hunches. One of those hunches became public and that lead to an opportunity to be on the radio. It wasn't really a decision to go public, it sort of just happened."

"But going public is what brought you two back together, isn't it? It makes you wonder where luck ends and destiny begins," Ellen says.

"I don't know if it's luck or destiny, but I know I'm not letting go of this special lady again," Doug says. The audience gives another sigh. "Tonight is our engagement party, and Sophie is predicting a lifetime of happily ever after for us."

"Do you plan to make any other predictions? I'm sure our audience here would love to hear what you have to say." The crowd gives a cheer.

"Oh, no. I'm afraid my public reading days are over."

"Don't be shy Sophie, go ahead," Doug says.

"Yes, come on, Sophie!" Ellen says. "I know several people in our audience would like to hear what you have to say. There's also a group here in Victoria that's interested in what Sophie has to say. CISCOP, a skeptical organization devoted to the investigation of the paranormal is in town for a conference. They're the modern day X-file hunters. We've asked one of their members to join us today and evaluate Sophie's predictions. We'll be right back after this commercial break, live with Psychic Sophie Kintock and disbeliever Professor Nick McKenna!"

"And . . . we're out." The crew man yells and the lights click off. Wherever I look there's a white circle, a ghostly imprint of the spotlight. The clipboard Rotweiller is ushering Nick onto the set. I untangle myself from Doug and the quicksand cushions, pushing myself up to meet Nick at the edge of the set, blocking his way.

"What are you doing here?" I hiss at Nick.

"I was just going to ask you the same thing," he hisses back.

"I can't believe you are doing this," I say crossing my arms.

"Doing what? I got a call from the station saying they were having a psychic on and would we be willing to send someone over to present our viewpoint. Do you know how rare that is? Most of the time media outlets put psychics on as if it's the Gospel. The station is giving us a chance to show another side. This is what I do, I had no idea you would be the psychic."

"What happened to spending time with your new girlfriend? Shouldn't you be wining and dining her instead of making media appearances?"

"My new girlfriend?" Nick looks at me for a moment and then rolls his eyes. "You mean Cathie? You can rest assured that she is very committed to the skeptical cause."

"Well, how nice for her. I'm sure you two have a lovely time debating the merits of alien infestation."

"It has been lovely. In fact, I'm asking her to move to Vancouver tonight at the conference." My mouth pops open. *Mr. Sensible is asking her to move here?*

"I thought you two just started dating."

"We did, but I've known her for years. She's been down at the University of Oregon and I think it's time she moved up to

Vancouver so we can work together. We have a lot in common. She's done a lot of important work around psychic events."

"How nice for both of you. You're here to try to prove I'm a fake. You're going to make a fool of me in front of everyone just so the two of you have something to laugh about."

"Stop being ridiculous and making me the bad guy. You are the one getting married to the Neanderthal. Why are you doing the show? You told me you weren't doing any more readings, it was over. Have you considered the situation this puts me in? For crying out loud, it's not like I have to *prove* you're a fake, you *are* a fake."

"Is he bothering you?" Doug asks, suddenly appearing by my side. Nick rolls his eyes.

"Please, spare me your caveman, me-Tarzan-king-of-the-jungle speech. Sophie is perfectly capable of speaking to me without you playing the hero. Has it occurred to you that she doesn't need saving?"

"Look buddy," Doug says pushing him in the chest with one finger. "You just keep your distance from her. I don't know what you're up to, but I'm telling you for the last time to back off."

"Where do you get these lines? Do you watch nothing but Clint Eastwood movies? Do you practice them at home in the mirror while flexing your muscles? I'm trying to have a conversation with her. At least she's capable of stringing together a sentence made up of multisyllablabic words. Why don't you back off?"

"Okay, that's it." Doug pushes up the sleeves of his shirt and takes a step closer to Nick.

"Okay, you two, save it for the camera," the producer says pushing all of us back toward the couch. "We're back in three, two, one." The lights go on, the only thing brighter is Ellen's megawatt smile.

"Welcome back, we're here with psychic Sophie Kintock, her fiancé, Doug, and skeptic Dr. Nick McKenna. Is it fair to say the CSICOP hates psychics? Are you against true love?"

"This doesn't have anything to do with hate or love, it's about science. CSICOP is committed to the scientific investigation of claims of the paranormal. We believe in looking at things and practicing critical thinking skills. Psychic phenomenon is growing in popularity. We're asking people to take a hard look at what exactly is being said and to take a logical approach."

"What's logical about love, Ellen?" Doug asks interrupting Nick. "You can't measure it on any scientific instrument. Maybe there is more to life than something that can be measured."

"We're not talking about love. We're talking about psychics," Nick says through pursed lips.

"You're talking about the woman I love. Her psychic skills are what brought us together. When you attack her psychic abilities, you attack the very glue that bonds our relationship."

"I would prefer not to discuss your relationship at all. I would prefer to discuss the topic at hand, psychic claims, how these claims can be faked and how these claims can be hurtful to other people."

"Do you think Sophie is a fake?" Ellen asks "How would you counter the predictions she's made that have come true?

There are a host of listeners out there who are ready to disagree with you, not just the man in her life." Nick looks at me. This is it, he could bust me right here. All he has to say is that he taught me everything I know, that I've done the whole thing in an effort to get Doug back. Nick breaks the eye contact first, looking away.

"I can't prove that Ms. Kintock is a fake." Relief floods in and I take a deep breath.

"This isn't about logic and science, Ellen, this is about being a sore loser. Mr. McKenna has a crush on my Sophie," Doug says. "Do you deny you dated her? You chased after her like a puppy and when she came back to me you couldn't stand it. He's only here because he can't be with her." My tongue feels like it's dried out and I have an urge to crawl off the set and hide. Nick's nostrils flare; his face is growing red.

"It's Dr. McKenna, if you don't mind. The one thing that is logical is that she can clearly do better than settling for you," Nick fires back.

"This discussion certainly is heating up! Join us after this commercial break, when we have another guest who wants to weigh in on the issue of psychics, skeptics, love, and loss," Ellen says gleefully. The lights click off.

"Look, I don't have anything else to say. I think it would be best if I left." Nick tries to stand up but his microphone cord is caught on the couch tethering him down. Doug gives a snort and looks away.

I turn to tell Ellen that there's some kind of mistake, I'm not interested in doing any more readings, and we should just call it a day, but she is buried beneath a pile of makeup people who are covering her in a fresh layer of powder and lipstick. I could use some of that. I can feel a slick shine of sweat popping up on my forehead.

"Now, Nick, you can't leave. We've got another guest who's joining us," Ellen says, her eyes darting off to the side. I follow her gaze and my stomach lurches up my throat. Standing in the wings being helped across the sea of cables is Melanie. Doug's hand tightens on mine. Melanie sits on the couch next to Ellen. Her lips are pulled tight into what could be a smile or a snarl. It's a bit hard to tell at this point. Nick looks shocked and sits back down without another protest when the sound guy gently directs him to the couch. The lights click back on, and the temperature in the room heats up instantly.

"And we're back in three, two, one." The crew member points at Ellen, who breaks into her instant smile. She's starting to look like an evil jack-o'-lantern.

"We've been discussing psychics and skeptics and the story of psychic Sophie Kintock. Her abilities brought her and her estranged boyfriend back together, but that left a few people in the cold. One of them is Dr. Nick McKenna, whose lost love turned him skeptical, and the other is . . ."

"Melanie," I say in a flat voice. Ellen meets my eyes and smiles wider, I can feel one of the cameras rushing up to catch a close-up of Doug and me.

"That's right. Did you have a vision that she would be here?" Ellen asks. I swallow and shake my head. "For our audience, this is Melanie Feehan. She had been dating Doug. Sophie gave her a reading saying the two of them should break up, that they weren't meant to be together. That was the reading that led Doug and Sophie to reconciliation, but left Melanie alone."

"I figured you owed me another reading. The last one you gave me was correct, so I thought I would come back and see what else you had to say," Melanie says, each word cracking with ice.

"Melanie, fighting over me won't change anything" Doug says.

"It's not about you anymore. I came here because I want to hear what Sophie can tell me. You went back to her because you fell in love with the idea of her. The idea of her being psychic with magical powers. I think she's nothing but a fake."

"Well, Dr. McKenna, it looks like you aren't alone in your views. Maybe the two of you should get together." Nick starts when Ellen says this. He doesn't look reassured to have Melanie as his skeptical backup. Doug looks like he's still trying to understand how the universe stopped revolving around him.

"As you know, Ellen, I'm a journalist," Melanie says in a smooth tone. "I pride myself on my critical thinking skills, although I didn't see myself as a skeptic, per se. As embarrassing as it is, I'll admit to being taken in by Ms. Kintock. I've always been someone who believed it was important to be open. Unfortunately, in this situation I left myself open to a con woman. She faked being a psychic in an effort to steal Doug back. She knew the only way to get him back was to resort to dirty tricks." The audience makes a booing sound. They've turned on me. This is how people end up lynched.

"Doesn't this really come down to a difference in opinion, a she said–she said kind of thing?" Ellen asks as if we are still having a reasonable discussion.

"I canvassed the people in our apartment building and did some investigation. Ms. Kintock was spotted on a number of occasions illegally entering the apartment building where both Doug and I lived. I believe she used those opportunities to 'case' the situation, gather information, and created her 'predictions' from that. The whole thing was calculated from the word *go*."

"This is ridiculous," I squeak, but no one seems to be paying any attention. On a screen to the left a grainy security video flickers on. It's the laundry room in Doug's old apartment building. The door opens and you can see me clear as day. I knew those lights in the laundry room were too bright. I guess they had to be, they were busy filming documentaries in there. The video has no sound but like a good silent movie you can still make out what is happening. You can see me poking around in the washing machines and dryer, carefully selecting socks and then diving under the folding table. Melanie and Doug had their scene. Then you could see Nick enter and help me out from under the table. The video stopped. Melanie is smiling smugly. She leans back and crosses her legs. I feel like an air mattress where all the air is slowly leaking out. It seems possible that I could ooze down and slip right off the couch.

"I'm not sure what to say," Ellen purrs, trying very hard to hide her smile. I hate her. She's become the Jerry Springer of Canadian TV. All that is missing are a few women in the studio audience taking off their tops, a fight, and the revelation that Melanie is secretly dating her dad's lover.

"Sophie? Can you explain this?" Doug is looking at me with wide eyes, like he's discovered I have a secret history as a stripper.

"Sure." I pause while I wait for an answer to come to me. I know there was always a chance I would have to tell Doug the truth someday. I just didn't expect to be telling him in front of a live studio audience that is ready to string me up using the light cables.

"Go on. Explain it. Explain to everyone how you faked the whole thing," Melanie crows. I look back and forth between her and Doug. This is it. When I tell the truth everything will be over. Doug will go back to her, heck, he might force me to pry the ring off my finger right here and hand it over to her.

"I can explain," Nick says, breaking the silence. Everyone pivots to look at him, we had forgotten he was there.

"I hired Ms. Kintock to be a fake psychic. I was planning on writing a paper on beliefs and how easily people are duped into believing in things like psychic predictions. It wasn't her idea at all, it was mine. I have to take responsibility for this situation."

"You're lying," Melanie says softly.

"I'm afraid not. If you check the business records of Stack of Books, where Ms. Kintock works, you will note the transaction. For someone who prides themselves on their investigative reporting abilities I must say you didn't investigate very much. It's all there in black and white. I believe the account is even paid in full. Feel free to call right now, I'm certain the documents could be faxed here to the station if additional proof is required."

"But, why was she spying on Doug, then?" Melanie asks. Nick shakes his head slowly, as if deeply disappointed in her. I'm interested to hear the answer, too.

"She wasn't spying on Doug, she was spying on *you*. This is the problem of leaping to conclusions without doing any critical thinking. Once you decided she was stalking Doug you interpreted everything you learned through that filter. It skewed reality and gave you the picture you wanted to see. For the record, I also live in the building. I knew that you were a reporter with the paper. The fact that you became involved with her ex-boyfriend was nothing more than an unfortunate coincidence. At the time, she begged me to stop the experiment, but it was going so well I was unwilling. When she and Doug got back together she told me that she wouldn't be able to continue, and we called an end to it. She has been nothing but honorable and upstanding in this situation."

"Why didn't you tell me?" Doug asks looking at me.

"She couldn't. I had her sign a confidentiality agreement," Nick says before I say anything and blow our story. I look at Doug and shrug *what's a girl to do?*

"So this was designed to trick me?" Melanie whispers.

"It wasn't a trick, it was a test. You were presented with someone who stated they had psychic abilities. Instead of investigating, asking questions, *anything* for that matter, you bought it lock, stock, and barrel. You presented it to the public as fact. Even when the story started to fall apart you didn't question the most outrageous part, that she was a psychic. The part you questioned was her motivation. You thought the whole thing was some type of elaborate scheme to get her boyfriend back. That is laughable. The fact that you're so gullible is criminal for someone in your position."

"You make it sound like believing in something outside our understanding is a waste. Wouldn't it be a bleak world without any wonder or magic?" Ellen asks.

"Do you know what I find amazing? What I find wonderful?" Nick looks around at the studio audience. "Do you know how to suspend thousands of tons of water in the air without any visible means of support? Do you?" Everyone on the set and most of the studio audience shake our heads no. A few people look up into the rafters as if they might spot a ton of water levitating above the set. "You build a cloud." He pauses while we think about that. "Science is amazing; you don't need magic to find the world magical. The people we meet, the relationships we build, are what makes it special. The universe is an amazing place by itself. It doesn't need paranormal events to make it interesting."

"You don't find paranormal phenomena interesting?" Ellen asks.

"You know what I find interesting? I find it interesting people believe that there are aliens who possess the technology, and interest, to travel light years to come to this planet for no other reason than to do anal probes on some hick from backwater Tennessee. That they have no other way to communicate other than buzz the fields and create crop circles with strange shapes and designs. If they had the ability to travel here, wouldn't they do something more valuable than create intergalactic graffiti?"

"But—" Melanie gets out before Nick interrupts her.

"I find it interesting that people believe that the dead return to communicate and have nothing more to say than 'things here are fine.' I find it fascinating people think spending money on NASA is a waste, but fully support some guy wearing fatigues wandering around the forest in search of Yeti. Even when someone comes out and admits that he wore a monkey suit and faked it, nobody believes him. Oh, no, by all means the giant monkey boy is real. I find it interesting that people overlook the people in their lives that matter and focus on the fictional."

"It sounds like you don't believe in anything, Dr. McKenna," Ellen says softly.

"I believe this whole thing has been blown completely out of proportion. Ms. Feehan came here to try and do a 'sting' operation on Ms. Kintock. The problem is, there's no conspiracy."

"I think what you've done is mean. I think it was spiteful, all this to prove a point," Melanie says.

"Congratulations, it's nice to know you can think. At least you've proved something," Nick fires back. Melanie's eyes grow wide. She stands up and rips the microphone off her blouse and tosses it in Nick's direction and stomps off the set. The crew guy is waving madly and the clipboard assistants are buzzing around behind the camera. I'm getting the idea this is the most excitement this set has seen since the last miracle makeover segment.

"It seems the mystery behind psychic Sophie Kintock has been solved, but the mystery of the paranormal in general will take more time to solve then we have today. Thanks for joining us today on *Live at 11* with me, your host, Ellen Bigham."

"We're out," the crew lead yells out. Ellen shakes everyone's hands and is then swallowed up by her crowd of clipboard-carrying lackeys.

"So you two were never really dating?" Doug asks, talk about missing the big picture. Nick shakes his head no.

"It was a business relationship," Nick says. "You didn't think she would really go out with me, did you?"

"No, but then I figured she might have been upset over my leaving." Doug reaches a hand out and shakes Nick's hand. His other arm gives him a manly slap on the shoulder. "Sorry about the misunderstanding, I hope there are no hard feelings. I feel like a bit of a horse's ass for the way I've behaved."

"No hard feelings, I'm sure you can't help being an ass."

"Beg your pardon?"

"Just a joke. Sorry, eccentric professor humor." Nick unclips his microphone and steps off the set. "I hope you both have a great party, congratulations again." I watch him slip between the cameras and walk away, his shoulders bent.

"Hang on, I have to ask him something," I say to Doug, and then I dash after Nick. I catch him by the door. I grab him by the arm.

"Wait for a minute. How can I thank you? You were brilliant. I thought the situation was hopelessly screwed up. You won't get in trouble with CSICOP, will you?"

"A few people will be upset. The group as a whole promotes a very rational approach to debating psychics. Hiring someone to be a fake isn't an approach we've typically employed. I'll issue a statement later making sure it's clear it was entirely my idea, no reflection on the association. A few others will find the whole thing to be a lark."

"I didn't want you to have to be involved. I feel bad."

"Don't—I was here because I wanted to be here. In the end, the situation most likely worked out for the best: CSICOP got some press coverage and you and Doug are still together."

"I'm sorry he's being a bit of a bore. He has a set way of looking at things." I can't seem to find the words to explain the feeling in my chest. "I thought what you said was beautiful, how science is the real miracle, your belief in logic and reason. How normal things are what is special."

"I do believe in one thing that is illogical and irrational."

"What's that?"

"I believe in you." He kisses me softly and then slips out the door. I reach out and touch it; it feels cold and hard. I want to run after him, but that doesn't make any sense. I hardly know him, and besides, he's dating someone. I wonder what Cathie is like. I picture her as the sexy librarian type. She probably does math equations for fun. The two of them most likely lay in bed discussing quantum physics and making risqué jokes involving scientific terms. They belong together. I take a deep breath and turn back toward Doug. It's time for me to do the rational thing, to stay with the person I've loved for years, who has loved me. Doug and I may not be perfect for each other, but you don't walk away from our kind of stability. Love isn't all fireworks and excitement. I paint a smile on my lips and walk back to him.

Forty-two

VIRGO
Taking everything at face value may cause you to miss out on
something very special. Follow the clues in your life and you will
discover a new treasure that has been waiting to be found. If you
don't act fast, your coach will turn back into a pumpkin.

Doug and I walked the seawall along the harbor after we left
the studio. He said he wasn't mad, but I could tell that he was.
He was trying to decide which is worse: when he thought Nick
and I were dating, or the idea that I kept a secret from him. I
knew he wanted me to plead for forgiveness, even though I
technically didn't *do* anything. Okay, technically, I stalked him
and faked being a psychic to get him back, but as far as he
knows the only thing I did was keep quiet about something I
had promised to keep secret. In fact, if you look at it that way,
I did the only noble thing I could—I kept my word. Does he
want me to turn into one of those people who just say anything
to anyone? I still said I was sorry. I cried a bit, too, and promised I would never keep something like that from him again.

Doug's official story is that he suspected I wasn't a psychic
all along. My original thought was to cry out "liar, liar, pants
on fire!" but I managed to hold that in. Instead I told him how

much I appreciated the fact that he didn't push me and that he must have instinctively known that I wouldn't keep a secret from him unless it was important. We kissed and made up and promised never to pretend to have paranormal powers to one another ever again.

Jane finds the whole story hilarious. I keep telling her it wasn't funny at all, but she interrupts me to call the station to find out if she can get a copy of the tape.

"I just have to see Melanie's face when Nick tells her that he's proud of her for thinking. That would have been priceless."

"I still can't believe Nick did it, saying the whole thing was his idea."

"I can, I keep telling you he's crazy about you."

"He kissed me."

"What! Why didn't you say anything?" Jane scoots across the hotel bed until we are sitting knee to knee.

"It was more like a kiss good-bye. He's seeing someone. He's asking her to move up to Vancouver tonight."

"What are you going to do?"

"I'm not going to do anything. I'm going to get ready and go to my engagement party." Jane gives a dramatic sigh, but helps me get dressed. I know she has more to say, but thankfully she keeps her thoughts to herself. All the shopping was worth it; the dress is perfect. The fabric catches the light and drapes in just the right places. It makes me look at least ten pounds lighter, which by itself makes it worth every penny. Jane does my hair for me in an updo and for once, as if sensing the importance of the event, my curls behave instead of jutting out of my head. It's the kind of outfit that you fantasize about owning. It has a put-together look I usually try for and fail at miserably.

The party is everything I ever imagined. The hotel ballroom looks magical and I'm surrounded by a few hundred of my closest friends. Technically, most of these people aren't my closest friends. In fact, I don't even know the majority of them. Ann set up a receiving line and for the past hour I've stood between Doug and Theodore being kissed by total strangers. I tried sticking with a friendly handshake, but they were having none of that, they'd just lean in and grab some lip action. Apparently now that Doug and I are officially engaged, I'm available for public displays of affection by everyone in the Chase family's general circle.

Ann rented a string quartet to play for the evening, and the sounds of the music weave in between the conversation. At least I think she rented the quartet. It's possible she purchased them and the whole group will have to live out the rest of their lives in her garage, plinking on their strings while they wait to be needed again. It's my party, you'd think I would be enjoying it, having a drink, dancing, eating, doing something besides standing next to the door. My feet are starting to hurt. The spiked heels that look perfect with the dress were clearly built for fashion instead of function. They're "drop me at the door" kind of shoes. I can feel a blister erupting off the side of my little toe. At present, the blister is the same size as my toe. Based on its current growth pattern, I would estimate that within the hour it will double in size and be in the process of taking over my foot like some kind of blister blob.

My dad and Sharon came through the line about twenty minutes ago. I could see my dad looking around and being shocked at the surroundings. I've long suspected he thought I was going to end up marrying someone named "Jed," who would hit him up at the wedding reception for a down payment on a trailer that we would park on an abandoned lot. The Empress Hotel and the guests dripping with money were a pleasant surprise for him. Sharon was annoyed. I made sure to give her a nice, long look at my ring. It might be gaudy, but it's large-diamond gaudy.

"You look lovely," my dad says.

"Thanks, I'm glad you could come."

"I wouldn't dream of missing my daughter's engagement party."

"You do know we can't help you pay for this. I hope you weren't counting on that. We have Lindsey, our oldest, starting university this year," Sharon says. I grind my teeth. Dad puts his hand on her arm. It seems even he is a bit embarrassed. Perhaps in the presence of real class, he can recognize the fake.

"Doug's family was kind enough to host the party, but thanks for the thought."

"We're just glad you could join us," Doug says, ever the warm and welcoming host. "I'd be interested in hearing more about your business, Mr. Kintock. Sophie's told me so much about you. I was thinking there may be some way your business could help us out. My company has a regional office in Chicago."

"Really? Well, that would be interesting. We'll have to talk later. After all, I'm going to have to get to know the man who's stealing my baby girl." I smile and try not to notice that my dad is clearly more interested in a business deal than who I'm marrying. All these years I've wanted his approval, and now that I have it I would have thought I would be more excited.

Sharon leads my dad directly over to the bar, where it looks like she plans to make use of the open-bar hospitality.

I was cheek-kissing another business acquaintance of Theodore's when I see my mom standing in the corner. She looks fascinated with her mini-appetizers, as if doing an in-depth study on how long it takes to have the grease leak through the napkin. Her dress is too long. I suspect that she borrowed it from one of her friends. She would be loathe to spend a bunch of money on a dress she wouldn't wear again. The too-large dress makes her look small and frail. I whisper my apologies to Doug and make my way over to my mom.

"How long have you been here?" I ask giving her a big hug. "Why didn't you come through the receiving line? I didn't even know you had arrived."

"Well, someone has a pretty inflated view of herself, thinking her own mother should wait in a line to see her." She kisses my cheek. "You look absolutely beautiful."

"Thanks, Mom." I find myself breaking into a huge grin. My mom isn't the kind of person who gives a compliment unless she really means it. She doesn't believe in the idea of social niceties. When I was about fourteen, I saved up my baby-sitting money to get my hair done at a fancy hair salon in the mall. When I came home preening and asked for her opinion, she told me it looked like I cut it myself. When I told her she was mean, she pointed out she had been nice enough not to mention it looked like I cut it myself after being on a bender, with blunt scissors and closed eyes. I didn't speak to her for a week. I've got the pictures, and it turns out she was right.

"This sure is quite the party." She looks around the room.

"I see your dad is in his element. You better be careful or he'll start rubbing against the people here. He can smell the money on them the way cats smell fish."

"Mom! You promised to be on your best behavior." I try not to smile, my dad is at the bar practically crawling into the pocket of several of Theodore's associates. Sharon is next to a growing pile of empty glasses.

"I'll behave, but it takes all the fun out of everything." She takes a deep drink of her wine. "What does the Boy Wonder think of the party?" My mom has called Doug "the Boy Wonder" ever since she met him for the first time. I've never mentioned this endearing nickname to him.

"Stop calling him that."

"He looks like he should be varnished." She glances at me. "Sorry, being cynical comes naturally to me. He seems nice, and he clearly cares for you."

"I love him, Mom. I do."

"You don't have to convince me. You're the only one who needs to be convinced. Besides," She pauses. "Never mind."

"You were going to give me the 'love is not enough' speech again, weren't you?" My mom is famous for this speech, in the same way Abraham Lincoln is known for his 'four score and seven years ago' spiel. The short version of the talk is that love is good, but love doesn't pay the bills, heat the house, or keep you from getting hungry. My mom distrusts flowery discussions of true love. "You're a skeptic."

"I like skeptics; if they believe in something it's because they know it's true, not because of some fleeting feeling. People who doubt, but still choose to believe, well that's a person you can count on." She goes back to chewing on the pile of appetizers she has on the plate in front of her. I suspect before the night is out she'll wrap up parcels of food in extra napkins and stick them into her purse.

"Don't you think I should marry Doug?" My voice comes out all whispery and soft, not strong and forceful the way I imagined it in my head. My mom looks around the room and then whispers back to me out of the side of her mouth as if we were spies meeting to trade military secrets.

"Are you having doubts?"

"No, of course not. Just prewedding jitters. Doug and I have been together for a long time. He is everything I ever wanted in a man. I've been wanting to get married for so long it's just natural to be nervous now that it's actually happening. Right?" My mom doesn't say anything, she just looks at me. I'm about to say something else when Jane appears out of the crowd and takes my arm.

"Doug's mom wanted me to find you. She wants to have a couple of toasts and then the staff will start serving dinner."

"Sure." I let Jane lead me to the head table. The wait staff is pouring champagne into tall flute glasses and I find myself standing next to Doug holding one aloft, looking out over the crowd.

"This is a day I'm sure Sophie thought would never come," Doug states; the crowd gives a good natured chuckle. "I thought I might escape the bonds of matrimony, but I find myself tonight tied up tight. Thanks to all of our friends and family for joining us this evening. We look forward to seeing all of you again at the wedding." Doug raises the glass as if about to drink and then stops. "And the next time we see you, we expect presents!" The crowd breaks into laughter and everyone drinks. The music starts up again and people began drifting toward their tables. The wait staff appear at the doors of the room each holding a silver tray.

"You're not eating your chicken," Doug notes as everyone is finishing up their dinners. I give the bird carcass on my plate another poke. It retreats to the far side of the plate and is stacked on top of my asparagus. My stomach feels tight and hard. There isn't any room in there for dinner. "You haven't had anything to eat all day; you rushed out to the spa this morning without stopping for breakfast."

"I'm not feeling very well. Besides, the spa gave me grapes," I mumble.

"Don't be ridiculous, you can't possibly be sick." So much for "in sickness and in health," I guess.

"Excuse me for a minute." I leave the table and head toward the bathroom. At first it's strictly for show, but about halfway there it strikes me I might actually throw up. I manage to keep a tight smile past the tables of all of our guests. Just a happy bride-to-be on her way to the ladies room, nothing to look at here. I try to avoid running the last few steps.

The bathroom door swishes shut, and the noise of the party is silenced. The bathroom is done with heavy carved-wood paneling, plush, flocked wallpaper, and a creamy marble sink. On the counter there are complimentary cotton balls, hairspray, lotion, and tissues. I love this bathroom; I can't believe I never spent any time in here before, it's gorgeous. I sit in the stall for a while. Pressing my face against the side of the wall, I feel hot and cold all at the same time. I don't understand why when I'm getting everything I want, it feels like I'm losing.

I step outside the bathroom and look at the bank of pay phones hanging on the wall. I dial before I think about it for too long. Does it mean anything that I know the cell number by heart?

"Nick?" I say when he picks up after only one ring.

"Is everything okay?"

"Sure. I just wanted to give you a call and say thanks again." There's a pause, and I wish I could see his face.

"No problem." I'm not sure what I planned on saying but I had hoped the conversation would be going a bit better than this.

"What did Cathie say about the idea of moving to Vancouver? I imagine she's thrilled."

"I haven't asked her yet. She's not really the type to be emotional. In fact, she's—" Nick pauses. "She's wonderful, but she's more the detached, reasonable type. We're well suited that way, logic before passion, after all." I feel my throat tighten up.

"I realized we didn't invite you to the party. You could come if you want." As soon as the words are out of mouth I want to kick myself. I can't imagine Nick at this kind of event, standing between the silver spray-painted willow branches.

"I don't think I can, I've got the conference here. I wouldn't want to miss out on the Big Foot debate."

"Did you get in trouble over the TV show?" I ask. Nick laughs.

"A conference benefits from a little controversy. Don't worry about it."

"I wish I would have met you at a different time."

"We need a time machine, I guess." There's another pause. "You should probably go back to your party."

"Yeah, I should. I guess you should get back to Cathie and your skeptical crowd."

"Yes. Take care of yourself," Nick says quietly and clicks off. I hang up the phone. The party is really heating up. *Who says the rich don't like to get down and party?* People were up from the tables and dancing. By dancing, I mean actually dancing, as opposed to swaying back and forth to the music. I can't tell you if it was a waltz or the Foxtrot, but it clearly had defined steps.

"You've got to stop disappearing," my dad says, grabbing at my elbow. "You're the hostess of this party, you know. You're embarrassing me." I wrench my arm back from him. *Embarrassing him?* That's a hoot. I weave between guests stopping every so often to say hello again and make sure that they're having a good time. It seems like with the exception of myself, everyone is having a heck of a time. Doug spots me and makes his way over.

"Where did you go? We had to wait to cut the cake because I couldn't find you."

"We have a cake?"

"Of course there's a cake." Doug breaks off and pulls me to his side. I think for a minute that he's overcome by passion, but then I realize there's a photographer. "Smile, for god's sake. You look all washed out and miserable. What are people going to think?"

The flash goes off and Doug pulls away instantly. "Come on, we should dance."

"I don't really feel up to it. Honestly, Doug, I'm not feeling great. I think I need to sit, maybe even lie down for a few minutes." Doug gives a sigh as if I'm personally torturing him.

"My mom has been planning this party forever." He sighs again.

"I don't want to ruin the party."

"Good. Then let's dance. If you still feel bad then, we'll cut the cake and you can go up to the room and lie down for a while. It won't matter if you're around after that, no one will notice."

"Well, as long as I can be sick on a convenient schedule for you," I say, but he misses the sarcasm.

"Thanks, baby, you're a good sport." Doug smiles to the quartet, raising a finger and they start up again. The crowd clears a space for us and Doug pulls me close. He spins me around to face different cameras. The flashbulbs keep going off in my eyes and I'm having a hard time telling which way is up. The lights start to narrow, and the strange thing is that I don't hear the music anymore, just this rushing noise, like the ocean is pouring into the room. I can see flashes of black and white off to the side, it's like the pod of whales is in the room with us. They must have followed us from the ferry dock. It seems like we're on the *Titanic* and we're going down. I try to say something to Doug so he knows we are in danger. He's looking at me strangely, and I hear him say my name but it sounds like he's yelling it from across a cavern. I take a step back but there's nothing there, and I fall.

Forty-three

LIBRA

Everything seems upside down, backward, and inside out. Look for your guiding stars and don't get distracted. If you follow your own star, you'll find your way home and discover that it's not just fairy tales that end in "happily ever after."

I come to lying on the floor of the ballroom. Someone has folded up a tablecloth and put it under my head. There's a cold, wet napkin on my forehead. My mom and Jane are kneeling next to my side. My mom is holding my hand and Jane is waving her hand over my face as an ineffective fan. Just beyond them I can see the rest of the guests, circled around. Well *this* has given them all something to talk about at the country club next week other than how hard it is to get good servants. I really hope when I passed out I managed to keep my skirt down and spared them all a view of my control-top panties required by this dress. I try to sit up, but the world does a slow spin, tilting to the left. My mom presses my shoulder back down.

"She's okay now," my mom says. Doug leans in and looks at me like I'm a science project. I have the urge to point out that I told him I was sick.

"Can she get up? She's making a show of herself down

there," he says. *Ah, my hero.* Glad to know he's worried about how it looks as opposed to how I might actually be feeling. My mom swats his hand away.

"Give her a minute." She looks down at me. "How are you feeling?"

"I think I passed out," I manage to say.

"I think that is something we can agree on," Mom says, helping me up into a sitting position. "Just rest there for a minute, don't move too fast, you took quite a fall."

"You should have seen yourself, you went down hard. I think everyone heard your head smack the floor," Jane offers, ever the helpful friend. My hand reaches up and touches the side of my head. I can feel a bump forming. "Did you see stars?" When she says this, my breath holds for a minute. I did see something. I look at her, my mom, and then Doug. I can see it perfectly, a flash-forward to my own future, but the future isn't here yet. I've been acting like everything is predestined, but that isn't true. I can change my future. I'm not wearing a watch. I wonder how late it is, I wonder if it's too late. I can picture Nick sitting next to Cathie and leaning over to whisper in her ear. I lean forward and try to stand up. My legs seem to have lost the ability to coordinate with the messages my brain is sending them. I end up having to roll onto my knees and then push up from there. I stand swaying for a minute, trying to take several deep breaths. I look around. The tables all have candles on them and the hotel has dimmed the lights in the room to create mood lighting, but suddenly everything is clear.

"Mom, I did see something. I had a dream." She leans forward to hear me.

"C'mon, Sophie, let's get you upstairs so you can lie

down," Doug says. He looks annoyed. This is not how the party should be going. For one thing, he is no longer the center of attention. He isn't looking for a wife, he's looking for a second-in-command and I'm not so sure I want to be up for only supporting actress roles anymore.

"What did you see, Sophie?" my mom asks, stepping in front of Doug.

"I don't know, maybe it was nothing, it just seemed for a minute . . ." My voice trails off and I shake my head, trying to clear out the cotton wool that seemed to have taken up residence in there.

"I thought you got out of the prediction business," Doug says. His words act like smelling salts, resulting in utter clarity. It's not about what I dreamed about, what things look like or what other people think. To worry about that would be illogical. There's only one thing, one person that seems logical.

"I thought I had, too." I look at my mom. She was smiling, she knew what I was thinking; she'd read my mind. Suddenly I have this image of her dressed up like a fairy godmother.

"You can take my rental car. It's parked out front, some kind of hideous SUV thing. You can't miss it, it's orange. It's as large as school bus. It was all the rental company had when I arrived," she says, handing me the keys.

"You can't go anywhere. What about the cake?" Doug practically squeals.

"I have to." I look at him, his tie is crooked. "I'm sorry, Doug."

"When will you be back?"

"I won't." Everyone is silent, it seems like my words are still bouncing around the room.

"You cannot be serious." He looks around. "You'll regret this." Doug's lips are growing tighter.

"I might; then again, I might not." I take the keys from my mom. The one thing I am certain of is that I will have bigger regrets if I don't try. I look at the crowd of people. I have the urge to make an announcement. "I want to thank you all for coming, sorry about all the drama. I've realized something. Many of you know I had a brief career as a psychic, foretelling the future and all that. Turns out you don't have to know the future. All you have to do is make choices that lead you in the direction you want to go and with the people you want to go with." No one says anything. I thought this was fairly profound and I was hoping for a bigger reaction. My mom gives me a small push toward the door.

It's raining outside, fat drops that drip from the sky and plink onto the driveway of the hotel. My mom's rental car is parked off to the side. I scurry past the valet and jump in. I drive a Volkswagen Beetle—I could park my car inside of this one and still have room left over. I turn it over and race the engine. The fresh air has revitalized me, and suddenly I have to be there now, not a minute later. I need to find Nick before he talks to Cathie. Once he's taken that step it will be hard for him to change, he's too much of a gentleman. I put the car into drive and race for the driveway. The valet dashes in front of the car waving madly. I suspect Doug sent him in a bid to stop me but I will not be thrown from my course that easily. I pull the wheel to the right to avoid him and race under the hotel overhang.

I notice a small sign that reads "6 FEET" a second before I drive under the overhang. I have a split-second thought; *I wonder how tall this thing is?* The sound of grinding metal screams out. Then I know the SUV is at least six feet one inch tall. I've wedged the SUV in tight, like a mastodon in a tar pit. I pop it into reverse and try to back out, more metal screaming and then a loud groan, freedom. I feel something bounce off my hair and look up. The sunroof has torn free, another screw bouncing down before the whole apparatus hits the hood and then slides to the ground. The rain starts to plink into the car. I turn the car off and cock my face up to the rain for a second.

"Lady, are you crazy?" the valet yells. I don't answer. It seems to be the kind of question that doesn't require an answer. I step out of the car to see if it looks as bad from out there. The hotel overhang is curled down, like a melting candle. The top of my mom's rental car looks bashed in and the sun roof is laying there like roadkill. *Who knew these things were so shabbily installed?* It's raining into the car. I can't have that.

"Do you have any duct tape?" I ask in what I think is a calm voice.

"*Tape*? Lady, you drove your car into the hotel!"

"I didn't drive it into the hotel. This is clearly some kind of overhang. It was added later, anyone can tell that. If you ask me it ruins the line of the hotel, anyway. Now, do you have tape and something like a garbage bag?" He storms off and I suspect he may be calling for backup, but he comes back with the requested items.

"I'm not going to help you with whatever you've got in your head. My job is strictly parking cars." He crosses his arms. Talk about difficult people.

"I didn't ask you to. Look, would you be willing to give me a leg up, at least?" He sighs and makes a stirrup with his laced hands. I kick off my shoes and use him to vault onto the top of the SUV. It's quite slippery up here, actually. The rental place must wax these cars on a weekly basis. I yank my dress up, straddle the roof of the car, and scoot up to the open hole in the roof. My hose catches on a piece of metal and tears. I curse until it occurs to me that this is the least of my troubles. Using the sleeve of my dress, I do the best I can to dry off the roof of the car and carefully tape the garbage bag over the hole. Repair complete, I roll onto my stomach and slide slowly off the side of the car, my dress hitching up around my waist. I can just picture what a show this is giving everyone of my panties.

I hit the ground and pull the dress down. I turn and see that the majority of our guests have come to the hotel entrance to see what's going on. I guess a car wedged into a hotel over-hang is not an everyday occurrence for them. I give a small wave to Ann who looks like she is having some kind of stroke and jump back into the car. I give the valet a thumbs-up, back up the car and go out the driveway. I realize that I've left my shoes there, but it seems more trouble than it's worth to dou-ble back for them. In my mind I can picture Nick and Cathie sitting across from each other discussing the benefits of home-opathic medicine. Nick takes her hand, tells her how he enjoys these talks, and that he hopes it doesn't have to end when the conference ends. This image alone makes me press more firmly on the gas, and the SUV surges forward.

The Laurel Point Inn is only a few minutes away from The Empress Hotel. I pull into their driveway and jump out. I toss the keys to their valet and jog inside. I catch a look at myself in the mirrored back wall. The products Jane used in my hair did not mix well with the rain—it's hanging in chunks, my mascara has run, I'm shoeless, and my hose are ripped. My brand-new dress looks a bit worse for the wear, as well. It isn't giving off the sexy, sophisticated vibe anymore. They just don't make things the way they used to. I take a moment, run my finger under my eye to clear the mascara, and pull my skirt down, in an attempt to look a little less crazy-Lady Macbeth-like. Let's hope that Nick makes his choice based on more than looks.

"Excuse me? Can you tell me where the skeptics conference is?" I ask the concierge, who is staring at me like I levitated into the room. He seems incapable of speech, so he simply points. I give him a smile and jog down the hall, my feet making smacking sounds on the tile floor. I can hear voices. There's a registration table outside the room. One of the people working it has a *Star Trek* sweatshirt on and the other is wearing a shirt with some kind of math equation joke on it.

I step past them and into the conference room. The room is full of people. At the front there's a table with various people sitting at a head table. I can see Nick, he is at the end with a small cardboard sign in front of him that reads, "Dr. McKenna." Someone else is speaking and showing slides on the PowerPoint projector. A few people turn and look when I enter. They poke and whisper to the people next to them, so much for making a subtle entrance. Nick looks up and when he recognizes me, his eyes widen. He looks to either side of him as if to seek confirmation that I'm really standing there. The presenter finally notices that the attention was off of him, and stops speaking.

"Sorry to be a bother, could I speak with you for just a minute, Nick?" Nick stands, sits down, and then stands again.

"In private," I clarify. Nick nods and says something quietly to the person seated next to him and then shuffles off the stage.

"What happened, Sophie?" he asks as he draws close to me. "Are you all right?"

"I'm fine. I need to know have you talked to Cathie, yet?"

"What?"

"Cathie, have you talked to her?" Nick shakes his head no, and the tight band around my stomach lessens slightly. This might not change anything, but I know I have to try. "I needed to talk to you, to tell you something."

"Sure, of course." Nick leads me to the back of the room, the presenter resumes talking. It's something about alternative health methods and improper research studies. I can't tell if people are listening to him or watching us. Maybe I should have taken the time to change.

"I shouldn't have interrupted your conference. I'm sorry." My throat feels tight. I pat my hair down, trying to make it take some type of shape. "I would like to tell everyone how the psychic thing was my idea. Asking you to cover for me is not fair."

"It's fine. Honestly, it doesn't matter."

"Remember at the at the TV station, you said something." Nick looks at me; we are exactly the same height. I always wanted to date tall men, but I never realized how nice it would be to look directly into someone's eyes. "You said you believed in me." He nods. "You are the first person to do that in a really long time. I didn't even believe in myself. I wanted to say I believe in you, too." Nick picks up my hand; his hands are warm and dry.

"Sophie, I'm a short, Scottish immigrant. I work in academia, and my yearly salary is most likely the same as Doug's clothing budget. I enjoy reading books on topics like the time-space continuum and the history of obscure figures. I don't do exotic hobbies and I shun social parties. I like to argue about the existence of Bigfoot and even more humiliating is the fact that I have the DVD of every season of *Buffy the Vampire Slayer*. Is this what you want?" I nod. His face breaks into a smile. "What changed your mind?"

"I had a vision."

"A vision?"

"A prediction."

"Uh-huh. What kind of prediction?" He raises his eyebrows.

"I predicted that we belong together. It was a vision of happily ever after." I look down. He lifts my chin, looking into my eyes.

"Now that is a prediction I could believe in." He kisses me. The conference room breaks into applause. Even skeptics can believe in true love. I look around the room to see if I can see a devastated librarian-type lurking in a corner.

"What about Cathie?" I ask. I hope *she's* that librarian. What if she's a burly, lumberjack-type? She is from Oregon after all. What if she asks me to go out behind the conference hall and beats me up?

"I thought I would still ask her to move in with me." I pull back from his arms. *Now just when I think everything's perfect, he's going to admit to some kind of weird perversion?*

"You want her to move in," I repeat, so he can hear what a bad plan this is.

"I thought so." He's giving me this huge smile and I know somehow the joke is on me, but I can't figure it out. He turns me around so I'm facing the front of the room again, then I see the banner: CATHIE—Critical Analytical Thinking for Higher Institutions of Education. "It's a curriculum program to teach critical thinking to college students. It was piloted down at the University of Oregon, but I'll be rolling it out up here."

"Cathie is a *what*, not a *who*?"

"Pretty much. I couldn't have you thinking I would be all by myself, pining away for you, could I? A guy has to have his pride. After racing over here in a vain attempt to drive Cathie and me apart, would you be willing to share with her?"

"I could get used to her. As long as she knows her place."

"It's a deal, then. If it's going to be happily ever after, then I'm guessing I'll get you to join me for season tickets at the opera?"

"I'm skeptical on that issue," I hedge.

He laughs and kisses me again. At last, something I have no doubts about at all.